Beware of the scandalous woman...

USA TODAY Bestselling Author

NICOLA CORNICK

Notorious

"A riveting read."
—*New York Times* bestselling author Mary Jo Putney on *Whisper of Scandal*

ISBN-13: 978-0-373-77583-5

Praise for *USA TODAY* bestselling author Nicola Cornick

"Ms. Cornick is first-class, queen of her game."
—*Romance Junkies*

"A rising star of the Regency arena."
—*Publishers Weekly*

"Nicola Cornick creates a glittering, sensual world of historical romance that I never want to leave."
—Anna Campbell, author of *Untouched*

"A wonderfully original, sinfully amusing and sexy Regency historical by the always entertaining Cornick."
—*Booklist* on *The Confessions of a Duchess*

"Fast-paced, enchanting and wildly romantic!"
—*SingleTitles.com* on *The Scandals of an Innocent*

"Witty banter, lively action and sizzling passion."
—*Library Journal* on *The Undoing of a Lady*

"RITA® Award–nominated Cornick deftly steeps her latest intriguingly complex Regency historical in a beguiling blend of danger and desire."
—*Booklist* on *Unmasked*

"If you've liked Nicola Cornick's other books, you are sure to like this one as well. If you've never read one—what are you waiting for?"
—*Rakehell* on *Lord of Scandal*

"Cornick masterfully blends misconceptions, vengeance, powerful emotions and the realization of great love into a touching story."
—*RT Book Reviews,* 4 1/2 stars, on *Deceived*

Don't miss the rest of the latest Scandalous Women of the Ton trilogy, available now!

Whisper of Scandal
One Wicked Sin
Mistress By Midnight

Also available from Nicola Cornick and HQN Books

Deceived
Christmas Keepsakes
"A Season for Suitors"
Lord of Scandal
Unmasked
The Confessions of a Duchess
The Scandals of an Innocent
The Undoing of a Lady

Browse www.Harlequin.com for Nicola's full backlist.

NICOLA CORNICK

Notorious

ISBN-13: 978-0-373-77583-5

NOTORIOUS

This edition published by arrangement with Harlequin Books S.A.

For questions and comments about the quality of this book please contact us at Customer_eCare@Harlequin.ca.

www.HQNBooks.com

Printed in U.S.A.

Dear Reader,

The Scandalous Women of the Ton are back! Or in this case, perhaps it should be the scandalous *Men* of the Ton...

James Devlin, cousin to Alex, the hero of *Whisper of Scandal,* has been one of London's most shocking rakes. Now settled into a life of riches and respectability as the fiancé of a beautiful society heiress, Dev is terminally bored. Enter Caroline, Lady Carew, a woman with a mysterious past who knows enough about Dev to ruin his engagement and all his future prospects. But Lady Carew also has secrets to keep, for she is none other than a notorious match breaker, paid by rich parents to end unsuitable engagements....

Reading through the letters and accounts of the Regency period, I sometimes come across cases where fathers or trustees have paid off a man or a woman they consider unsuitable. Perhaps a son has fallen in love with a courtesan and wishes to marry her, or an heiress has taken a fancy to a poverty-stricken scoundrel and threatens to elope. In many instances, the parents or guardians are absolutely ruthless in removing the threat. In my imagination it was only a small step from there to the idea that a rich and determined parent might hire a heartbreaker to seduce their son away from his unsuitable fiancée. And so the idea for *Notorious* was born....

Notorious was huge fun to write and I very much hope that you enjoy it, too!

Nicola Cornick

Notorious

CHAPTER ONE

"He who does not burn with desire grows cold."
—Seventeenth-century proverb

JAMES DEVLIN WAS TWENTY-SEVEN years old and he had everything that he had ever wanted. He had a place in society, he had a beautiful, rich fiancée and he had a title of his own. Yet on the night that his former wife walked back into his life after nine years absence he was bored; as bored as it was possible for a gentleman to be at a ton ball at the height of the London season.

It was another night of lavish excess and hollow entertainment. The Duke and Duchess of Alton threw the best parties in the ton, opulent, tasteful and frightfully exclusive. For Dev it was also another night of fetching lemonade for Emma when she became thirsty, of finding her fan when she misplaced it and of fawning on Emma's mama, who could not stand him and probably did not even know his name although he had been betrothed to her daughter for two years. Once upon a time Dev had had to brave the elements on the rain-lashed deck of a ship of the line, scramble up rigging and fight for his life. Each day had brought new dangers, new excitement. It had only been two years but it felt like a century ago. These days he did nothing more dangerous than check the set of his coat and pass Emma her reticule.

"Jealous, Dev?" His sister Francesca put a hand on his sleeve and Dev realized that he had been frowning at Emma across the dance floor, glaring at her as she twirled through the steps of the waltz in the arms of her cousin Frederick Walters. Chessie was not the only one who had noticed his grim stance. He saw the sideways glances and covert amusement. Everyone thought that he was possessive, resentful of the time that Emma, a consummate flirt, lavished on other men. If he had been the jealous type he would have spent his days on the dueling field but the fact was that one had to care in order to be jealous and Dev had long ago realized that he did not care a jot if Emma flirted with every man in London.

He straightened up and smoothed the frown from his brow. "I'm not jealous in the least," he said.

Chessie's blue gaze appraised his face, looking for signs that he was trying to fool her. "It is no secret that the Earl and Countess of Brooke prefer Fred as a suitor for Emma," she said.

Dev shrugged. "The Earl and Countess would prefer a distempered hound as a suitor for Emma but I am the one that Emma wants."

"And Emma always gets what she wants." There was the very faintest edge to Chessie's voice now.

Dev shot his sister a look. Chessie had not yet got what she wanted and she had been waiting a long time. Fitzwilliam Alton, only son and heir to the Duke and Duchess, had been paying Chessie marked attention for some months. Such public notice could only end respectably in a proposal of marriage but so far Fitz had not declared himself and now the ton was starting to gossip. Society, Dev thought, had not been kind, talking scandal about him and Chessie in particular from the first. They had breeding of sorts, but precious little of it and no money. He had at least carved out something of a Navy career for himself before he had resorted to hunting a fortune. Chessie had had to make an impression through her beauty and her vivacious personality alone. It was always harder for a woman.

"You don't like Emma," Dev said now.

He felt rather than saw his sister's scornful glance. "I don't like what she has done to you," she said. "You've become one of Emma's pets, like that fluffy white dog or her bad-tempered monkey."

Ouch.

"It's a small price to pay for what I want," Dev said.

Wealth. Status. He had hunted them for the last ten years. Born with nothing, he had no intention of going back to the poverty of his youth. Now everything was within his grasp and if that meant he had to be Emma's lapdog for the rest of his life there were worse fates. Or so he told himself.

"You are no better," he said to his sister, aware that he sounded perilously close to the tit for tat banter of their childhood. "You have caught yourself a marquis."

Chessie flicked her fan in a gesture that conveyed total disdain. "Don't be so vulgar, Dev. I am completely different from you. I may be a fortune hunter but at least I love Fitz. And anyway—" a tiny frown marred her brow "—I have not caught him yet."

"He'll propose soon," Dev said. He had heard the trace of uncertainty in Chessie's voice that revealed how wafer-thin was her confidence. He wanted to reassure her, even though he thought Fitzwilliam Alton nowhere near good enough for his sister. "Fitz loves you, too," he said, hoping he was right. "He is only waiting for the right moment to tell his parents the news."

"That will never happen," Chessie said dryly.

"You must love Fitz very much to be prepared to endure the Duchess of Alton as a mother-in-law," Dev said.

"And you must love Emma's money very much to be prepared to endure the Countess of Brooke," Chessie said.

"I do," Dev said.

Chessie shook her head slightly. "It will not serve, Dev," she said. "In the end you will hate her."

"I'm sure you are right," Dev said. "I already dislike her very much."

"I meant Emma," Chessie said, her eyes on the shifting patterns of the dance, "not her mother. Though if Emma becomes more like her mother as she grows older that will be hard to bear."

Dev could not deny that it was not an appealing prospect.

"If Fitz becomes more like his mother you will have to squeeze money out of him like a lemon," he said. The Duchess of Alton had a sour disposition and a mouth like the tightly drawn drawstring of a purse. It gave fair warning as to her character.

Chessie gave a spontaneous giggle. "Fitz will not become like his parents." The laughter faded from her face and she fidgeted with the struts of her fan, her gloved fingers pulling at the lace. Lately, Dev thought, she seemed to have lost some of her sparkle. Now he could see her searching the crowded room for Fitz. She was wearing her heart on her sleeve. He felt a rush of protective concern. Chessie was pinning everything on the prospect of this betrothal and Fitz, genial enough, but arrogant and spoiled in equal measure, was aware of her regard and was toying with her reputation. Chessie deserved better than that. Dev clenched his fists at his sides. One step out of line and he would ram that silver spoon Fitz had been born with right down his throat.

"You look very fierce," Chessie said, squeezing his arm.

"Sorry," Dev said, smoothing out his expression again. He smiled at her. "We haven't done badly," he said, "for two penniless orphans from County Galway."

Chessie did not reply and he saw that her gaze had returned to the waltz, which was now spinning to a triumphant climax. Fitz, tall, dark, distinguished, was at the far end of the room, almost lost in the shift and sway of the dancers. He was partnering a woman in a shimmering silver gauze gown, a woman who was also tall and dark. They looked magnificent together. Fitz had always had a weakness for a pretty face, just as his cousin Emma wanted a handsome trophy of a husband. But this woman was different from Fitz's usual flirts and there was something about the way that she moved, the lilt and cadence of her steps that shot Dev through with recognition even though he could not see her face.

"Who is that?" he said, and his voice sounded a little hoarse. Something strange—premonition—was edging up his spine. He was the least superstitious of men yet he felt the cold air breathe gooseflesh along his skin even though the Duke and Duchess of Alton's ballroom was stiflingly hot.

He could see that Chessie felt something, too. She was strung as tight as violin, her face pale now. He saw a shiver rack her body.

"Someone rich," she said bitterly. "Someone beautiful and eligible whom Fitz's parents will have introduced to him tonight in order to distract him from me."

"Nonsense," Dev said bracingly. "She will be yet another horse-faced, inbred poor relation—"

"Dev," Chessie reproved, as a dowager rustled past them on a wave of disapproval.

The music finished on a resounding flourish. There was a ripple of applause about the room. The pattern of dancers broke up. Fitz was escorting his partner across the floor toward them. Evidently he intended to introduce her to Chessie. Dev was not sure whether that reassured him or worried him.

"Dev!" Emma had also arrived, breathless and flushed by his side, dragging Freddie Walters with her by the hand. "Come and dance with me!"

For the first time in as long as he could remember, Dev did not respond immediately to Emma's imperious demand. Instead he was watching the woman at Fitz's side. She was not in the first flush of youth, closer perhaps to his age than Chessie's. Age, or experience, or both, gave her an unconscious confidence. She walked with the same elegance that Dev had seen in her in the waltz, a fluid grace that was accentuated by the sinuous swirl of the silver gauze gown. It caressed her breasts and hips, wrapping itself about her like a lover's kiss. There was not a man in the room, Dev thought, who was not staring at her, his mouth drying with lust, his mind a rampage of images as to what it would be like to unwrap that gown from those curves.

Or perhaps those were just his fantasies.

She was very pale with the kind of translucent skin dusted with freckles that was a feature of the Celtic races. The contrast between her vivid green eyes and her black hair was shocking, exhilarating. It made her look fragile and fey, like a kelpie or dryad, too exotic to be human. Her black curls were piled up on her head in a tumble of ringlets held by a dazzling diamond comb. Matching jewels sparkled about her slender neck and adorned her wrists. Not a poor relation then. She looked magnificent.

She also looked familiar.

Dev's heart missed a beat then started to race. For a moment it felt as though everything had stopped; the music, the chatter, the breath in his body. For one long moment he could neither think nor speak.

It was almost ten years since he had seen Susanna Burney. His last memory of her was not one he was likely ever to forget: Susanna gloriously naked and fast asleep in the bed that they had shared for their brief, passionate wedding night. As he had blown out the guttering candle he had had no notion that he would never see her again.

In the morning she was gone, and with her his marriage. She had left him a note—it had all been a terrible mistake, she had said. She had begged him not to come after her, had said that she would sue for an annulment. Young and full of pride, angry, hurt and betrayed, he had let her go.

It had been two years later when he had returned

from his first full tour of duty with the Royal Navy that he had reconsidered his abandonment of his wayward wife and had traveled to Scotland to find her again. He had told himself that it had been for curiosity's sake alone and to ensure that their annulment had indeed been granted. He had plans for the future, ambitious ideas, and they did not involve the girl he had seduced, married on impulse and let go. Sweat broke out over his body now as he recalled knocking on the door of the rectory and confronting Susanna's uncle and aunt. They had told him that Susanna was dead. He could recall the fierce punch of shock that had made a mockery of his bravado. He had cared for Susanna a great deal more than he had pretended.

Susanna Burney looked very much alive to him.

Anger and shock warred within him. He met her indifferent, unrecognizing gaze and a second wave of fury beat through him. She was pretending that she did not know him.

"Dev!" Emma was tugging on his hand, reclaiming his attention. A frown marred the pretty regularity of her features.

Emma, his rich, beautiful, well-connected fiancée…

Emma, the woman who was bringing him everything that he had ever wanted…

He had never told Emma about his first hasty, ill-fated marriage. There were many things that he had not told Emma. He had pretended that it was because all his past indiscretions were long gone, unimportant and forgotten, but the truth was that Emma was jealous and possessive and he could not predict how she would react to any revelation, and he did not want to put that to the test and endanger the entire house of cards he had built for himself—and for Chessie.

A cold prickle of tension edged its way down Dev's spine. The damage that Susanna might do was incalculable. If she revealed even a hint of his past, Emma might break their engagement and everything he had worked for would be lost.

He watched as Susanna drew closer. Her hand was resting on Fitz's arm in the most confiding gesture, their dark heads bent close together. She was smiling at Fitz as though he was the most fascinating man in the universe. Fitz, Dev thought, looked completely dazzled, flushing like a youth in the grip of his first infatuation.

Susanna looked up again and her gaze met Dev's for one long, long moment. He could not read her expression. There was still no flicker of recognition in her eyes and no trace of nervousness in her manner.

Dev felt cold, very cold. He straightened, squared his shoulders and prepared to be introduced to the wife he had thought was dead.

CHAPTER TWO

SHE DID NOT RECOGNIZE him until it was too late to run and equally impossible to hide. Not that hiding was her style.

The Duke and Duchess of Alton's Midsummer Ball was the most terrible crush and the press of guests had obscured Susanna's vision. The room was hot and airless, so noisy she could barely hear what Fitz was saying to her as he escorted her across the floor. Something about meeting some of his friends, she thought, which had been kind of him since she knew no one in London. And then the crowd had fallen back and she was looking at James Devlin and all the breath left her lungs in a rush and her head spun and she thought she might faint. It was only through sheer self-discipline that she did not.

Fitz had not noticed her discomfort. He was not, she thought, an observant man. Handsome, charming, spoiled, arrogant… She had ascertained all those facts about him within five minutes of their introduction. Within ten she had learned that he was devoted to his horses and his wine cellar. Within fifteen she had realized that he was susceptible to a beautiful woman, which would be useful since she was both beautiful and pledged to seduce him.

Fitz was still speaking as he drew her closer to the group of people about James Devlin. She had no idea what he was talking about; fortunately it seemed to require no reply on her part. All she could see was Devlin. All she was aware of was his height, the breadth of him and the coldness in his blue eyes as they rested on her with absolute disdain. She supposed she could not blame him for that. She was the one who had walked away from him, left him before the ink was dry on the marriage lines and whilst the bed was still warm from their lovemaking.

Susanna raised her chin and straightened her spine. She had been playing a part for so long that surely it could not be too difficult to wipe all expression from her face and conceal the fact that she was shaking inside. Yet it seemed inordinately hard to do. She let her gaze travel over Devlin again in slow appraisal. The calculated coolness of her stare was in direct contradiction to the nervous bumping of her heart against her ribs.

There was such authority and innate confidence about Devlin now, a poignant contrast to the dazzling youth of eighteen that she remembered so well. He had had brilliance and dash even at that age but there had been something eager and untried about him as well, as though the world, with its sharp edges, had not yet hardened his soul.

He had certainly filled out in the intervening

years. His shoulders were broad, his chest deep. He was taller, more muscular, most definitely a man rather than a boy, and so handsome that he would have been within a hairsbreadth of looking pretty had it not been for the square jaw and high cheekbones that robbed his face of any softness at all. Susanna felt a sudden and totally unexpected pang that the boy she had known had grown into so formidable a man. She would never have guessed it. But she had made her choices years ago. It was far too late for regrets now. Life had taught her that regrets were no more than self-indulgence.

She saw the little blonde girl hanging on Devlin's arm. That was one thing that had not changed then. Not that she cared a jot after nine years. But there had always been women hanging around James Devlin like bees to the honeypot. He knew he was handsome and he knew very well the effect that had on women. The arrogant self-assurance in the tilt of his head said so.

He was watching her. He had not taken his gaze from her from the moment that she had crossed the floor on Fitz's arm. She risked meeting his eyes again and was almost scalded by the look she saw there. Instead of the indifference that she had expected she saw angry challenge and a turbulent sensual heat that seemed to call a response from so deep within her that she visibly shivered. Her stomach tumbled. The polished wood of the ballroom floor seemed to shift beneath her silver slippers. She could feel her racing heart accelerate still further and saw Devlin's gaze shift to the hollow of her throat where a beautiful borrowed diamond drop rested on her frantic pulse. Suddenly Susanna's skin felt hot and damp; she knew the color had come into her face, knew, too, that Devlin had seen the betraying glitter of the diamond as it moved in response to the hammer of her pulse. She saw the corner of his mouth turn up in a smile of masculine satisfaction that he had been able to discompose her. That was something else that had not changed then: his conceit.

She raised her chin and gave him a look of profound dislike spiced with defiance. Too much was at stake here for her to draw back now, though every instinct she possessed prompted her to flee.

The girl to Devlin's left, the one to whom Fitz wanted to introduce her, was clearly Dev's sister. They shared the same coloring and bone structure, the same blue eyes and tawny gold hair. Susanna caught her bottom lip briefly between her teeth. This was the girl the Duke and Duchess of Alton were employing her to separate from Fitz. This was the girl whose life she was to ruin, whose future husband she was to steal, whose world she would leave in tatters. What an utter, confounded nuisance that the woman the Duchess had referred to, dismissively, as "Fitz's little fancy," should turn out to be Devlin's sister.

"Lady Carew." Fitz, smiling, was drawing Devlin's sister forward. "May I present to you Miss Francesca Devlin? Chessie, this is Caroline, Lady Carew, a friend of my parents who has recently come to London from Edinburgh."

Susanna felt rather than saw Devlin stiffen as he heard her name but she forced herself not to look at him. Francesca Devlin curtsied very prettily. The candlelight picked out the strands of bronze and copper and gold in her hair. Her blue eyes were very warm, her greeting even warmer. Susanna admired her tactics. When a handsome, eligible marquis whom you have a fancy to marry introduces a beautiful woman to you, pretend to be delighted to make her acquaintance...

That one was straight out of the adventuress's handbook. Under other circumstances, Susanna thought, she might have enjoyed befriending Miss Francesca Devlin, with whom she had more than a little in common. Unfortunately she was being paid a vast sum of money to inveigle herself into Fitz's affections and get rid of Francesca for good, which was not a promising basis for a friendship.

James Devlin shifted at his sister's side and Susanna met his eyes and saw naked antagonism there. Unlike Francesca he was not troubling to hide his hostility to her. Susanna felt the force of it ripple through her whole body. She supposed it was naive of her to imagine that Devlin would be indifferent to her sudden reappearance after an absence of nine long years. She had treated him badly; that was undeniable. He would want an explanation at the least, retribution at worst. Her mouth dried at the thought.

Devlin was not a man one would want as an enemy—he was too forceful, too determined—and her position was very precarious indeed.

Devlin inclined his head to her as though he had read and understood her thoughts. There was an edge of cynical amusement to his antipathy, a curl to his lips that threw down a challenge to her. The dangerous light in his eyes warned her that whatever game she chose to play, he would match her. Match her and surpass her.

She saw Devlin cast his sister a glance and move a step closer to her as though offering silent moral support. Chessie shot him a smile that was for one unguarded moment full of affection and gratitude. So Devlin was a protective older brother, Susanna thought. That was exactly what she did not need when she was set on spoiling his sister's life. Matters, complicated enough already, took a turn for the worse. Her heart sank lower toward her delicate embroidered satin slippers.

The other lady in the group, the little blonde, pushed forward in a flurry of blue silk and lace.

"You should have introduced me first, Fitz," she said, pouting. "I am a lady!"

By name if not by nature, Susanna thought as Fitz, apologizing profusely, introduced the girl as his cousin Lady Emma Brooke and the other gentleman as the Honorable Frederick Walters. Susanna was sharply conscious of Devlin's eyes upon her all the time, the narrow blue glitter of his gaze holding her captive. Emma dragged him forward like a trophy.

"This is my fiancé," she said proudly, "Sir James Devlin."

Fiancé.

Susanna's heart jerked. She had known that Devlin had come into a title. But she had not known that he was betrothed.

Jealousy, sharp, dark and hot, stole her breath. She wondered why she had never imagined him wed before. The thought had never crossed her mind and yet in the nine years since they had parted he could have been married twice over, three times, six times like Henry VIII for all she knew.

Except for the small difficulty that he was still married to her.

She really should have told him that they were still wed. She should have told him long ago.

Susanna's conscience, often troublesome, such a disadvantage to an adventuress, pricked her again. This, however, did not seem like the appropriate moment to break the news to Devlin, with his fiancée smiling at her with that possessive air and that warning glint in her eyes.

Susanna swallowed hard. She had intended to get an annulment within the first year of her marriage. She had written to Dev and promised him that she would. Then she had discovered that she was pregnant and her wedding ring and marriage lines had suddenly been the only thing standing between her and ruin. Alone and destitute, disowned by her family, she had clung to the very edge of respectability. And later, when she had remembered her pledge and had once again thought to end her marriage she had discovered that annulments, like many things in life, were both prodigiously expensive and a great deal more difficult to obtain than she had ever imagined. By then she had been spending every last penny she earned simply keeping body and soul together on the streets of Edinburgh. There was no cash to pay the lawyers. Sometimes she had barely managed to survive.

The memory of those dark days invaded Susanna's mind and she felt the familiar panic and fear rise in her throat. Her palms felt slippery with sweat within the elegant lace of her evening gloves. The candles felt too hot, the ballroom stifling. Everyone was looking at her. With a great effort of will she pushed the memories away and smiled at Emma Brooke.

"You are to be congratulated on your betrothal, Lady Emma," she said, "though not as much as Sir James is on his."

There was a slight pause whilst Emma tried to work out if this was a compliment and, deciding that it was, beamed. Susanna saw Dev's lips quirk into a smile.

"I am indeed the most fortunate of men," he said smoothly. "And you, Lady Carew," he added. There was a gleam of dark amusement in the depths of his eyes, shadowed by that ever-present anger. "It seems that you, too, must be congratulated, since the last time we met you were neither a lady nor were you called Caroline Carew, as I recall."

His tone was very courteous, his words anything but. A little ripple went around the group. Susanna saw a sharpening of speculation in the women's eyes and a different sort of interest in the men's. No wonder. Dev had just implied she was an adventuress at best, a harlot masquerading as a lady at worst.

The moment spun out. Susanna knew she had a choice and she had to make her decision fast. She could pretend that Devlin had mistaken her identity. Or she could take the fight to him. It was risky to claim that she did not know him because Dev would probably see that as a challenge. He was that sort of man. It was equally perilous to engage with him because she was not sure that she could win. But it was certainly too late to feign indifference. Everyone was waiting to see how she would respond to Dev's calculated remark.

"I am flattered that you claim to remember so much about me," Susanna said lightly. "I had forgotten all about you."

Dev's smile deepened at the setdown. The look he gave her sent heat searing through her.

"Oh, I remember everything about you, Lady… Carew," he said.

"You never knew everything about me, Sir James," Susanna said.

Their gazes locked like the hiss of blades engaging. Susanna's skin prickled with awareness. Too late to back down now…

"On the contrary," Dev said. "I remember, for instance, the very last time we met." There was a hint of devilry in his eyes. He was enjoying baiting her. Susanna saw it and felt a flare of anger.

Then her gaze fell on Emma's furious, pouting face and her anger dissolved into relief. This was just for show on Dev's part, to punish her for past sins and make her squirm. He had no intention of revealing the truth. It would damage him as much as it would her. Emma, she was already persuaded, was no meek and biddable betrothed. And Emma must surely hold the purse strings because Dev had never had any money at all.

Susanna allowed her gaze to consider the extravagant embroidery on Dev's white and gold waistcoat, the crisp quality of his linen and the unmistakable value of the diamond in his cravat pin. Then she let her eyes drift to Emma again. She saw Dev's gaze follow her. She knew he understood.

Finally, she smiled. "Well," she said, "I am sure you would not be so churlish as to bore everyone with the details, Sir James. There is nothing so tedious for others as old acquaintances harping on about past times."

"Did you know one another in Ireland?" Emma had clearly had enough of their conversation. She pushed between them, looking from Dev to Susanna with ill-concealed jealousy. She made Ireland sound like the back of beyond, a place fit only to leave.

"We met briefly in Scotland," Susanna said, "when Sir James was visiting his cousin Lord Grant one summer. It was a very long time ago."

"But now we have the happy opportunity to renew our acquaintance." The expression in Dev's eyes was in direct contrast to the smoothness of his tone. "You must grant me the next dance, Lady Carew, so that we may talk about the past without boring our friends."

In one sentence he had demolished her attempts to escape. Susanna mentally gritted her teeth. She recognized that determination in him. He had had the same single-mindedness at eighteen. He had seen something he wanted and he had taken it. She shivered.

"I have no desire to rake over the past," she said. "I fear I am promised for the next, Sir James. You must excuse me."

She turned pointedly to Fitz, allowing her fingers to brush his wrist in the lightest of gestures that nevertheless conveyed a hint of promise. She had almost forgotten about Fitz in the tumult of her feelings on seeing Devlin again. Already she had allowed herself to become distracted, which was not good enough when Fitz's parents' commission was all that stood between her and life on the London streets.

"Thank you for introducing me to your friends, my lord," she said. "I hope we shall meet again soon."

She scattered an impartial smile around the group, noting that Chessie's response was a rather less than friendly nod and that Emma failed to acknowledge her at all. Fitz seemed impervious to the strained atmosphere and kissed her hand with a gallantry that made Dev frown. Chessie turned away, as though she could not bear to watch Fitz's attentiveness to another woman.

Susanna started to walk quickly toward the ballroom door. Now that she had escaped Dev her heart was bumping against her ribs in reaction and she felt breathless and shaky all over again. She needed somewhere quiet to go. She needed to think, to try to unravel the tangle of deceit and confusion she was suddenly caught up in.

"May I beg a dance later in the evening, Lady Carew?"

Freddie Walters was blocking her path, his gaze insolent, assessing her like a thoroughbred horse, his touch on her arm more than familiar. His tone said that he already knew everything he needed to know about her, that she was a widow of questionable morals who was probably not averse to a light love affair. The blatant disrespect in his manner set Susanna's teeth on edge.

"Thank you, Mr. Walters," she said, "but I have decided to go home. I have the headache."

"A pity," Walters murmured. "Perhaps I could call on you?"

"You're making the lady's headache worse, Walters." It was Dev's voice, cold with a hard edge. Susanna saw Walters's eyes widen, then, as Dev made a sharp gesture, the other man scuttled off. Dev watched him out of earshot, then his gaze came back to Susanna's face and fixed there. She had wanted to scuttle away, too, but she had the lowering thought that Dev would simply grab her if she tried to run out on him now. He did not appear to care much for the conventions of the ballroom since he had accosted her in the center of the floor.

"Thank you for your assistance," she said coldly, "but it was quite unnecessary. I can look after myself."

Dev smiled. "I am aware," he said. His gaze, hard and appraising, traveled over her in a manner quite different from Walters's blatant sexual calculation. It was thoughtful, measured and infinitely more disturbing.

"I was not trying to rescue you," he added gently. "I wanted you to myself."

His choice of words and the look in his eyes made Susanna quiver somewhere deep inside. He had removed the feeble threat that Walters posed only to replace it with something far more dangerous. Himself. He was confronting her here, in full view of the Duke and Duchess of Alton's guests. It was audacious. It was impossible.

"I don't have anything to say to you." Susanna kept her voice steady. She had had nine years of learning how to protect herself. It had never been as difficult as it was now, trying to erect defenses against this man and his perceptive blue gaze and his forcefulness.

He laughed. "You can do better than that, Susanna. What the hell is going on?"

"I have no notion what you mean," Susanna said. Her pulse was racing. She looked around but there was no refuge. She started to walk slowly to the side of the dance floor. Dev took her arm, adapting his long stride to her shorter steps. To an observer it would look as though they were doing what everyone else did between dances, strolling around the floor, chatting with the casual indifference of social acquaintances. Except that there was nothing casual in the touch of Dev's hand.

"You owe me an explanation at the very least," Dev said. "An apology, even—" his tone was sarcastic "—if that is not too much to expect." For a moment Susanna saw something fierce in his eyes. A passing couple shot them a curious glance. They had caught the tone if not the content of Dev's words and had sensed the tension in the air.

Susanna deployed her fan to shield her expression.

"It was a long time ago." She aimed for disdain, cool and dismissive, and hit exactly the right note. "Yes, I left you, but surely you have managed to recover from the loss." She paused, smiled. "Don't tell me I broke your heart."

She had provoked him on purpose and she expected him to tell her she had meant nothing to him. Instead she saw the heat and anger in his eyes intensify.

"I came back to find you," he said, "two years later."

Susanna almost dropped her fan. Two years. She had never known. She felt a mixture of bitterness and regret. It would have made no difference. Two years was far too late. It had been too late from the moment she had run away from him. She could see that now, with the benefit of hindsight. She could see all the mistakes she had made—see, too, how pointless it was to regret them almost a decade later.

"I only wished to ensure that our annulment had been granted." Dev shot her a look, contemptuous, cold. "But when I called on your aunt and uncle they told me that you were dead." He spoke through his teeth. "An overstatement of the facts, it would seem."

Susanna was so shocked that she almost fell. For one long, terrifying moment the ballroom spun before her eyes, the music and voices fading, everything slipping away from her. She put out a hand and realized with blessed relief that they had reached the corner of the room and were standing beside one of the long, arched windows that opened onto the terrace. The cool pane of the glass was against her fingers and a breath of air stole into the overheated room.

She raised her eyes to Dev's face. His expression

was hard, his mouth a tight line. She could sense the elemental fury in him.

"Dead?" she whispered. It was true that her aunt and uncle had cast her out when she had fallen pregnant and refused to give up her child. She had been disowned, disinherited, dismissed. They had said she was dead to them. Evidently that was exactly what they had told everyone else, too.

The cold crept into her heart. Her family's callous cruelty had almost destroyed her nine years before. Now she felt their malice touch her again. She had not thought they could hurt her anymore. She had been wrong.

Dev was still speaking. "Was it really necessary to go so far?" he was saying with biting anger. "It was not as though I wished for a reconciliation."

He stopped. Susanna knew he was waiting for her reply but for a moment she could not find the words. There was so much to absorb, and so quickly; that he had come to find her, that her family had lied to him. It hurt much more than she would ever have anticipated.

"I..." Her chest was tight. She tried to breathe. She knew that she had to stop this now, before Dev realized that she had known nothing of her family's shocking lies to him. Already he was getting too close. An instant's slip on her part and she would give herself away. If he suspected the truth he would have endless questions for her; questions about the past, questions about what had happened to her and, more dangerous still, questions about her life now and why she was in London. She could tell him none of those things. She had to protect herself and her secrets at all costs or she would lose everything. Suddenly she was fiercely glad that she had never told him that their marriage had not been annulled. It could prove to be a useful weapon should she need to defend herself against him.

Susanna straightened, steadying herself. She drew in a deep breath, searching for the right words to drive Dev away from her. He forestalled her. His voice was thick and heavy with emotion, an emotion that even after the passage of nine years cut straight to the core of her and made her feel with an intensity she had not experienced in years.

"Hell and the devil, Susanna," he burst out, "you were my wife, not some strumpet I had tumbled in a ditch! Don't you owe me more than this? You walk out on me and then you ask your family to lie to me! Why would you do such a thing?"

There was such passion and honesty in his eyes. Susanna hated herself for what she was about to do, what she had to do in order to protect herself.

"I asked them to lie because I had to be sure to be rid of you," she said. She made her voice light and uncaring. The words seemed to stick in her throat but she forced them out. She knew she had to finish this and make sure that Dev would hate her so much that he would never question her again. There was no other way.

"I wed you because I wanted you to rid me of the burden of my virginity," she said. She dragged out a smile, made it vivid, convincing. She knew she was a good actress. She had had enough practice in those lean and bitter years after her family had disowned her, when her skill at dissembling was all that had stood between her and starvation.

"After one night of marriage I had everything I needed from you, Devlin," she said. "I wanted to know about sex. You taught me." She forced herself to meet his eyes. He was stony-faced, his jaw set hard as he listened to her cheapen the love they had shared. "It was delightful—" she gave a little shrug, matching the gesture to the dismissive tone of her voice "—but after I had seduced you I had no further use for you."

That, she thought, should be enough to make him despise her. No man would accept such a blow to his pride. She turned to walk away.

Dev prevented her escape by the simple expedient of catching her wrist and drawing her close to him. Her body stirred to his touch, every fiber of her being waking to him as though they had never been apart. The color flooded her cheeks, heating her skin so that every inch of her felt alive and responsive as never before. She saw Dev's gaze move over her slowly in precise and insolent appreciation of her state of arousal. His gaze dropped to the neckline of her gown. It had been chosen to ensnare Fitz, and for the first time that evening Susanna wished it was a little more demure. It felt as though the sweep of Dev's eyes across the curves of her breasts was a sensual caress.

"A moment," Dev said, and his voice was very soft amidst the hubbub of the ballroom, the tinkle of the music and the clamor of voices, soft but with an edge of steel. "This time you don't walk away from me until I am ready, Susanna. This time you stay at my pleasure."

CHAPTER THREE

DEV LOOKED AT HIS FORMER wife's exquisite, defiant face and felt his temper soar dangerously again. She was damnably beautiful and his body reacted to the temptation she presented even as his mind dismissed her as the most conniving, duplicitous little harlot that had ever lived. He wanted to kiss her; to take that wide, sensuous mouth with his own, to bite down on the full lower lip and slide his tongue into her mouth and taste her again with all the explosive passion they had known before. He wanted to prove her indifference to him to be a sham. He wanted to strip the silver gown from her pale limbs and plunder her body ruthlessly until she was utterly quiescent in his arms.

It was hell being a reformed rake. He had given up other women when he had become betrothed to Emma but Dev knew that he was not really reformed at all. He might as well admit it. This dangerous attraction he had to Susanna was proof enough. Given half a chance, a quarter of a chance, he would like to ravish Susanna, to take her with merciless abandon and revel in the experience. Never had chastity seemed so unappealing an option. Never had his betrothal seemed so dull and colorless in contrast to the appeal of his treacherous former wife.

He could feel Susanna's pulse hammering beneath his fingers. The silk of her glove gave her no protection from him. He knew that she wanted him as much as he wanted her.

And yet he was also ready to strangle her. Disloyal, deceitful Susanna Burney, who had seemed so radiantly innocent, had taken him royally for a fool. He had thought that he had seduced and wed a naive young girl. Instead she had been using him to gain a little worldly experience.

Dev exerted absolute self-discipline to keep himself under control. He felt a raw edge of anger as cutting as a blade. A moment before, when he had challenged Susanna about her family's duplicity, he had felt a fleeting uncertainty. He had seen the shock in her eyes and thought that she must have been in ignorance of their vile pretence. Her mocking words had swiftly put paid to that idea. Instead of being a victim she had been at the heart of the plan to deceive him.

He looked at her. She was watching him and despite that fierce attraction that locked them together there was also a derisive glint in her green eyes. He wondered how it was possible to be so mistaken in a woman. The Susanna Burney he had known at eighteen had seemed so shy and sweet. It was difficult to see how she could have changed into this brazen creature. On the other hand he had to accept that it was almost ten years ago, he had been eighteen years old and perhaps not such a man of the world as he had liked to imagine. Doubtless he had been the one who was naive. His judgment had certainly been spectacularly flawed when it came to his adoring bride.

"There was no need to wed me if all you wanted was to be rid of your virginity," he said grimly. "You should have told me. I would have been happy to oblige you—without the benefit of clergy."

Their eyes tangled. He saw the sensual heat flare again in hers, turning them a darker green, bright as emeralds. In a split second he was transported from the bustling ballroom to the intimate darkness of their marriage bed. They had had one night only, one night of sweet desire and passion richer and deeper than his most vivid dreams. She had been the first and only woman he had loved. That sense of intimacy had been more frightening than the reckless pleasure he had found in her arms. That emotion had been strong and profound enough to bind him to her forever. Then she had run out on him the next day and ripped everything apart.

Now she stood looking at him with cool disdain, the desire banished from her eyes.

"You misunderstand," she said. "Marriage was a necessity. I had no wish to be a whore."

Dev looked her over with studied contempt. "In

your case I am struggling to tell the difference," he said.

Susanna's eyes narrowed to an inimical gleam. "Then let me explain it to you," she said. Dev watched her slender, gloved fingers trace a pattern on the windowpane. "It was so tediously dreary in my uncle's house," she said, "and we were poor and I did not care for it. I knew I was pretty and clever enough to seduce a rich man into marriage but I needed experience as well as beauty. No one was going to look twice at me buried away in that village, the dull schoolmaster's little niece." She moved slightly and the diamond necklace at her throat sparkled, rich and malevolent. "I was afraid that I would be stuck there forever, expiring with the boredom of it all." Her hand moved to caress the glittering stones at her neck. "So I contrived a plan. To wed you, learn what I needed from you and then move on to better things." Her gaze came up to meet his.

"You were no one, Devlin," she said gently. "You had no money and precious few prospects. But I could see that you could be useful to me." Her eyes were bright and hard. "I wanted to be young and beautiful and intriguing enough to lure a very rich man into marriage. It was not good enough to be a courtesan. I had to be respectable enough to catch a husband—" her luscious mouth turned up in a little, private smile "—but improper enough to know how to please him in bed." She turned away from him so that all he could see was her reflection in the glass of the window and that lingering smile.

"I flatter myself that I was rather good," she said. "I posed as a widow. I had many suitors."

Dev could believe it. She was beautiful enough to tempt a saint and there was a knowing air to her, a sensual allure that was provocative enough to make any man want to please as well as possess her. Of course she would set her sights much higher than merely being a courtesan. That would have been a course from which she could never have regained respectability. Instead, as a beautiful widow she would have drawn suitors like moths to the flame. They would have begged for her notice. Only he knew the venal heart beneath her lovely facade.

"So you killed me off as well as yourself," he said coldly. "How very tidy of you."

"Oh, I never mentioned your name," Susanna said. "No one ever asked about my first husband. I suppose that if they had I could have admitted to the annulment and painted our marriage as a youthful indiscretion." She raised her brows as though inviting his congratulations. "Yes, it was a neat plan, was it not?"

"I'm still having trouble with the difference between a courtesan and a woman who buys herself a rich husband with her body," Dev said.

Susanna shrugged, apparently indifferent to his disapproval. "You are too particular. We all use the advantages we are given."

She had been given plenty, Dev thought grimly. That angel's face, that lissome, lovely body—and a grasping nature that cared nothing for the pain she inflicted on others. It was a pity he had not been able to see past the obvious when they had first met but he had been a youth confronted by a beautiful girl. He had not been thinking with his head but with a different and far more basic part of his anatomy.

He felt cold at the sheer calculating callousness of Susanna's plan. She had been an adventuress from the first. She had wed him, learned from him the arts she needed to please a man in bed and then left him to pursue bigger, richer prey. Armed with her annulment she would indeed be free to remarry. He could see how much the combination of her youth, beauty, wit, experience and the tiniest hint of a mysterious past might appeal to a wealthy older man. Hell, it was obvious that Fitz was already in thrall to her. Even he could barely look at her without wanting to plunder every inch of that exquisite, perfidious body, and he knew what a lying, conniving strumpet she was.

"You mistake if you think that you are not a whore," he said. "You have whored yourself out for money whether it is by marriage or not."

The candlelight shimmered on some expression in Susanna's eyes that was, for one tiny second, utterly at odds with her brazen words. But then it was gone and all that was left was contempt.

"You should know, Devlin," she said. "Are you not doing precisely the same thing, catching an heiress with your good looks and charm?" Her perfect brows arched. "If I am a whore, what does that make you?"

Dev took a furious step toward her—and stopped when he saw the triumph in her eyes. She was glad she had been able to goad him into near-indiscretion. He drew in a deep breath.

"You are also mistaken if you think you learned all there is to pleasure a man in one night at my hands," he ground out. "But should you wish to extend your experience I am, of course, at your disposal."

"As you were nine years ago." She smiled, not one whit discomposed, as cool as spring water. "I thank you but there is no need. I have addressed the deficiencies in my education in the past few years."

Dev was sure that she had. There had been her remarriage to Carew, who had presumably been an affluent baronet. Perhaps there had been other lovers as well, or even previous marriages. And now she truly was a rich widow and he suspected she was hunting another trophy. A marquis, perhaps…

He had been played. He had been used—comprehensively, ruthlessly. Susanna had seen him as a mere stepping-stone to better things. He, the fortune hunter, should appreciate her strategy. He did not.

Suddenly he could see Chessie's hopes for the future vanishing like mist in the sun. He could see just how vulnerable both he and his sister were with no more than foothold in the ton. One false step, one piece of bad luck, could send them tumbling back into the void of poverty and despair that had been their childhood on the streets of Dublin. Dev had experienced both unimaginable wealth and abject poverty several times; as the son of a compulsive gambler he had known the extremes of rich and poor before he was barely out of short trousers. That fear, that knowledge, had driven him ever since. He could not permit Susanna to steal Chessie's future or ruin his own plans. He would have to keep her close, watch her every move.

Susanna inclined her head to him with mock civility. "Good evening, Sir James," she said. "I wish you good luck with your fortune hunting."

"Do you?" Dev said, politely incredulous.

She smiled. "About as much as you wish me luck with mine."

Dev watched her walk away, her figure a silver flame in the sinuous dress, the diamonds sparkling in her hair and the heels of her silver embroidered slippers tapping on the floor.

Keep her close… In some ways it would be no hardship. In others it would be the most dangerous thing that he could do.

SUSANNA WAS STILL SHAKING as she climbed into the carriage. She did not expect Dev to come after her again—she had made very sure that he would not—but the antagonism of their encounter still beat through her blood with primitive force. It was impossible to believe that once upon a time she and Dev had made love with such exquisite tenderness. Now there was nothing left.

She remembered Dev's bitter condemnation of her, the disgust in his eyes, and she felt shot through with regret. There had been no other way to drive him away from her. She could not afford for anyone to uncover the truth about her past, not now when so much was at stake. This was her last job. With the money the Duke and Duchess of Alton would be paying her for separating Fitz from Chessie she would at last have sufficient funds to settle her debts, return to Scotland and provide a home for her twin wards, Rory and Rose, the children of her best friend. The three of them needed to be together, to be a family once again as they had been in the beginning. Susanna's heart ached with a sudden fierce pang that made her breath catch in her throat. She hated this life, hated playing a role, hated the deception and hated most of all the fact that there was no one who knew, no one she could confide in. She was on her own. She always had been, from the moment her aunt and uncle had thrown her out, pregnant, destitute, seventeen years old.

She touched the diamond necklace at her throat. They were borrowed plumes, like the carriage and the house in Curzon Street, the beautiful gown and the silver slippers. Nothing was real. She was a counterfeit lady, a Cinderella whose carefully constructed world might vanish in a puff of smoke if anyone found out the truth. She touched the dress gently, almost reverentially. When she had been selling such gowns for a living, her head spinning with tiredness from the long hours working in poor light, her fingers sore from the needle and cut by the thread, she had dreamed of wearing such a beautiful creation and being the belle of the ball. Tonight she had been that fairy-tale princess, yet beneath the layers of silk and lace she was still little Susanna Burney, a fraud who feared discovery.

Once again Dev's face rose in her mind's eye, hard, unyielding, his expression full of scorn. He was the one of whom she had to beware. If Dev had suspected for a moment that she had been thrown out onto the street, disowned, disinherited, abandoned, he would start to ask all the difficult questions she wanted to avoid. He would uncover her past and ruin the future that was so close within her grasp.

Susanna leaned her head back against the cushions of the seat and closed her eyes. If only… If only she had not run off to marry Dev secretly in the first and last impulsive action of her life. If only she had not had the idea of going to Lord Grant, Dev's cousin, the next morning, to confess and ask for his support for them. If only she had not run back to the perceived security of her aunt and uncle's house and had tried to pretend nothing had happened. If only she had not been pregnant with Dev's child… One disastrous decision had set in train a course of events that had led to the poorhouse and to places in her own mind that were so full of despair that she never wanted to go there again. The tiny body of her child wrapped in its pitiful shroud, the words of the priest, the gray dawn mist creeping over the Edinburgh graveyard...

With a gasp of pain Susanna buried her face in her hands, then she let them fall and stared into the darkness, her eyes dry. She must never think of that again. Never. The dark clouds hovered like beating wings. She pushed them away, closing her eyes, breathing deeply, until she felt the panic subside and the calm seep back into her mind. She had lost her own daughter but she had Rory and Rose to care for and she clung to them with the fierceness of a tigress. She had given her word to their mother, there in the bitter dark chill of the poorhouse, in the cold hours before Flora's death, and sometimes it seemed that the gift of the twins was both penitence and blessing to her. She had lost Maura but she could make amends now and she would never, ever let Rory and Rose down, which was why it was imperative that Dev must never learn the truth and scupper her plans.

Sighing, she kicked off her pretty silver evening slippers and flexed her toes. Her feet ached. Cinderella's slippers were all very well but they were not comfortable. Her headache, which had originally been an excuse to escape Frederick Walters's importunities, was a reality now. All she wanted was to be home.

The carriage passed a group of young bucks noisily drinking and carousing in the street. Hot summer nights reminded Susanna of Edinburgh in the days when she had dragged herself out of the poorhouse to work as a tavern wench and ballad singer. She had such a checkered past, she thought, with a rueful smile. The tavern, the gown shop… It had been through good looks and sheer luck that she had fallen into her extraordinary work as a heartbreaker, paid by parents to ruin the unsuitable matches of their rich and titled offspring.

Susanna rubbed her temples where the diamond clasp was pulling her hair. The night had started so well. The Duke and Duchess of Alton had introduced her to Fitz and he had seemed intrigued by her and definitely more than a little interested in taking their acquaintance further. She had sparkled, flirted, playing the mysterious widow to perfection. She and Fitz had waltzed together and she had allowed him to hold her a little closer than convention dictated. Everything had been going smoothly. She had even started to plan the next step—another meeting with Fitz, one that would appear to happen quite by chance but would in fact be the result of the Duke and Duchess paying their son's valet some extortionate amount to disclose the details of his master's diary. That was how she was always one step ahead of the game; before she even met her victim—or her assignment as she preferred to think of him—she would know every last thing about him, his likes and dislikes, the places he frequented, his interests, his weaknesses.

The weaknesses were especially useful, whether they were for women, gambling, drink or all of the above in combination. It was her tried and tested method. Size up the man, learn everything there was to know about him, flatter his opinions and mix in a touch of seduction. No one had been able to resist.

That was the way that the acquaintance should have gone with Fitzwilliam Alton. A chance encounter in the Park, an invitation to ride with him, the promise of a dance at the next ball, a little dalliance, until Fitz was dazzled, hers to command. If necessary she would go as far as a betrothal, before breaking it off with all due regret a month or so later. That was the way she had intended it, before James Devlin had appeared and threatened all her plans.

She thought of Dev, his blue eyes full of anger and loathing as he watched her.

A shiver racked her. She was sure that he had already worked out that she was intent on spoiling his sister's plans to catch Fitz. He would assume that she wanted Fitz for herself, of course; it was most unlikely he would uncover the true nature of her work as a matchbreaker, for this was the first time she had come to London or worked in such exalted social circles. It was a risk, but she should be safe from exposure. Whether she was safe from Dev revealing the truth of their previous relationship was another matter but she guessed that he had no wish for his winsome heiress to know the truth. Lady Emma

Brooke had not seemed a particularly pliable fiancée and she was surely the one with the money.

Which brought her back to the annulment. Guilt squirmed in her stomach again. She knew that she should have formally ended her marriage a long time ago. Once the Duke and Duchess's commission was complete and she and Rory and Rose were safe, she would pay for the annulment and leave Dev free to wed Emma. He would never know.

She opened her reticule and took out a rather squashed pastry cake that she had purloined from the refreshment room at the ball. Her bag was full of crumbs. She had ruined more reticules this way than any other. She took a bite and felt instantly comforted as the sweet pastry melted on her tongue. Eating had always made her feel better whether she was hungry or not. She tended to eat as much as she could whenever food was laid out before her, a legacy of the time when she had not known where her next square meal would come from. It was surprising that she had not split her sensuous silver silk gown as a result.

Despite her attempts to push the past away, the memories rippled through her again: Dev holding her hand before the altar as the minister intoned the solemn words of the marriage service, Dev smiling at her as she stumbled a little over her vows in shyness and fear, even then expecting the church door to slam open and her uncle to march in to reclaim her. Dev's touch had been reassuring and the warmth in his eyes had steadied her. She had felt loved and wanted for the first time in many long cold years.

For a second she was shot through with regret so sharp and poignant that it made her gasp. First love had been very sweet and innocent.

First love had been hopelessly naive.

Susanna turned her shoulder against the rich velvet cushions of the carriage and let the memories slip from her like sand running through the fingers. It was stupid and pointless to have regrets or to dwell on the past. What she had had with James Devlin had been a girl's fantasy. Now he had nothing but contempt for her. And soon, if she were successful in her plan to take Fitz away from Francesca, Dev would hate her even more.

CHAPTER FOUR

THE HACKNEY CARRIAGE put Miss Francesca Devlin down in front of a set of anonymous rooms in Hemming Row. She stood on the cobbles feeling a little drunk with a mixture of guilt, fear and a giddy excitement that was making her head spin. This was a part of town she had visited for the first time only two weeks ago. It was an unfashionable quarter where she knew no one and no one knew her; that, she had been told, was the beauty of the place. Her reputation was quite safe. No one would ever know what she had done.

After her first visit she had promised herself that it was just the once and it would never happen again. She had gone through the motions of her daily life exactly as she had done before. Nothing was different. Yet everything was different.

The second summons had come this very night, at the Duke and Duchess of Alton's ball. Chessie had tucked the note into her reticule, hidden it beneath a white embroidered handkerchief and had spent the rest of the evening in an agony of impatience mixed with anticipation. She had known from the moment she unfolded the note that she would go. Like her brother she had inherited a streak of recklessness, a need to gamble, and this was the greatest game of her life. If she won she would secure everything that she had ever desired. If she lost… But she did not want to think about losing. Not tonight.

Gambling was in Chessie's blood. Her childhood had been stalked by poverty, the furniture pawned to pay her father's debts and no food on the table. Those moments had been interspersed with rare occasions when they had been so rich it seemed to Chessie that she could not quite believe the grandeur of it all. On one occasion her father had won so much that they had ridden around Dublin in a golden carriage pulled by two white horses like something from a fairy tale. That day she had eaten so much she had thought she would burst. She had gone to sleep between silken sheets and in the morning she had woken and the carriage and horses had gone and her mother was crying, and within a week the silken sheets had gone, too, and they were back to coarse blankets. And then when she was six, her father had died.

Through it all there had been Devlin, four years older than she, tough, protective, grown harder than any child should have to be, determined to defend her and his mother, too, no matter the cost. Chessie knew Dev had worked for them, had very probably begged, borrowed and stolen for them, too. It was Dev who, after their mother died, had gone to their cousin Alex Grant and made him take responsibility for them. The experience had bound them as close as a brother and sister could be. They had had no secrets—until now.

Chessie paused on the doorstep and almost ran back to the house in Bedford Street where Alex and Joanna thought that she was safely in her bed, back to the world she knew. Except that it was too late, for she had already taken the steps that would leave that world behind. She had done things that a fortnight ago she would not have dreamed of—gone out unchaperoned at night, traveled alone in a hackney carriage, things that other people did all the time but which were forbidden to a young girl of unimpeachable reputation. She smothered a laugh that had a wild edge to it. Young girls did not indulge in games of chance with a gentleman. Nor did they pay with their bodies when they lost.

The door opened silently to her knock and then he was drawing her into the candlelit room where the gaming table was already set up and the cards waiting. Chessie thought about winning and felt a rush of excitement that lit her blood like fire. Then she thought about losing and shivered with a different sort of excitement. He was kissing her already, with a passion that stoked her desires and soothed her fears. This could not be wrong because it felt right. Her gamble was not really on the cards but on love, and surely love conquered all. He released her; smiled.

"SHALL WE PLAY?" he said. "This is no place for a lady." Susanna jumped and almost hit her head on the wooden rail of the stall. She had been kneeling in the straw to examine the horse that Fitz had picked out for her at the latest Tattersalls' sale. Even at a distance she had known it was a poor choice. It looked beautiful with a shiny bay coat and bright eyes but its chest was a fraction too narrow and its legs just a little too short. Naturally she had not told Fitz any of those things. She had congratulated him on his judgment and had watched him preen.

Only a moment before, Susanna had been congratulating herself, too, silently applauding how well her plans were progressing. It had taken her four days only to gain Fitz's undivided attention to the point that he was now probably prepared to buy her a horse never mind simply recommend one to her. He had already tried to buy her emeralds but Susanna knew exactly what he would expect in return for those and had refused them, prettily, regretfully but very finally. She had played the virtuous widow to perfection. Becoming Fitz's mistress was definitely not part of the plan.

Instead she had treated Fitz as a friend, deferred to his opinion, leaned on his advice and flattered his judgment. He had helped her to buy a carriage and now a riding horse. They were using his parents' money, but of course he was unaware of that. Susanna could see how much the role of confidant confused Fitz—he was not accustomed to viewing beautiful women in a capacity of friendship, not unless they had occupied his bed first. He was puzzled, bewildered and intrigued, which was exactly as Susanna wanted him to be. His parents were delighted to see their son so thoroughly distracted from his courtship of Francesca Devlin, which made them generous. All had been set fair, but she might have known that Dev would reappear to put a spoke in her wheel.

Susanna sat back on her heels. There was a pair of very elegant riding boots now in her line of vision, radiant with a champagne polish. Above those were muscular thighs encased in skintight pantaloons, and above that she dared not look. How tiresome to be kneeling in the Tattersalls' straw at the feet of James Devlin.

"Mr. Tattersall welcomes ladies to his auctions," she said, raising her gaze to meet Dev's and trying to keep her eyes firmly focused on his face even though it gave her a crick in the neck to do so.

"The only females welcome here are the ones whose pedigrees are better than those of the horses," Dev said. "Which rules you out, Lady Carew."

He made no move to help her to her feet. Susanna was acutely aware of the prickling discomfort of the straw through the velvet skirts of her riding habit and the strong scent of horse that surrounded them. God forbid that the bay gelding would choose this moment to relieve itself.

For a second she thought she would be obliged to

scramble up of her own accord, flushed, undignified and covered in hay, but then Dev leaned down and grabbed her arm, pulling her to her feet with rather more strength than finesse. The maneuver brought her into his arms for one brief moment and the scent of leather and cedar soap and fresh air on his skin overlaid that of horse and set Susanna's senses awry. She could feel the hard muscle of his arm beneath the smooth blue superfine of his coat. He felt like a man whose body was in prime physical condition. Evidently waiting on Lady Emma must be more physically punishing than she had imagined.

Susanna experienced the oddest sensation, as though the layers of clothes between them had melted away and she was touching Dev's bare flesh, warm and smooth under her fingers. Never had she been so acutely aware of a man and so swiftly, her defenses shattered by simple proximity. Her cheeks flaming, she freed herself hastily from Dev's grip and saw him smile, that wicked, sardonic smile she remembered.

"Feeling the heat, Lady Carew?"

"Suffering as a result of your discourtesy," Susanna snapped.

He raised a brow. "There was a time when you did not object to being held in my arms." He straightened, driving his hands into the pockets of his coat. "But of course, I forgot—that was for educational purposes only, was it not?" His voice was heavily laced with irony. "That horse has a chest that's too narrow and legs that are too short," he added, running an eye over the bay in the box.

"I know," Susanna said crossly. She dusted the palms of her gloves slightly self-consciously and started to pick the straw off her velvet riding skirts. "I suppose you are an expert on horseflesh?"

"Not particularly." Dev's admission surprised her. "Not all the Irish grow up in the country, able to whisper horses from birth." His expression darkened. "I grew up on the streets of Dublin. The only horses there were drays and sad creatures pulling rich men's carriages."

Their eyes met and the breath caught in Susanna's throat. Her heart skipped a beat, two. She thought how odd it was that life could still trick her after all she had experienced, that it could trip her up unexpectedly like a false step in the dark. She remembered being seventeen, lying in the summer grass with the stars whirling overhead and Dev turning away her questions about his childhood with light answers. She had not known anything about his early life other than that it had been poverty-stricken like her own. They had not talked much about anything, she thought now, with a sharp stab of regret. They had laughed together and had kissed with sweet urgency. They had both been so eager and so young.

"You never told me much about your childhood," she said, and regretted the words as soon as they were out of her mouth.

Dev's expression hardened into coldness. "That hardly matters now."

Susanna winced at the rebuff and the sharp reminder that none of Dev's life was any of her business now. He and Francesca had climbed high, she thought. She had known that Dev's parents were impoverished gentry; for him to be betrothed to the daughter of an earl and for Chessie to aspire to marry a duke's heir was fortune hunting of the highest order. Except that Chessie would not now be Duchess of Alton. It was her job to make sure of that.

Susanna felt a wayward pang of sympathy for Miss Francesca Devlin. Normally she was able to console herself that her assignments were better off separated from the object of their desire. The gentlemen she was engaged to lead astray were so often libertines or wastrels or simply weak-willed and unworthy. And it was true that she had no great opinion of Fitz, who seemed to embody all the vices of his class and none of the virtues: arrogance, self-centeredness and profligacy in just about everything. But even so, even if Francesca could do so much better than Fitz, Susanna admired her enterprise in trying to catch the heir to a dukedom. In some ways Francesca was an adventuress just as she was and it was a pity to ruin her chances.

Awkwardness hung in the air. Dev, whilst showing no desire to converse with her, also showed no inclination to leave. Across the yard Fitz was deep in conversation with Freddie Walters as they admired a glossy black hunter.

"Your sister does not accompany you today?" Susanna asked politely, slipping out of the stall.

Dev shook his head. "Francesca is shopping in Bond Street with our cousin Lady Grant. Some last-minute purchases for a ball tomorrow, I believe."

"Lady Grant?" Susanna said. She could hear the odd note in her own voice and feel the sudden dryness in her throat.

Dev had heard her tone, too. He gave her a sharp look. "My cousin Alex remarried a couple of years ago," he said. He paused. "You lived on Alex's Scottish estate—presumably you knew he had lost his first wife?"

"No," Susanna said. She could hear a rushing sound in her ears. For a second the sunlight seemed too bright and too hot, dazzling her. So Amelia Grant had died. Amelia, who had befriended her, advised her and ultimately ruined her future. But it was futile to blame Amelia for her own lack of courage. Lady Grant had merely played on fears that were already in her own mind. She had exploited Susanna's youth and her weakness, that was true, but Susanna knew that the ultimate responsibility for running away from Devlin was hers and hers alone.

"I thought your aunt and uncle might have kept you informed of news from Balvenie," Dev said.

"My aunt and uncle died a long time ago," Susanna said.

Dev's lips twisted. "Am I supposed to believe that, or will they resurrect as swiftly as you have?"

Susanna ignored him and turned away, stroking the silky neck of the gelding. "You have a sweet nature," she said to the horse, "but I don't think you would make a good mount." The horse whickered softly, pressing its velvet nose into her gloved hand.

"Too lazy," Dev concurred. "I suppose Fitz picked the horse out for you." His gaze came to rest on her, bright and mocking. "He never sees beyond the obvious. For him it is all about show and he has as poor taste in horses as he has poor judgment of women." He smiled. "Are you going to flatter him to the extent of paying good money for a bad horse?"

"Of course not," Susanna said. Dev's words had stung, as they had been meant to do. She could see the dislike in his eyes, chill and unyielding. Nothing could have made it clearer to her that it was far too late for regrets and far too late to go back. Dev believed her to be conniving and duplicitous, which was no great surprise since she had made sure he would believe it by spinning him a pack of lies.

For a moment she wanted to cry out to him that it had not been her fault, to take back all the things she had said three nights ago at the ball and pour out the truth. The strength of her impulse shook her deeply. But she could not do it. Whatever had been between them was dead and gone anyway and now she had a job to do, the only thing that stood between her and penury. She had not fought every inch of the way to save herself and the twins in order to throw it all away now. The thought of losing all she had worked for terrified her. Their lives were on a knife-edge as it was.

Nevertheless her heart shriveled, cold and tight, to see the contempt in Dev's eyes. The only defense she had was to pretend he did not have the power to hurt her anymore.

"You have read the fortune-hunter's rulebook, too," she taunted. "You know full well I shall thank Fitz for choosing me such a fine beast and compliment him on his discernment whilst pleading my privilege as a female to change my mind and hold on to my money. My choice," she added, "would be that mare over there." She pointed to a spirited chestnut that was being shown around the ring.

"You have a good eye for quality." Somehow Dev managed to make even that compliment sound like an insult. "Mares can be a handful," he added, his gaze dwelling thoughtfully on her face. "But perhaps you are looking to ride something more exciting than a steady gelding this time?"

His meaning was crystal clear beneath the thin veneer of civility. Susanna's gaze clashed with his and she saw the challenge in his eyes.

"I prefer a horse with spirit and attitude," she said. "Whereas you—" she tilted her head thoughtfully, eyes narrowed on him "—would probably pick something as unsubtle as that stallion simply as a fashion accessory. All muscles and no brain."

Dev gave a crack of laughter. "I wouldn't throw away that much money on something that might kill me."

"You have changed then," Susanna said politely. Then added, as he raised his brows in quizzical challenge, "Wild-goose chases to Mexico in search of treasure, ludicrously dangerous missions for the British Navy, a preposterous voyage to the Arctic during which you boarded another ship as though you were a pirate..." She stopped as the look in his eyes turned to pure amusement.

"You have been following my career," he murmured. "How flattering and unexpected. Could you not quite let me go, Susanna?"

Susanna had in fact followed every step of Devlin's career but she did not want him to know that. It would only feed his conceit, as well as raising awkward questions about why she had cared, questions she could not and did not want to answer.

"I read the scandal sheets," she said, shrugging. "They convinced me that you were as reckless as I had always believed you to be."

"Reckless," Dev said. There was an odd tone in his voice. "Yes, I have always been that, Susanna."

At seventeen Susanna had loved that wildness in him, such a counterpoint to her staid and predictable life. She had been dazzled, blinded by the thrill of it all, swept away. Their secret meetings had been breathtakingly illicit. The risk had transfixed her. Even though a tiny, sensible part of her mind had argued that Dev was too handsome and too exciting ever to belong to her, she had wanted to believe that he could. Even though she had secretly suspected he had only proposed to her because he wanted to sleep with her, she had wanted to believe he truly loved her. For one brief day and night she had given herself up to pleasure, feeling alive for the first time in years, lit up with love and excitement. But in the morning had come the reckoning and after that she had paid and paid.

She swallowed what felt like a huge lump in her throat. It was too late now to regret her lack of courage or faith. She did not know why she should feel this misery, as though she had let something valuable slip away, because over the years Dev had surely proved himself exactly as irresponsible and rash and dangerous as she had known he would be.

"I am not Susanna anymore," she said. "I am Caroline Carew, remember?"

Dev's hand came out and caught her sleeve. She looked up, startled, to see the spark of pure anger in his eyes.

"So you jettisoned your name along with everything else," he murmured. "You could not rid yourself of your old life fast enough, could you?"

Susanna shrugged. "One moves on from past mistakes. And Caroline is my middle name." She paused. "I hope I can rely on you to remember that I am now Caroline Carew?"

For a long moment Dev looked into her eyes and

Susanna almost flinched from the dark anger she saw there. Her heart was racing, her chest tight. Her skin prickled with awareness.

"I would hate you to think that you can rely on me for anything," he said pleasantly. "Is not ambiguity the spice of life?"

"Servant, Devlin." Fitz's bored, aristocratic tones cut across them and Dev dropped Susanna's arm as though it was a hot coal, straightened, turned and sketched Fitz a bow.

"Alton." His voice was very cold.

Fitz's gaze darted from him to Susanna's face. She pressed her gloved hands together to prevent them from shaking. There was something about Devlin's potent physical presence that got through to her every time. Over the years she had built up such a strong protective facade that she had thought it could withstand anything. Dev demolished it with one look or one touch.

"Lady Carew," Dev said, and Susanna heard the emphasis he put on the name, "is trying to decide whether to accept your recommendation, Alton."

Susanna saw the frown that touched Fitz's forehead at the suggestion that his judgment of horseflesh might not be sound.

"He is a beautiful horse, my lord," she said quickly, to repair the damage, "but I am in two minds—I can always hire a riding horse from the livery stables. Would it not be more fun to own a racehorse instead?"

She thought she heard Dev snort—but it could have been one of the horses. Fitz's face cleared miraculously.

"A racehorse!" he said enthusiastically. "Capital idea, Lady Carew! Capital!"

"I am sure," Susanna said, slipping her hand through his arm, "that it would be vastly exciting to watch it run—and to gamble on it, as well, of course."

"Only if you are plump in the pocket," Dev said dryly. His gaze traveled over her, lingering on the neat fit of her riding habit as it emphasized the lush curve of her breasts. "But I forgot—you are very well endowed, are you not, Lady Carew?"

His direct gaze brought the blood up into Susanna's face. She could remember more than Dev's gaze lingering on those curves.

"I do apologize for Devlin," Fitz said. "His cousin sent him to Eton but education don't make the man, I am sorry to say."

"No, indeed," Susanna said. Her gaze clashed with Dev's cool blue one. "I am, as you say, endowed with many advantages that you lack, Sir James, including good manners."

"Once a knave," Dev murmured, without any hint of apology. There was a glimmer of wickedness in his eyes. "But you knew that about me already, Lady Carew. You know all my secrets."

"I have no ambition to know anything about you, Sir James," Susanna said coldly. Her heart was beating a warning; how much would he risk, how much would he reveal?

"You must think yourself fascinating indeed to make yourself the subject of the conversation," she said.

She could see what Dev was trying to do: he wanted to suggest to Fitz that there was more to her than met the eye, that she had a checkered rather than a romantically mysterious past, that she had been his mistress, even. He wanted to imply that whilst she might be a rich widow now she was not the sort of person a marquis would marry, especially when there was the far more suitable virginal debutante Miss Francesca Devlin waiting patiently in the wings...

"Lady Emma not with you today, Devlin?" Fitz asked pointedly. He tightened his grip on Susanna's arm. Susanna found she did not like it but resisted the urge to pull away, instead smiling sweetly at Fitz and moving close enough to brush her body against his.

"No," Dev said. "Emma dislikes horses unless they are doing something functional such as pulling her carriage." He bowed, a sardonic light lurking in his eyes. "I can see that I am de trop here. I will leave you to throw your money away on a racehorse, Lady Carew."

"How thoughtful of you," Susanna said. "Good day, Sir James."

She could feel the tension in Fitz's body as they stood together watching Dev stroll away.

"I say, Lady Carew," Fitz said, turning to look down at her, "Devlin is most frightfully disrespectful to you. Are you sure there is nothing more between the two of you than old acquaintance?"

Mentally cursing Dev and his meddling, Susanna plastered on her most convincing smile. "I met Sir James on his cousin's estate at Balvenie in Scotland when I was little more than a child, my lord," she said. "I am afraid I did not like him and I made the mistake of letting it show. Even then Sir James was insufferably conceited and wanted all the ladies to fall at his feet. He has never forgiven me that I did not."

She had not fallen at his feet; she had fallen into his bed. But Fitz was smiling, she saw with relief. "Grant's estate, eh?" he said. "Sound fellow, Grant, but barely a feather to fly. The whole family is ramshackle. There's no breeding to speak of and bad blood in the Devlin family."

Susanna was surprised to hear him dismiss Chessie thus, especially when his attentions to her had been so marked and could surely have been nothing but honorable. But it augured well for her own plans. Chessie was as good as defeated already and none of Dev's interference could change that.

She smiled prettily, squeezing Fitz's arm. "I wonder if you have the time to accompany me to the wine merchant, my lord?" she said. "I require to purchase a special gift of champagne and I know you have a knowledge of the best vintage."

Fitz looked gratified and Susanna, her gaze falling on one of the shovels used to clear out the horse-boxes, wondered just how thickly she would have to lay on the flattery before he became suspicious of her. Dev's stringent wit and intelligence would have demolished her in an instant but there seemed to be no limit to the Marquis of Alton's self-regard.

"Delighted, Lady Carew," Fitz said. "And afterward perhaps we may celebrate with a glass together, eh?" His smile was vulpine. "I should enjoy that a great deal, just the two of us."

"That would be splendid, thank you," Susanna murmured. "I very much appreciate having a friend to lean upon when I am so new to London." She slipped her hand from Fitz's arm and walked a little ahead of him so that he could appreciate the sway of her hips beneath the luxurious fall of the velvet riding habit. She could feel Fitz's eyes on her—and sense, too, his frustration that once again she had taken a step back from the intimacy he was trying to create between them. Frustration bred eagerness, and that was exactly what she wanted from him. Smiling, she turned the corner of the yard and walked straight into Devlin, who was lounging against the doorway, an appreciative gleam in his eyes.

"Beautifully done, Susanna," he whispered. His breath stirred the tendrils of hair that had escaped from beneath her hat. She felt them brush her cheek with the lightest caress. "What a lot of practice you must have had in the art of seduction."

"Endless amounts," Susanna agreed. She saw that Fitz had stopped for a final word with Richard Tattersall and cursed the delay. The last thing she wanted to do was reengage with Dev again and to give him another opportunity to undo all her good work.

"I thought that you had gone," she seethed.

"Alas, I could not tear myself away," Dev said. "I felt an almost overwhelming desire to see in action the methods employed by the modern adventuress." He smiled straight into her eyes. "You are a consummate professional, Susanna."

"And you are a damned nuisance," Susanna snapped.

Dev kissed her fingers. She tried to withdraw her hand but he held her tight. His touch seared her even through the material of her glove. Her palm tingled.

"Choose another victim," he murmured. "You could have anyone. Leave Fitz alone."

"No," Susanna said. "It is Fitz that I want."

Something flared in Dev's eyes, something dark and dangerous and hot. It held her captive whilst her pulse raced and her stomach tumbled.

"Liar," he said. "It's me that you still want."

Susanna raised her chin. It might be true that she was still damnably susceptible to him but it was also time to give him a magnificent setdown. "You are mistaken, Sir James," she said sweetly. "You are so conceited that you have come to believe yourself irresistible." She flicked her hand from his grasp. "You might do very well for Lady Emma Brooke as she is clearly too young to know any better," she continued. "But I assure you that rich widows can do a sight better than a penniless fortune hunter."

"I did not mean that you wanted to marry me—again," Dev said pleasantly. His gaze fell to her mouth, lingered there. "I meant that you wanted to—"

"To see the back of you," Susanna said. "Very quickly. Don't make trouble for me," she added, "unless you wish me to do the same for you."

Dev laughed. "I look forward to it." He nodded to her. "Good luck, Lady Carew."

"I don't need luck," Susanna said. "I have skill. Hurry back to your winsome heiress," she added, "before some other unprincipled adventurer steals her from you."

Dev nodded. "Advice from the best." He bowed. "Your servant, Lady Carew."

"I do not believe that for a moment," Susanna said.

The laughter fled Dev's eyes. "Once I was yours to command, Susanna," he said. "All yours and no one else's." He raised a hand in farewell and walked away, leaving Susanna feeling shaken by a minor earthquake. For in that moment she knew Dev had spoken the truth. He had been hers and she had destroyed everything that had been between them and she would never have that again.

CHAPTER FIVE

THERE WAS NOTHING, DEV thought, quite like a group of ill-assorted people who did not enjoy one another's company pretending to be having a marvelous time. It was raining, they were in St. Paul's Cathedral and they were looking at tombs because Susanna had expressed a wish to see some of the more esoteric sights of London. Dev had wondered what the hell she was playing at—until he had overheard Fitz praising her for her intelligence as well as her beauty. Cunning jade. Fitz was pretty stupid himself, Dev thought, but he liked to consider himself cultured and what better way than to show the dazzling Lady Carew around this historic site that was the burial place of heroes.

"Remind me what we are doing here again?" Chessie grumbed at him. "I was supposed to be attending Lady Astridge's musicale this afternoon. Instead you bring me to this mausoleum so that I can watch Fitz dance attendance on Lady Carew." Her pretty face screwed up into a tighter expression of disgust. "If I had wanted to torture myself I would have stayed at home and read an improving book."

Dev drew his sister behind one of the huge pillars

that supported the soaring roof. He wanted to tell her to stop being so childish and petulant, but he supposed she did have an excuse. For the last fortnight it seemed that Susanna's name—or at least her assumed name—had been on everyone's lips. The ton was full of the arrival of the beautiful, rich widow in their midst, the papers followed her every move, the London gown shops reportedly sent her dresses hoping she would wear them to the nightly balls she attended. And Fitz was now behaving as though he could not quite remember whom Chessie was, so dazzled was he by his new inamorata. To Chessie, fathoms deep in love with Fitz and now thwarted and ignored, it must be unbearable. Dev felt a pang of sympathy for his little sister, who had been so close to her fairy-tale betrothal and was now slighted. Chessie was pining visibly, losing weight, appearing thin and wan, all her vivacious sparkle lost. The ton was laughing at her. Emma had told Dev all about the gossip and had, he thought, derived a certain pleasure from doing so.

"We are here to thwart Lady Carew," he said calmly, "and you will not do so by flouncing around like a child in a temper."

A spark of interest came into Chessie's eyes. "Tell me how I am to achieve that then," she said.

"By being everything that Lady Carew is not," Dev said.

Chessie's mouth drooped. "You want me to be ugly and stupid? I cannot see how that will help."

Dev stifled a grin. It was true that Susanna was both beautiful and intelligent and no matter how much he detested her it was pointless to deny it. Very few men would be indifferent to Susanna. Some might dislike her wit, but with them she would be clever enough to pretend to be stupid. It was difficult to identify her weakness but he was determined to find it. Find it and use it against her.

"You are younger than Lady Carew," he said. "That will do for a start."

Chessie arched her brows. "Is that the best we can do? I am a year or two younger?"

"Four years," Dev said, without thinking.

Chessie frowned. "How do you know?" Her gaze was a little too penetrating for Dev's liking. "Did you know her very well in Scotland?"

Intimately.

Dev glanced across to where Susanna was perusing her guidebook, head bent, a very pretty picture of beauty and scholarship combined. Superimposed on the image of the bluestocking was another, that of the wanton beauty who had lain in his arms for just one night. In the heat of their lovemaking her cool reserve had dissolved into the most fierce and passionate desire. She had refused him nothing and he, drunk with the need to possess her, had ravished every last exquisite inch of her. His body tightened on the thought and he slammed the memory back down into darkness where it belonged. Reigniting that flame, feeling himself burn again for her, was not something he could ever tolerate. He was in control now. He was not that headstrong boy who had fancied himself in love.

"Dev?" Chessie's gaze had become even more quizzical.

Dev shrugged the question away. "I'm just guessing," he said. "And she is a widow—"

"Which Fitz likes," Chessie said gloomily. "He prefers the older, more sophisticated woman."

"Only as a mistress, not as a wife," Dev said.

Chessie sighed. "Do you think that all she wants is an affaire? Perhaps if I wait—"

"You're too good to sit around waiting for Fitz whilst he takes another woman as a mistress," Dev snapped. He felt very grim and it was not simply all the tombs that were lowering his mood. He knew Susanna had set her sights on Fitz and he was certain she was not simply interested in an affaire. Watching his former wife become Fitz's mistress would have been bad enough, evoking in him the sort of primal anger that Dev did not want to examine too closely, but seeing her become Marchioness of Alton evoked an equally strong reaction in him compounded of the same white-hot possessiveness and a fury that Susanna could so easily, so carelessly, ruin Chessie's hopes. He clenched his hands within the pockets of his coat. Possessiveness was misplaced when his short-lived marriage to Susanna was as dead as ashes. Fury would not help, either. Cold, hard calculation was what was needed now to stop Susanna in her tracks.

"Perhaps I could become Fitz's mistress instead," Chessie was saying. "Beat her to the job—"

Dev grabbed her. "Don't even say that in jest, Chessie," he said through his teeth.

For a second he saw fear reflected in Chessie's eyes. Her eyes swam with tears. "It was only an idea—"

"A very bad one," Dev said. He let her go; tried to lighten the mood. "Apart from anything else," he said, "I would have to put a bullet through Fitz and then Emma wouldn't want to marry me anymore."

Chessie gave a little watery giggle. "That would be no loss other than in the financial sense."

"I used to like Fitz," Dev said, "before he started behaving like an ass."

"That is because you and he had so much in common," Chessie said with the sort of unflattering truth that only a sister could get away with. "You both like women and gambling and sport and drink. Or at least you used to," she added. "When you were permitted to do so. Before Emma."

"One thing I don't like is sightseeing in a mausoleum," Dev said. Susanna had wandered across the aisle now and was looking up at the mosaics that rioted across the cathedral's dome. As he watched, a beam of watery sunlight cut through the gloom to pin her in a ray of light. She looked bright and ethereal, though anyone less like an angel would be difficult to imagine. Fitz, however, looked as though he had been struck by a vision.

"You should find someone else," Dev said abruptly.

"It was difficult enough finding Fitz," Chessie said. "Had you not noticed, Devlin, that I do not have suitors queuing up at the door?"

"You have a good dowry," Dev said. Alex, their cousin, had put ten thousand pounds aside for Chessie's future.

"A modest dowry," Chessie corrected. "No one is going to take me for that when there are heiresses to catch. Not when I have no eligible connections."

"You have me and Alex and Joanna," Dev said.

"That," Chessie said, "proves my point. No eligible connections and plenty of scandalous ones."

Dev drew her hand through his arm. "Come along. I will distract Lady Carew whilst you ask Fitz a question about Restoration architecture or something."

"Could you not do that permanently?" Chessie said hopefully. "Take Lady Carew away from Fitz, I mean. You could pretend to be in love with her. Or you could just seduce her. You used to be quite good at that sort of thing, so I heard."

"That is not the sort of thing one wants one's sister to hear," Dev said. "Or to suggest, for that matter."

"Don't be stuffy," Chessie said. "Do it for me."

Seduce Susanna…

The temptation grabbed Dev like the grip of a vise. To pursue Susanna ruthlessly, to tumble her into his bed, to sate his desire in that cool, untouchable body… He had always wanted what he could not have. Already the lust drove him at the mere thought.

He took a deep breath and the carved faces of the cherubs on the tombs swam back into focus. This was, Dev thought, a most inappropriate place to harbor such carnal thoughts.

"It wouldn't work," he said. "Lady Carew is too clever—she would realize what I was about in a moment. And Emma would probably notice, too."

"Where is Emma today?" Chessie said. "Usually she sticks to you like glue. It is very peaceful without her," she added.

"Emma is at home with the earache," Dev said. "Which is why, just this once, I can help you by distracting Lady Carew."

"You will be the one with the earache when Emma hears of it," Chessie said frankly. "And Freddie will make sure she does hear. He is a frightful gossip and malicious with it." She looked at him. "Freddie will do all he can to spoil matters for you, you know. And he will do it for fun, no better reason."

"I'll talk Emma round," Dev said.

"Your life's work," his sister said coolly. "That is your future, Devlin—charming Emma into good humor for the next forty years, all for the sake of her money." She sailed across to where Fitz, Susanna and Freddie were gathered around the tomb of Sir Joshua Reynolds and slipped her hand through Fitz's arm.

"I fear all this culture is giving me the headache,

my lord," she said. "It may well do for intellectuals like Lady Carew—" she shot Susanna a limpid smile "—but you know that I am not bookish. What do you say that we go to Gunters for refreshment instead?"

Dev grinned. There was something to be said for the direct approach and Chessie was, after all, only following his advice in being the opposite of Susanna. It had worked, too. Fitz was looking relieved at the prospect of escape and just for a second Susanna looked absolutely furious before she smoothed her irritation away and smiled in agreement with the plan. Chessie, having captured Fitz's attention at last was hanging on like a limpet and when it looked as though Fitz were about to offer his other arm to Susanna, Dev stepped forward and placed himself between them.

"I see you have the guidebook, Lady Carew," he said. "Can you tell me if Lord Nelson is buried here?"

Susanna was obliged to pause and Fitz and Chessie moved past them, walking together toward the door. They were already deep in conversation, Chessie smiling up at Fitz with sparkling eyes, all her vivacity apparently restored now that she had his attention.

In contrast, Susanna's green eyes were bright with anger rather than pleasure as they contemplated Dev's innocent expression.

"Lord Nelson is not only buried here," she said politely, "but he is spinning in his grave at the thought that a former Naval captain might not know it." She looked up at him, her body taut with annoyance, her tone fizzing with frustration. "You already knew the answer to that question, did you not, Sir James?"

"It was the best I could think of on the spur of the moment," Dev admitted, without a trace of apology. "I wanted to speak to you—"

"Again?" Susanna snapped. "I hardly flatter myself that you have an inclination for my company."

"Perhaps it would be more accurate to say that I wanted to delay you," Dev conceded.

His blunt honesty was rewarded with another glare.

"I am aware of that," Susanna said. "I understand your strategy perfectly."

She ignored the arm that he offered her and started to follow Fitz and Chessie toward the door. One of the guides was already running to call them a hackney. The fine weather had broken abruptly and the sky outside was now a dull, pale gray and rain dripped from the guttering to pool on the pavement outside the cathedral.

"I am afraid that you will have to share a carriage with me, Lady Carew," Dev said, very politely, as Fitz helped Chessie up into the first vehicle. "Unless you would prefer to ride with Mr. Walters, of course?"

"Hobson's choice," Susanna said. The quick tap of the guidebook on the palm of her gloved hand betrayed her annoyance.

"Think of me as the lesser of two evils," Dev said,

smiling at her. "Unless," he added, "you would prefer to walk to Berkeley Square in the rain? I regret I do not have an umbrella to offer you for protection."

Susanna shot him an exasperated look.

"Try not to keep the horses standing," Dev added as she hesitated.

Susanna gave an irritable sigh. "Oh, very well!" She accepted the hand Dev proffered to help her climb in, touching him with as much reluctance as though he had some contagious disease. Once inside the dark, poky interior, she released him abruptly and moved to the corner, as far away from him as possible. Dev sat opposite, stretching out his legs and crossing them at the ankle. His boots brushed the hem of her gown; Susanna moved her skirts aside with great deliberation as though he might contaminate her.

Dev smiled lazily at her through the darkness. "Fitz is easily distracted," he said. "You are going to have to exert a greater hold on him if you wish to have his sole attention."

Susanna turned her gaze on him. "Fitz is like a small child in a confectionery shop," she said. She made no effort to hide her exasperation and Dev found he almost liked her for it. There was no artifice in her—no pretence that she had any regard for Fitz other than for his title, and Dev had a reluctant admiration for that honesty. If she had pretended to any affection for the Marquis he would have despised her hypocrisy.

"An apt metaphor," he said. "Sweet and pretty confections do catch Fitz's eye." He allowed his gaze to travel over her appraisingly. "No doubt he sees you as a particularly nicely wrapped treat."

"Well, he won't be helping himself to this treat anytime soon," Susanna snapped.

"I imagine not," Dev said. "If you withhold your favors for a while you are likely to gain far more from him."

That won him another flash of those vivid green eyes. "Thank you for the advice," Susanna said. "I assure you I prize myself far too highly to become Fitz's mistress too easily." She turned her face away from him, gazing instead out of the grimy window at the rain-streaked streets. Her profile was exquisite beneath her saucy little feathered hat, eyelashes thick and black, the line of her cheek pure and sweet, her lips tilted always as though on the edge of a smile. A cluster of ebony curls nestled against her throat, so silky and black that Dev felt a physical urge to run his fingers through them to see if they were really as soft as they looked. It was extraordinary, he thought cynically, how someone as venal as Susanna Burney could look so alluring, extraordinary that her ruthlessness did not spill out in some way, spoiling the pretty picture of the captivating widow. Yet that, he supposed, was part of her skill. She did not attempt to compete with the innocence of debutantes. Her appeal lay in her sophistication and charm. In truth she was little different from a courtesan, a very high class, very talented, very beautiful courtesan, but available to the highest bidder all the same, as long as it was marriage he was offering.

"Do you intend to seduce Fitz into marriage?" he asked.

Her gaze came back to his face, mocking him. "What a very vulgar question, Sir James. I have no intention of answering."

"As you have said yourself, a widow may use certain experience to her advantage."

A smile touched Susanna's lips beneath the shadow of the bonnet. "Very true," she said. "Just as a rake may use his knowledge and skill to trap a debutante heiress."

There was silence between them, thick and taut, in the dark, enclosed world of the hackney coach. The rain drummed hard on the roof. The wheels splashed through the puddles on the road outside.

"You're staring," Susanna said coolly. "Try the window instead."

"I see London every day," Dev said. "I was admiring you."

Susanna laughed. "I doubt that very much."

"I meant in the aesthetic sense," Dev said. "You are very beautiful. I'm not telling you anything you don't know," he added.

"You can spare me the compliments," Susanna said dismissively. She smoothed her skirt with a gloved hand. "I am quite comfortable with silence."

"I was trying to play nicely," Dev said.

She cast him another glance, disdainful. "I doubt you do anything nicely, Devlin."

"I make love very nicely indeed," Dev said. "Do you not remember?"

"No." She turned her face away again so that he could not read her expression. Her voice was cold but Dev sensed some emotion beneath her words. Discomposure? Discomfort? Surely so experienced an adventuress as Susanna could not be embarrassed by a reference to their mutual past so perhaps she was simply annoyed to have given him the opportunity to raise the subject of their passionate, shameless lovemaking. He felt a sudden strong urge to bait her further.

"You must surely remember it," he said. "You were as wild and wanton in your response to me as any woman I have ever met."

For a moment he thought she would win the encounter simply by ignoring his provocation but this was too blatant for her to let it go. He saw her eyes flash as she rose to his challenge and felt a stab of triumph to be able to force a reaction from her.

"How sweet of you to recall it after all this time," she said cuttingly. "But I am afraid that for me it was in no way memorable."

Liar.

The word hung on the air between them. Dev saw a tinge of color sting her cheeks as though he had spoken aloud. He shifted on the seat, shrugging.

"Perhaps the experience has been superseded by

so many others that your memory fails you," he said politely.

She looked at him with contempt. "Perhaps you confuse my romantic past with your own, Devlin. I heard that you were scarcely fastidious in your choices before your engagement to Lady Emma. Quantity over quality was your motto, so I believe."

Touché. He had indeed been an enthusiastic rake-hell.

"Once again I am flattered by the attention you give to my life," Dev said. "Are you very interested in my romantic career?"

"Of course not!" Susanna said. Her face was very pink now; hot, angry, animated.

"All evidence to the contrary," Dev said. "It is perhaps an odd preoccupation for my former wife—"

"You always did have good opinion of yourself," Susanna interrupted. "Or perhaps I mean a boundless conceit."

"I plead guilty," Dev said. "But there are some things at which I do excel."

Susanna rolled her eyes. "Why do men feel the need to brag of their sexual prowess?"

"I could demonstrate my prowess rather than simply talk about it if you prefer," Dev offered blandly.

Now it was Susanna's smile that was edged with scorn, her eyes vivid with challenge. "You would try to seduce me? I don't believe you would have the nerve, Devlin."

Dev laughed. "It's dangerous to dare me."

Susanna shook her head. "You are all talk. You would not do anything to put your betrothal with Lady Emma at risk."

"She wouldn't know," Dev said. He'd behaved like a monk for the past two years not, he was obliged to admit, for reasons of honor but simply because Emma would give him hell if she heard any rumors of infidelity. Emma would never tolerate the discreet liaisons with courtesans to which other wives and fiancées turned a blind eye. She was far too possessive. Her demand of fidelity was, Dev knew, nothing to do with her feelings but another sign that she had bought him and could dictate his behavior.

But Susanna was the one woman who could never betray him because he knew too many of her secrets.

The idea stole his breath. He liked it; he liked it far more than he ought. When Chessie had suggested earlier that he should try to take Susanna away from Fitz he had not entertained the idea seriously. Now he did. To make love to Susanna again, to uncover her body to his gaze and his touch, to press his lips to that silken skin, to taste her again and feel her response… His body hardened again at the mere thought of it.

"I would tell Lady Emma you tried to seduce me," Susanna said, her words cutting through his most intimate fantasies.

"I know too much about you," Dev said. "You'd never denounce me for fear I would betray you."

Their eyes locked in mutual dislike and an equally blistering and sudden mutual desire. It seemed to heat the small dark carriage, scalding the air between them.

"You don't like me," Susanna said. There was a thread of something in her voice now that made Dev's blood burn. She could deny an attraction to him for as long as she wished but he knew better. He had wanted her from the moment he had seen her walking across the ballroom toward him and he knew she felt the same.

"I don't like you," he agreed. "What is that to the purpose?"

"You would make love to a woman you don't like simply to demonstrate to her what she has been missing?"

"I could do that, certainly," Dev said. "But that is not how it would be with you, Susanna. I would make love to you because I want you and you would respond to me for the same reason."

He saw the ripple of disquiet shiver along Susanna's skin. She wanted to refute his words but something held her silent. Dev took her hand, peeling the silk glove from her fingers, tugging so that it came away and left her skin bare. Her hand lay in his now, gentle, warm and soft, all the things that Susanna was not. Dev brushed his lips against her fingers. He wanted to make her tremble. He wanted to prove to her that she was not indifferent to him, prove it so that she could never deny it again. He turned her hand over and pressed his lips to the pulse at her wrist. It was racing, yet her face was expressionless and her hand in his was quite still.

"You seem agitated," he murmured against her palm.

"Not at all." Her voice was cool. "I am merely curious to see how far you would take this charade."

Dev licked her palm with one sly stroke of the tongue. Her skin was smooth; she tasted delicious, salt and sweet together, a taste that kicked his awareness of her up another notch.

"I'd take it much further than this," he said. He released her and felt the frisson of relief that shook her. "I was only kissing your hand," he said gently. "Did you like it?"

"No, I did not." Her tone was firm but Dev had felt the tremor that coursed through her.

"Yet you are shaking," he said.

He leaned across to touch the fall of ebony ringlets at her throat. Instantly her hair curled confidingly about his fingers, entrapping him in a sensual mesh. It felt more slippery than silk; the faintest scent of honey rose from the dark strands, teasing his nostrils, wrapping about his senses.

Beneath the tumble of curls, his knuckles grazed her throat, gentle against softer skin. Her breath caught, a tiny sound but enough to betray her. He traced the vulnerable hollow of her collarbone, then his fingers dropped lower to the rich lace that edged the neckline of her gown. He followed it down. The filigree lace was whiter than the creamy skin beneath, both framing and concealing the swell of her breasts, designed to incite carnal need whilst appearing irreproachably innocent.

A sudden fierce urge seized him to tear that lace aside and slide his hand beneath the silk of her gown, to cup her breast and feel the nipple harden against his palm. The game that had started as challenge and provocation had suddenly changed. Now he, for all his experience, was the one feeling as primed and lust-ridden as a youth and she looked as cool as spring water, only the flutter of her pulse and the shimmer of heat in her eyes betraying her desire.

He slid his index finger down to the valley between her breasts and felt her shiver under his touch. They were very close now. He could hear her quickened breathing and see the color that ran up under her skin, heating it from the inside out, stinging her pallor with arousal. Her lips were slightly parted and she bit down on her full lower lip and his body clenched. He knew nothing other than that he had to kiss her—he had to kiss her now—but he retained enough shreds of sanity to know that despite her apparent quiescence if he tried she would probably stab him with a hairpin.

He was not going to take that risk. Quick as a flash he wrapped the cord of her reticule about her wrists, binding them together. She gave a little gasp of shock but he held the thread tight, forcing her hands down and in her lap.

"I'm tying you up so you can't hurt me," he said. He scarcely recognized his voice, rough and hoarse with need.

She might bite him, of course, but he might enjoy that. That was a risk he was prepared to take.

He saw her eyes flash with fury but beneath the anger he also saw a reluctant fascination that made the hunger roar through him.

"You're a brigand," Susanna said. Her voice was not quite steady.

"A pirate," Dev said. "You know it." He tugged on the cord of the reticule. The movement jerked Susanna's wrists and brought her closer to him. He bent his head and took her mouth with his.

Her lips were very lush and they trembled beneath his like a debutante receiving her first kiss. It felt unpracticed, uncertain, as though she had not kissed anyone for a very long time. Dev hesitated, completely thrown by her response. He had not for a moment supposed that she was an innocent. Her history contradicted it; she had denied it in her own words, and yet her lack of finesse spoke for itself. There was no pretence between them, either. It was as though the moment he had kissed her all the barriers between them had dissolved and there was no anger and no resentment left, nothing but longing and sweet, aching need. For a moment Dev felt swamped by dangerous emotion and then Susanna opened her lips beneath his and she tasted so shockingly familiar, so enticing, that his senses spun. He forgot everything, releasing the cord about her wrist so that he could draw her into his arms and kiss her with hunger and passion and an ever-deepening tenderness.

His tongue tangled with hers, coaxing it into a potently carnal dance. Desire leaped to greater desire within him like a fierce flame. Soon, he knew, he would be lost to everything other than the need to make love to Susanna here and now in a flea-infested hackney carriage in broad daylight on the streets of London. He struggled to remember that he could not yield to this seduction. He was supposed to be proving something to Susanna, not losing himself in her. Yet it seemed he could not resist. He did not want to need her but he could not help himself.

He brushed aside the ebony curls with fingers that shook, and pressed his lips to her throat. Her skin was cool beneath his touch and Dev felt like a starving man offered manna in the desert. His self-control hung by a thread. He slid the gown down a little and nipped at the curve of Susanna's shoulder, biting softly, tasting her. The scent of honey was on her skin, faint and sweet. Dev had never eaten honey in his life but he wanted to eat it now. He wanted to lick her all over. He felt almost light-headed with the craving.

The bodice of Susanna's gown rustled softly as it slipped another inch lower. Dev felt the filigree lace rough against his lips and Susanna's breast soft beneath it, inciting him to rip the material away so that he could take her in his mouth. He groaned.

Susanna put one hand against his chest and pushed him away. Dev was so surprised that he let her go.

"Have you finished trying to make a point yet, Sir James?" She sounded slightly bored.

It took Dev a moment to cut through the clamor of his body and to focus. When he did, it was to see that Susanna was adjusting that provocative lace and was patting her hair back into place beneath the saucy bonnet, which had been knocked askew in their embrace. Her face was perfectly blank, pale, composed, the indifferent mask of a lady of fashion.

Shock and disbelief raked through Devlin that he should feel such an intensity of desire and, more disturbingly, such a treacherous sense of affinity with her when to Susanna it seemed it had been nothing but a dare.

"You were pretending?" he said.

Her green eyes were expressionless. If anything, she looked slightly puzzled. "Of course I was," she said. "Weren't you?"

"I…" There was an odd emptiness beneath Devlin's heart. "That innocent response," he said. His throat felt dry. "It was feigned?"

She smiled. It was a smile that made him feel a naive fool. "Men seem to like it," she murmured.

"And you always give men what they want," Dev said. He could feel the bitterness rising like bile in his throat.

"If it gains me what I want."

Dev took her by the shoulders, searching her face for any clue that she lied, looking for even a hint that the storm of sensation that had racked him had touched her, too. She met his gaze defiantly.

"I don't believe you," he said. "You wanted me, too."

Susanna shrugged and turned her face away from him.

"Your opinion is not important to me," she said. "You were trying to prove a point. You failed."

Dev let her go, sinking back onto the seat. The taut desire had drained from him now and he felt chilled and empty. Susanna's words were no more than a salutary reminder of how cynical she had become.

"I find I would rather walk than suffer any more of your…conversation," Susanna said. She rapped sharply on the roof of the carriage. The hackney jerked to a halt.

Dev sat back. "As you wish." He smiled mockingly. "Running out on me so soon, Susanna? I had barely begun the seduction." He held her gaze with his. In the darkness of the carriage her eyes were soft and dark now, unreadable.

"I believe I know your weakness now," he said. "You pretend indifference to me but it is not true."

"I believe your weakness is still vanity," Susanna said coldly. "Good day, Sir James." She opened the door and stepped down into the street. The carriage door banged shut behind her. Dev laughed aloud.

As the carriage moved off he caught a glimpse of her. She was standing at the side of the road looking fragile and in need of protection, like a fairy-tale princess turned out in the rain. Already two gentlemen were advancing on her, purposefully unfurling their umbrellas. Dev shook his head, a sardonic smile on his lips. Yet he was just as susceptible to Susanna's wiles. He could still smell the scent of her skin and feel the warmth of her lips against his. It sharpened his desire and made him feel hollow with unfulfilled lust, even though he knew it for a sham. He had wanted to believe her honest and their passion unfeigned and when he had realized that it was all an act on her part he had felt a naive fool all over again. He had tried to prove Susanna's weakness. Instead he had uncovered his own.

CHAPTER SIX

SUSANNA WALKED QUICKLY along Ludgate Street and on down Ludgate Hill toward Holborn. Dark gray clouds chased overhead. The rain, light, summery but still penetratingly damp, lay slick on the road and spattered the shoulders of her pelisse. She knew she was going to look like a drowned rat by the time that she arrived home, the feather in her saucy bonnet drooping. She had had no desire to accept the offers of protection from either of the gentlemen who had come to her aid. She knew from experience that they would ask for something in return. As it was they had almost come to blows over assisting her; umbrellas at dawn. She really should not have been so hasty, leaping out of the hackney into the rain, but all she had wanted to do was escape from Dev's provocation.

I believe I know your weakness...

It seemed impossible, foolish, infuriating that after all this time she should still be so vulnerable to Dev's touch. She should be supremely indifferent to him after the passing of so many years and yet she was not. She was dangerously susceptible to him. Other men had touched her, kissed her occasionally if she deemed it absolutely necessary for her work, but the experience had always left her indifferent. Yet it seemed that Dev need only look at her with that intensity that was all his own and her stomach would knot and her body tremble and she would be throwing herself at him with the same abandonment as the most hen-witted debutante. And how demeaning that was when he had toyed with her only to demonstrate her weakness to him. She pressed her fingers to her lips and felt a wave of heat engulf her from her toes upward. Oh, she was weak indeed. She had wanted to carry on kissing Dev forever, to surrender to that delicious pleasure, to feel his hands on her body and rediscover the joy she had found in his arms all those years before. She despised herself for that need. She had tried so hard to kill her love for Dev in the past. She was not going to falter now.

James Devlin. He was the thorn in her flesh. He was there at every turn. He would do all he could to thwart her plans to ensnare Fitz. Susanna wondered just how far Dev would go to stop her from ruining Chessie's chances and shivered beneath the damp wool of her pelisse. The material felt clinging and cold.

In the beginning she had told herself that there would be nothing Dev could do to stop her. Now, less than a fortnight later, she was not so sure. It was true that he could not reveal the details of their previous relationship without harming his own engagement to Emma, but there was plenty else he could do and she had a lowering suspicion that he would do it. She should never underestimate Dev. He was a dangerous adversary.

A faint, rueful smile touched her lips. Between them, Dev and his sister had certainly won this round. Francesca Devlin had blatantly stolen Fitz from beneath her nose and then Dev had stepped in to thwart her further. Here she was trudging home in the rain with no umbrella whilst Francesca was probably already ensconced in a booth at Gunters, sharing an ice with Fitz. Susanna's mouth watered at the thought. She longed for an ice or a cream bun or even a bonbon. She needed something sweet to comfort her and reassure her that she would not fail, for the Duke and Duchess of Alton would be furious when they heard what had happened this morning. Some kind soul would be bound to tell them, Freddie Walters, probably. He was a poisonous creature and had been looking daggers at her ever since she had turned him down. Susanna sighed as the summer rain trickled beneath her bonnet and down her neck, plastering her hair wetly against her throat. Since her future livelihood depended upon pleasing the Duke and Duchess and on severing the connection between Fitz and Francesca entirely, she would have to raise her game.

Dev most certainly could not be permitted to outwit her again with his games of false seduction. He still had her glove. She ripped off the other one in a fit of annoyance. The pair had cost her ten shillings and she could not afford to waste money like that. So she was left with a ruined bonnet and half a pair of gloves. It seemed to sum up her morning.

By the time she reached Curzon Street she was indeed soaking wet and the bonnet's feather was as drab as a pheasant caught in a thunderstorm. The deferential footman who opened the door to her smothered a grin to see it. Her maid, provided by the Duke and Duchess of Alton along with the house and all its contents and everything else, was less respectful.

"Heaven help us, milady," she said, on seeing Susanna, "what's become of you?"

"I was caught in the rain, Margery," Susanna said. She put down her glove on top of the waterlogged hat. The maid's brows shot up.

"You dropped a glove, as well?"

"I lost it somewhere along the way," Susanna excused.

The maid gave her a hard stare. She was a young girl, thin, plain and practical. Susanna had liked her from the start. There was no artifice to Margery and a great deal of plain speaking.

"I'll fetch some tea, milady," Margery said. "Looks like you could do with it. There are some letters," she added. "More invitations and the like. There's no room on the mantelpiece. You're the toast of London, madam."

"I'd like some cake, as well, please, Margery," Susanna said hastily. "Sponge. With cream and jam. Lots of it."

She took the pile of cards from the shining walnut hall table and went into the drawing room, closing the door behind her. The room was small and as elegantly appointed as the rest of the house and as lacking in character. Pale sunlight dappled the thick carpet, chasing away the summer rain. The drapes stirred in a lazy breeze from the window. A vase of lilies sat on a table by the window. Susanna had not arranged them herself; she had absolutely no aptitude with the feminine arts. Like everything else in the house they were set dressing, the perfect background for the dazzling rich widow Lady Carew.

The toast of London… Susanna's lips twisted into an ironic smile. If only they knew. Little Susanna Burney had been born in an Edinburgh tenement, given away by her mother when her father left to join the army and never returned. There had been too many mouths to feed and no money and she, the youngest and prettiest, had been given a new life with her childless aunt and uncle. A life she had thrown away when she had eloped with James Devlin. With a sigh Susanna dropped down into a deep Chippendale armchair. There was no trace of her personality in this house, no clue as to the real Susanna Burney. She kicked off her shoes and let her stockinged toes sink into the carpet. It felt deliciously soft and rich. She loved that feeling of opulence because beneath it was the memory of bare floors and cold stone and rain falling like tears. It did not feel so wrong to relish all this luxury when before she had had so little. Sometimes, though, she was almost seduced into believing her own fairy tale.

From beneath the pile of invitations to balls, soirees and musical evenings, she extracted three letters. The top one, she knew, was from the schoolmaster with whom her young ward Rory McAlister lodged in Edinburgh. A shiver of fear racked her. No news about Rory was ever good. At fourteen, he was wild, ungovernable and not particularly given to study. Susanna had had to pay over the odds to persuade Dr. Murchison to take the boy into his family as well as to educate him but she had hoped—prayed—that living with a family might suit Rory better than being sent to boarding school. He had run away from his two previous schools.

Susanna paused, aware of a very strong urge to leave the letter unopened and put off the moment of truth. Rory and Rose… She loved the twins as fiercely as though they were her own, bound to them through a life forged in the struggle for survival and the promises she had made their mother as Flora McAlister had lain dying in the poorhouse. Flora had given her the gift of children after her loss and she would not fail them. Blinking back the sudden sting of tears she opened the letter.

Rory, Dr. Murchison wrote, more in sorrow than in anger, had run away again. After a week they had found him living rough on the streets of Edinburgh, filthy, hungry, furious but safe.

Susanna dropped the letter onto her lap and

pressed her fingers to her temples where a headache threatened. Rory thought he was tough and clever and able to take care of himself but he was only a boy. And he was such a dear boy and she loved him and knew he loved her, too, but at times like this she also knew she had not done enough to help him. She felt it deeply, miserably and with an aching heart. The guilt tugged at her, a sick feeling in her stomach. So many times she had tried to keep her small, inherited family together. It had proved impossible. She could not provide for the twins unless she worked and if she worked she could not keep them with her. She had tried so hard but hunger and fear had stalked her world. Twice she had been robbed of those who were most precious to her. First she had lost Devlin and then she had lost their child. Now she would do everything in her power to protect the twins and see that they were safe. And in a couple of months she would have completed her work and the Duke and Duchess of Alton would have paid her and she would at last be free to visit the twins and even possibly make a fresh start with them.

Her hands shaking, she picked up the letter again. Although Dr. Murchison had covered the entire page there was little further news, but halfway down the tone of the letter changed. Rory, Dr. Murchison said, was a burden. It was with a heavy heart that he had to ask for more money for Rory's keep as recompense, he wrote, for all the trouble the boy had caused.

In a fit of fury Susanna screwed the letter into a

ball, feeling the sharp corners dent her palm. At this rate all the money she had so carefully scraped together so that she and Rory and Rose might one day resume their family life would be whittled away on unscrupulous people who always wanted more and more and more.

Susanna ran an abstracted hand through her hair, scattering a few pins. She looked at the second letter. An uncomfortable instinct told her that it would not be good news. But she had always met trouble head-on so she opened it anyway.

It was not good news.

The moneylenders were enquiring, politely but firmly, whether she wished to extend her loan. She knew that if she did their terms, already extortionately high, would increase still further. But if she did not borrow she would not be able to pay the next installment of Rose's school fees. Her headache increased like a knot tightening. Shc could feel the panic choking her throat.

The third letter was written in a hand that was unknown to her. She opened it carelessly with her thoughts still preoccupied by her financial troubles, perused it once with little concentration and then read it again with a sinking feeling of disbelief.

"I know who you really are."

The letter slipped from her fingers and spun away across the carpet to flutter to a stop in a patch of sunlight. It was warm in the room now but Susanna felt cold and racked by shivers.

I know who you really are.

The words that no impostor ever wanted to read.

"Tea, milady. And lots of cake." Margery had come in bearing a tray with a pretty china cup and matching pot. "You look proper moped, madam," she added.

"I am," Susanna said fervently.

"Money, I suppose," Margery said. "Or a man. Or both," she added. She looked around the drawing room, with the sun shining now on the beautifully polished furniture, picking out the rich colors in the thick rug before the marble fire.

"Just so as you know, ma'am," she added, "I never was any good at pretending."

"Oh, dear," Susanna said, wondering what on earth was going to follow.

"All this is very pretty, ma'am," Margery continued, "but the underwear that you were wearing when you arrived here had been darned over and over again and the soles of your shoes were almost worn through. You arrived on foot, carrying your own portmanteau and I know for a fact all this stuff—" her gesture encompassed the room again "—is a job lot bought by the lawyers. I just thought I would let you know that I knew, milady," she finished.

"I see," Susanna said slowly. She could not stop the smile that twitched her lips at her maid's detective work. It seemed that her anonymous correspondent was not the only one who suspected her. "So you think I may be poor," she said. "An impostor, perhaps, pretending to be a rich widow?"

"I don't know what you are, ma'am," the maid said frankly, "but I used to work for Lady St. Severin, ma'am, who eloped with a French prisoner of war in a balloon. Nothing shocks me. And after her I went to work for Lady Grant's sister Lady Darent, before Mr. Churchward requested me for this post." She smiled. "I can keep a secret, ma'am," she said, "but I just like to know what secret it is I am keeping, if you see what I mean."

"Perfectly, thank you, Margery," Susanna said. She paused, thinking of all that the maid had said, and how lonely it was to be a fraud with absolutely no one to talk to. She gestured to the tea tray. "If you would like to bring another cup, Margery," she said slowly, "perhaps we could talk."

The maid beamed and sped away and Susanna felt comforted. In her work she never confided in anyone, never trusted anyone with her secrets, but she felt she could trust the little maid who was so practical and outspoken.

Money or a man or both, Margery had said. Susanna rubbed the faint marks on her wrist, feeling again Dev's fingers against her skin, his touch searing her. Blackmail and seduction... Surely, surely it could not be Devlin who had written that threatening note? He was the only one who knew her secrets. She knew that Dev was dangerous and unscrupulous, yet some stubborn instinct told her that he would not stoop to such measures. Yet could she be sure? How far would Devlin go to defeat her and to get what he wanted? She had a frightening premonition that she was going to find out.

MISS FRANCESCA DEVLIN stood in front of Mrs. Tong's House of Pleasure and literally shivered in her satin slippers. She had never been to a place like this before. In the past few weeks her worldly experience had been extended beyond her wildest imaginings but there were still certain shreds of innocence left to her. Setting foot in a bawdy house would take her further than she had gone before.

The set of anonymous rooms in Hemming Row suddenly seemed a long way away, safe and almost respectable. Chessie knew she was not the first woman her lover had met there but she shut her mind to the fact she was unlikely to be the last because that would be to recognize defeat, to accept that this, her very last throw of the dice, had already failed. She simply could not contemplate failure.

The porter who answered her tentative knock at the bawdy house door looked very bored. No doubt he had seen many things over the years, including young ladies who had until recently been irreproachably virtuous but were now creeping out to meet a lover. No indeed, she was nothing new.

"Are you coming in or not?" The porter was trying to see beneath the heavy veil that covered her face. Then, as she stumbled across the threshold into a world of bright light and violent colors, "Up the stairs, second room on the right." He paused. "Make sure you get the right room, missy." He laughed.

There was noise all around her; laughter, music, voices. It all felt too loud and garish. The cries she could hear emanating from some of the other rooms made her blush down to her toes. She fumbled with the door handle and then she was inside the room, shaking, feeling sick, but he was here now, waiting for her, smiling.

He put back the veil from her face, took her coat and bonnet from her. "Here, take this…" He pressed a cup of wine into her hand and it was sweet and heady and she started to feel better. He kissed her. That was better still.

"You were very brave to come here." He sounded amused. "You deserve a reward…"

Still kissing her, he drew her down onto the bed. When she finally opened her dazed eyes he had already stripped her of all her clothes and she was lying naked on the top of the vivid orange coverlet, her hair loose of its pins spread about her.

"Are we not to play cards tonight?" she asked. It had been a part of their arrangement, cards first, lovemaking later when she lost. She always lost.

He sat back on his heels, the same wicked amusement in his dark eyes, and she saw beyond him the faro table prepared for several players.

"This time we'll play later," he said. He touched her hair. "How pretty you look," he added lightly, whilst she ached for one word of love from him. "I have a treat for you here."

Chessie's eyes widened as she took in the rack on the wall of the room. Whips, crops… She gulped, imagining the sting of the leather crisscrossing her flesh. Would he ask that of her? Would that be her fate if she lost tonight?

She saw him lift the most extraordinary carved wooden object, which he now brought close to her face until its smooth curves kissed her lips.

Somewhere in her deepest heart Chessie knew that this was his reward, not hers, but she closed her mind to the thought just as she closed her eyes as she felt the dildo trace a cool path over the slope of her breast and down, to dip between her thighs.

She did not see the watchers behind the screen.

CHAPTER SEVEN

"FRAZER," DEV SAID TO his valet as he sat before the shaving mirror, "did you ever do anything particularly stupid when you were young that came back to haunt you years later?"

He was in his set of rooms in Albany, preparing for the night's entertainments. Albany was the most exclusive bachelor residence in London where neither women nor musical instruments were tolerated. Dev had been allocated his chambers because he was the cousin of Lord Grant, the famous explorer, and because he was betrothed to an earl's daughter. He could not afford them, of course. Like everything else in his life they were paid for by the future promise of Emma's fortune.

He felt the razor pause at his throat and immediately regretted asking the question when he was in so vulnerable a position. It was not that Frazer's hand was unsteady despite his advancing age. It was more that he was never very comfortable with another man's knife at his throat, an understandable reaction after a street brawl in a Mexican port a few years before.

"What have ye done, Mr. Devlin?" Frazer asked, after a moment. He always forgot to call Devlin "Sir James" and Dev never bothered to remind him. He had inherited Frazer as valet from his cousin Alex Grant who had said that Dev needed the former Navy steward, with his dour Scots spirit, to keep him on the straight and narrow. Since Frazer had known Dev when he was in short coats there was no fooling the man.

"Nothing," Dev said. "Not for nine years, anyway."

Frazer ignored him. "Have ye gambled away another thousand or two, perhaps?" He persisted. "Seduced a lady—or someone who isnae a lady? Set up a lightskirt in keeping?" The razor touched Dev's throat and he swallowed hard. The soap was running down his neck now. He was probably sweating it off.

"Frazer," he said, "you wound me." It was an image that was likely to become literal as well as figurative if this carried on. Dev shifted in the chair. "You know that I have lived an irreproachably chaste life these past two years," he said. No doubt that accounted for his severe sexual frustration, he thought. Boxing, fencing, various other legally sanctioned outbursts of violence had been the only outlet for his feelings. Until the previous morning... And now the memory of Susanna in his arms haunted him. He had wanted her before. Now he ached for her.

"No," Frazer said. He shook his head. Dev watched the deft scrape of the razor in the speckled mirror.

"No what?" he said.

"No, I didnae do anything stupid when I was young," Frazer said. "I was in Edinburgh gaol when I was thirteen. Not much chance of doing anything stupid locked up in there. They only let me out to join the Navy."

"Of course," Dev said, entranced by this vision of a youthfully criminal Frazer. "How foolish of me to imagine you would have done anything stupid in your younger days, Frazer."

"What did you do then, Mr. Devlin?" Frazer asked slyly.

"I?" Dev said. "Nothing. Nothing at all."

Frazer gave a snort of disbelief. "Ye always were a headstrong lad. Like as not you ran off with someone else's wife."

No, Dev thought. Only with my own. Except that he had not run off with Susanna. She had run off without him.

He could only be grateful that no one else knew about his youthful indiscretion. He had been staying in Scotland with his cousin Alex Grant when he had met Susanna. Neither Alex nor his first wife, Amelia, had suspected the affair. Dev was sure of it. Alex had never been the man to enquire too closely into his personal affairs and Amelia… Dev paused in his thoughts, remembering his cousin's first wife, so soft and sweet on the outside, so hard on the inside, like a bonbon coated in sugar. Amelia had been so absorbed in herself that she had surely had no space to think about anything or anyone else. He pulled a face. Frazer muttered a word of warning as the razor hovered over his throat.

"Keep still, Mr. Devlin, or you'll lose more than your shirt at play tonight."

Dev froze as the razor resumed its work. He wondered if Susanna gambled. It was one of the vices of many rich widows. He had not seen her at the card tables since she had come to London but then she had been so busy pursuing Fitz that she had not had much time for other hobbies. Fitz was a gambler, too, though, and perhaps he had introduced Susanna to the pleasures of playing high. Dev felt his fingers itch for the cards. Throughout his life he had fought a fierce battle with himself to avoid his father's obsession with gaming. Most of the time he could control the compulsion. Occasionally he could not. Now he acknowledged that he would like to fleece Susanna at faro—or at any other game of chance. That would be very satisfying. Except, of course, that she might win. Susanna might be as shallow as a puddle and as grasping as the greediest whore but she was damnably single-minded when she wanted something, clever, too. Engaging with her on any level was a risk. Being in debt to her would be intolerable.

Frazer finished, washed the soap away and handed Dev a towel.

"Ye still have all your vital parts," he said sourly. "I've told you before to keep still when I shave ye."

"Sorry," Dev said. "I have matters on my mind."

"Women matters," Frazer said, even more sourly. "I know that look of yours. Be careful, Mr. Devlin."

"I will," Dev said. He grinned. "Thank you for your concern, Frazer. It's good to know you care."

Frazer pulled a face that looked like milk in the act of curdling.

Thirty minutes later, with his cravat tied in the Irish, a style he had made his own in neat homage to his antecedents, his jacket eased over his shoulders by Frazer, puffing like a bellows, and a particularly dashing waistcoat of gold and green, Dev was ready.

"The playhouse tonight, is it?" Frazer asked with a long face. "Bunch of jessies." Frazer hated the theater and condemned anything to do with it as soft. Dev suspected that this went back to a voyage Frazer had made to the Arctic with Alex when the ship's company had become stuck in the ice and had been obliged to entertain themselves with theatricals through the long, dark winter, dressing up as women, playing the female parts as well as the male. That, Dev thought, would have been enough to drive any self-respecting Scotsman mad. Not that he was much fonder of the theater himself. In his case his aversion sprang from a visit some two years previously when he had had the ill luck to bump into a former mistress whilst in company with Emma and her family. It had been exceedingly awkward. Emma had quizzed him endlessly about it; who was the woman, when had he known her, how intimately had he known her, were there other mistresses of his she was likely to meet—to which the answer, unfortunately, was yes, there were plenty, but Dev had been wise enough to deny it—on and on until Emma had given herself the vapors and Dev had wanted to leap on the first ship that was leaving the docks.

"Tonight it is *The Plain Dealer* by Wycherley," he said, and saw Frazer's mouth turn down even more. "Emma likes the theater."

Frazer made the sort of noncommittal grunt that nevertheless managed to convey perfectly his disapproval of a man obliged to attend social engagements at the bidding of his fiancée. Dev sighed. He knew exactly what Frazer thought of his fortune hunting. He knew that Alex and Joanna disapproved, too, if it came to that. None of them understood the demons that haunted him, though; the memories of a boy who, before Alex had rescued him from the Dublin streets, had scratched a living from any errand he could run simply to help feed his mother and sister. Chessie was the only one who had shared the bewildering experience of their father's profligacy. Marrying Emma was a guarantee against such poverty and as such Dev thought it had to be worth the price.

The evening, starting with so little promise, was quick to degenerate even further. Chessie had not been invited since Lady Brooke had said pointedly that it was a family occasion. Dev found dinner extremely tedious. Emma was in a scratchy sort of mood and ignored him, flirting instead with Freddie Walters but watching Dev to make sure that he noticed. Meanwhile his future mother-in-law followed her daughter's lead by ignoring him and Dev was reduced to toying with his overcooked beef and making polite conversation with Lady Brooke's elderly companion. His future, he knew, would be filled with endless nights like this. It was a thought Dev preferred not to dwell upon.

At the theater the Duke and Duchess of Alton, Fitz and Susanna joined their party. This was something that Dev had not anticipated. He masked his initial astonishment to see Susanna at what had been described as a family gathering but he was astounded at how quickly she had insinuated herself into the Altons' inner circle. He wondered if Fitz had petitioned his parents to allow Susanna to join them. It was not odd, Dev thought grimly, that Fitz would fall for Susanna's artfully presented charms but it was strange that his parents seemed similarly enchanted. The Duchess was a high stickler when it came to rank and breeding, the Duke, unlike his son, surely too hard headed to fall for no more than a pretty face and captivating figure, even if they were accompanied by a fortune.

"Good evening, Lady Carew," Dev said, as greetings were exchanged. "What a surprise to have you join our family party this evening."

Susanna smiled. "It is no surprise to me, Sir

James, that the Duke and Duchess have been generous enough to include me in their family circle."

Which, Dev thought with grim amusement, rather neatly emphasized the warmth with which Susanna had been welcomed compared with the frosty treatment he still received after two years as Emma's fiancé.

Susanna stepped past him to take a seat at the back of the box. Fitz immediately objected and drew her forward to sit beside him on the front row. Dev admired her strategy. Such unassuming modesty and such pretty thanks. Fitz was as soft as butter in her hands. All the progress that Chessie had made the previous day on the trip to Gunters now counted for nothing. Susanna had regained the upper hand.

"Nicely done," he murmured under his breath and caught the edge of the smile she cast him. It was laced with triumph.

"I practice a great deal," she said lightly.

"Clearly," Dev said. The sarcasm felt bitter on his tongue. He felt angry, on edge. Someone had refined a particular form of torture for him, he thought, to sit here and watch his former wife work her wiles on the man his sister wanted.

He thought of the way he had kissed Susanna in the carriage the day before, with heat and passion and driving need. His anger tightened another notch. She had beaten him at his own game and left him aching for more. Fitz, he knew, was her real quarry. She was an accomplished schemer.

He could warn Fitz, of course, tell him that Susanna was not all she seemed, that she was a fortune hunter. The idea was intensely appealing. The thought of what Susanna might do for revenge, however, was not. And Susanna was so skilful, she played Fitz so well, that she might already have told him, sorrowfully, that there were those who would like to see her fall and who would spread malicious tales about her. Dev could well imagine the protective fury that would arouse in a stupid man like Fitz who already saw Susanna as his property. Facing the Marquis across the dueling ground was not in his plans at all. It would achieve nothing.

Dev watched as Susanna disposed herself elegantly in the chair. She was in a gown of gold net over cream tonight. It was cut modestly over her breasts—she would surely have no desire to offend the Duke and Duchess by dressing as the wanton she was—and yet by some trick of design the gown's very demureness seemed to emphasize every glorious curve of her figure. The flimsy gauze shimmered in the shifting light. Her thick black hair was plaited and set within a delicate gold coronet. She looked elegant, expensive, tempting. Fitz certainly looked tempted and even Freddie Walters had abandoned Emma in an unseemly rush to help Susanna divest herself of her diaphanous golden wrap.

"I would offer my assistance, too, Lady Carew," Dev said when Fitz moved away to exchange a few brief words with his aunt, "but as Fitz escorts you and Freddie has already undone you there is so little for me to do."

Susanna's green gaze snapped at his implication that she was intimate with Walters. "I have no wish for you to exert yourself, Sir James," she said sweetly. "I hear that doing very little is your speciality these days." She glanced up at him from under her lashes. Her gaze rested on Emma for a brief moment. "You are an explorer who travels only between St. James's and Mayfair, I believe. How singular of you."

Dev smiled grimly. "Once again you demonstrate that you have been following my every step," he said. "I must fascinate you."

He saw a flicker of irritation in her eyes. "Oh," she said, "scarcely that. But even in Edinburgh we heard that the famous adventurer Sir James Devlin had been bought by a society heiress for seventy thousand pounds and now he languishes at home, at her beck and call."

Dev's breath hissed between his teeth. He could feel the tension tight across his shoulders, straining the material of his jacket. God forbid that he should split the seams. He could not afford a new coat. He already owed his tailor some extortionate sum of money. But trust Susanna to get under his skin within five minutes of their meeting. She had a talent for it and Dev knew he should not rise to her provocation, yet he could so seldom resist.

"Whereas you," he said, "have traveled a long way, Lady Carew. Or, more precisely, you have climbed high already. From schoolmaster's niece to baronet's widow, and onward toward the dizzy heights of a marquisate…" He looked her up and down in the golden gown. "A nice conceit to match your gown to your ambitions."

Susanna laughed. "You are very bad tempered tonight, Sir James, to reproach me for fortune hunting when you are the professional. Was dinner with your little heiress such a trial?"

"I'll wager it was not so exciting as your assignation with Fitz," Dev said grimly.

"We went to Rules restaurant," Susanna said. She gave him a luscious smile. "We ate oysters, and as you know they are the food of love."

"How very nasty and slimy," Dev said.

Fitz reclaimed Susanna then, taking the chair beside her and pointing out to Dev, an edge to his tone, that Emma was waiting to be seated. Dev saw the shadow of a smile touch Susanna's lips as she took in Emma's cross little face and stiff figure.

The curtain was going up.

"Is that woman another of your mistresses?" Emma hissed at Dev, ignoring the fact that the play had started. Like many of her contemporaries Emma did not go to the theater to watch, but to see and be seen. In fact, she was quite capable of talking all the way through a play. Even so on this occasion her sibilant whisper caused several heads to turn.

"No," Dev said shortly. "Lady Carew is not my mistress and never has been."

It was true and yet he knew every inch of Susanna's lovely lissome body intimately. Dev swallowed hard. He had never had a particularly good memory, at least not for mathematics, navigation, geography, or any other useful subject. Ironic then that here, now, in the most unsuitable circumstances imaginable, he was remembering every silken slide of his hands over Susanna's pale skin, the way that she had arched to the mastery of his touch, even the way in which the green of her eyes had intensified with desire, drenched in sensual pleasure. He shifted in his theater seat. It felt rock-hard. He felt rock-hard. He hoped to God that Emma would not glance sideways and see his entirely inappropriate reaction. She was quite capable of screaming with outrage and causing a scene.

His senses seemed to be aware of nothing but Susanna. Her seat was placed in front of his, a little to the right, and he could see her out of the corner of his eye. She seemed enraptured by the play, her silken skirts rustling as she sat forward, the light playing over the gossamer gold gown and the slope of her shoulders beneath. Her perfume enwrapped him, verbena and honey, sweet with an edge of sharpness like Susanna herself. He could see the tiny hairs that escaped the coronet to curl at her nape. He wanted to reach out and touch them and run his fingers down the line of her spine. He wanted to feel the crisp silk of the gown under his hand and the warmth of Susanna's body beneath that…

Emma dug her fan sharply into his ribs causing him to catch his breath in a painful gasp. She was glaring at him for watching Susanna rather than the play and Dev could not fault her on the principle, only her methods. He tried to concentrate on the performance but all he seemed capable of doing was remembering the exquisite bliss of making love to Susanna. He could recall the sweet and salty scent of her skin as she lay curled against him in exhausted satiation; he could feel the tickle of her hair against his naked chest and the brush of her leg entangled with his under the tumbled covers. He could taste her kiss. He remembered that he had lain awake for hours listening to her breathing, tracing the pure line of Susanna's cheek and throat, his hand falling lower, over the curve of her shoulder, his lips following, drinking in the taste of her, down to her breast, until he had woken her with urgency and she had laughed in his arms as they had made love again. It had been so fragile but had seemed so sweet and honest, a small foundation on which he had thought to build a life together. He remembered the way her lips had parted beneath his and the small sound of surrender and acquiescence she had made in her throat when he had kissed her for the first time. He had felt magnificent then, such a man, ready to take on the whole world…

Grief and regret pierced him, shocking in their intensity. It had all been built on a lie. All his tender feelings, all his hopes for the future had been founded on no more than his imagination and Susanna's deceit. She had used him. He had been no more than a means to an end, her first step on the path that would take her eventually to a Dukedom.

Dev turned his head slightly and saw that Fitz had possessed himself of Susanna's gloved hand and was peeling the material down to press a kiss on the pulse at her wrist in much the same way that Dev himself had done in the hackney carriage. He felt a kick of white-hot possessiveness that startled as much as displeased him. It was not edifying to lust after his former wife. It had to stop. Their relationship, such as it was, had been over a very long time.

He watched as Susanna withdrew her hand far too slowly for her action to be any kind of discouragement. She was laughing, scolding Fitz softly for distracting her from the play. It was clever of her, Dev thought, to combine such sophistication with such a natural enthusiasm for the performance. Amongst this jaded crowd of theatergoers, who attended only because it was fashionable to do so, Susanna's pleasure in the evening seemed charming and fresh. And in Dev's opinion it was as false as her regard for Fitz.

The curtain swept across to mark the interval and the chatter in the theater swelled to deafening proportions. Emma smiled prettily at him, her bad temper apparently banished. Fitz and Susanna did not appear to have noticed that the first act had ended, so engrossed were they in one another. Dev watched as Fitz bent forward to whisper in Susanna's ear, so close it looked as though he was within an inch of kissing the delicate line of her throat above the ruby necklace. He paused there, allowing his breath to feather across her skin and stir the tendrils of hair by her ear. Dev felt the anger tighten inside him again like a taut rope. He watched as Susanna's lips curved up in the most tantalizing smile. She half-turned her head so that Fitz caught the flirtatious edge of that smile and then she playfully pushed him away with her fan. Fitz snatched the fan from her hand then held it out of her reach as she laughingly tried to reclaim it. Dev wanted to punch him. He balled his fists at his sides. The ostentatious flirtations of the ton went on all the time but this one grated on his nerves. His frustrations were purely on Chessie's behalf, of course, or so he told himself. He could see her chances of becoming Marchioness of Alton slipping away like water through the fingers and all because Susanna was a scheming hussy and Fitz was spoiled and arrogant and used to getting what he wanted.

Susanna caught his gaze. Again she smiled, this time with mockery in the depths of her green eyes and Dev pointedly turned away. He wanted to strangle her, wanted it with a violence that was deeply disturbing. He was actually glad when Emma put a hand on his arm and very demurely asked him to escort her to speak with her friend Miss Daventry in the next box but one. They went out together and joined the crowds of theatergoers moving from box to box to greet their friends and acquaintances.

Once, Dev remembered, this had been the part of the night that would appeal to him the most. Emma had introduced him to endless useful contacts, to a stratum of society that had once been out of his reach and had glittered and tempted him beyond all reason. He had been at the height of his celebrity when he had first met Emma, a hero returning from a treasure-hunting voyage to Mexico, the darling of society. He had relished the notoriety of his name and had used both his celebrity and Emma's connections shamelessly to mountaineer up the ton. Susanna had been right to call him a fortune hunter. Not only had he sought money, he had sought advancement and all the advantages that his position could bring.

Tonight, though, for the first time the process felt pointless and a dead bore. Perhaps it was because he was so close to achieving all he had ever wanted and so there was no element of challenge anymore. Dev thought about the future as Emma's husband and this endless, elegantly monotonous round of life, season after season, year after year, with no real purpose at all, and found that he was almost yawning. He realized that the Dowager Lady Daventry was standing directly in front of him and turned the yawn into a bland smile.

"Good evening, ma'am..." He took her hand, bowing with supreme elegance, pressing a kiss on her glove in an old-fashioned gesture of gallantry.

The older ladies always liked that, complaining as they did about the lack of manners in the younger generation. Lady Daventry blushed and fluttered.

"Emma, my dear," she cooed, "you must snap up this young man in marriage at once before I elope with him myself!"

Dev smiled mechanically and said all the right things as Emma dragged him from group to group, her hand feeling more and more like a manacle on his arm as they went along. This, he reminded himself, was one of the reasons he had proposed to her. She was beautiful, rich and well-connected and he…

And he did not appear to care anymore.

Dev froze where he stood. This, he reminded himself, was everything that he had ever wanted: money, success and status. And yes, he still wanted money, success, fame, status and all the trappings of wealth but as Emma tugged his arm again it felt as though the price was becoming extortionately high.

"Dev! Dev!" Emma was whispering in his ear. At first Dev thought that she was trying to prompt him to respond to some urgent social inquiry, then he realized with shock and dawning horror that Emma had taken advantage of a brief moment's privacy behind a marble pillar to press her body hotly against his and put her lips to his ear.

"Come to me tonight," she whispered. Her tongue darted wetly into his ear in what Dev could only assume was an innocent's attempt to be erotic. "Meet me in the walled garden behind the house. I want you." This last was accompanied by another thrust of her body against his.

She released him as Freddie Walters approached, and spun away, throwing a little come-hither smile at him over her shoulder. Dev found himself unable to move for several seconds. Unless he had utterly misinterpreted the situation—and he could not see that it was open to a great deal of misunderstanding—his virginal fiancée had just propositioned him to seduce her.

He waited to feel something. Triumph would be a good response; he had played a waiting game with Emma, treating her with the cut-glass respect that a sheltered heiress demanded. True, this had been more out of the knowledge that if he seduced Emma or eloped with her, her parents would in all probability cut her off without a penny and then he would be stuck with a spoiled brat of a wife and no money to soften the pain. But now she was trying to seduce him and Dev thought he could succumb gracefully, go to Emma's parents and tell them that after two years of abstinence he and Emma had been carried away by their love for one another… He would press for the wedding to be held soon and he did not think at this stage, with Emma's reputation at stake, Lord and Lady Brooke would cavil at his suggestion.

There was only one drawback with this masterly plan.

He did not want to do it.

He felt not a flicker of desire for Emma and he

was not even sure that he could seduce her if he wanted to.

The sweat broke out on his forehead. He thought about ravishing Emma; thought about it in bright, vivid detail in the same way that he had remembered making love to Susanna. This time his body remained stubbornly unresponsive. He slammed his palm against the marble pillar in sheer exasperation. Hell and the devil, he was supposed to be a rake. This was a gift to him, the prize he had been waiting for. He should be primed and ready to exploit it, leap into the walled garden and ravish Emma in the gazebo or against a tree or on the garden bench or all three. He should make love to her until she was so swept away by sensual pleasure that she demanded to marry him there and then. He should be eager. Emma was, after all, deliciously pretty as well as being deliciously rich.

He looked down. Nothing disturbed the smooth fit of his pantaloons. He was not eager. He was moribund.

Another wave of unease assailed him. Suppose he was to press ahead with Emma's seduction and when it came to the point, still he could not perform? He had never had that problem in his entire life. Or only once or twice when he had been too drunk. Sexual anxiety was hardly his style.

The conclusion was inescapable. He did not want Emma. Not one whit; not at all. What he wanted…

Something flickered across his line of vision, a

woman in a gown of golden gauze that sheathed her body so tight and so close that he wanted to grab her and unwrap her like a gift, burying his face against her naked skin and inhaling her scent, tangling his fingers in her silky black hair and losing himself in her over and over again until they were both sated.

His senses stirred. His body leaped to attention. He watched Susanna as she slipped from the room and away along the corridor, the golden gown shimmering like gossamer.

He did not want Emma, his beautiful, rich, well-connected fiancée. He wanted Susanna, his beautiful, perfidious former wife.

He was in deep trouble.

CHAPTER EIGHT

SUSANNA WAS TIRED. NEVER before had an assignment caused her as much trouble as Fitzwilliam Alton was doing. Normally she enjoyed the challenge, but now her head ached, her feet in their adorable golden slippers ached and, rather oddly, her heart felt as though it was aching, too. Fitz's attentions were becoming very marked, very quickly, which was going to be a problem. She wished he were not quite such a rake. Rakes were a great deal more difficult to control than other men. They required more effort, more careful handling and a great deal of fending off.

Fitz's purpose, Susanna knew perfectly well, was to lure her into his bed as soon as possible. The fact that she was, nominally at least, an acquaintance of his parents, would not stop him. It was a game they were playing, the courtship dance that he thought would end in a most satisfactory affaire and Susanna knew would not. Fitz was, she had divined, a man of very simple desires, and at the moment he desired her. He was also extremely indulged, pampered from birth, accustomed to having everything that he wanted served up to him on a plate.

He would not be having her.

Her purpose was to fascinate Fitz but simultaneously thwart him. It was similar to the job of a juggler in a traveling circus, keeping all the balls in the air, not dropping a catch as she had done yesterday when Devlin had successfully distracted her. Susanna closed her eyes and pushed away the prickle of irritation that the memory had evoked. She could not allow Dev to get under her skin again. She had had to work very hard to make up the lost ground and gain this evening's invitation.

She had no intention of becoming Fitz's mistress. She had absolutely no inclination to take him as a lover, and anyway this was business not pleasure; there would be a danger that her power over Fitz would wane if he sated his lust. He could easily turn back to the virginal charms of Miss Francesca Devlin and then all would be lost. She had to seduce him into marriage, not into her bed. The way she always worked was to extract the marriage proposal, accept gracefully and then, after a couple of months, ruefully confess that she had acted hastily, she had changed her mind, and it was all a mistake. It had worked successfully in the past and there was no reason to suppose that Fitz would not be the next victim of her carefully calculated heartbreak.

Except that the fly in the ointment was Devlin. She did not want to admit to doubts but this was her most tricky case yet and conducting a flirtation with another man under Dev's stony gaze was proving to be very difficult. Susanna sighed, pressing her fingers to her temple where her headache pounded. Really, Dev should bottle that stern disapproval and sell it to chaperons. He would make a fortune and then he would not need to tout himself around to rich heiresses.

She watched Fitz from her seat. He had detoured from fetching her iced lemonade—which would be lukewarm by the time it reached her—in order to greet some family friends in the box opposite. Wherever he went the ladies fluttered for his attention like a host of brightly colored butterflies basking in the warmth of the sun. From the theater box he made his slow progress along the curving corridor back toward her. Now she could see that he had been waylaid by one of the demimonde's most notorious courtesans; in a flicker of an eyelash he had leaned in to whisper something in her ear, the woman had nodded and moved on with a murmur of silken skirts. A cynical smile deepened on Susanna's lips. Perhaps Fitz was cleverer than he seemed. He had certainly realized he would not be sharing her bed tonight and so had made other arrangements in order to satisfy his carnal desires.

"I see that Fitz spurns your charms for those of Miss Kingston, Lady Carew."

The voice was familiar, annoying so. Susanna looked up. Dev was standing before her, looking supremely elegant in his slashed white and gold embroidered waistcoat and his pristine white linen and his diamonds so bright they almost dazzled. She had heard that when Dev had first returned to London from his seafaring adventures he had worn a pearl in his ear. The ladies had apparently adored it. He had toned down that extravagant excess now, or rather transmuted it into something more tasteful and expensive. But there was still an edge of flamboyance to him and in his eyes was more than a hint of the old piratical James Devlin, the man who had taken three enemy ships in one engagement, won a treasure chest in a game of chance and, if the rumors were true, seduced an admiral's daughter up against the mainsail of his ship.

She met the sardonic glint in his eyes. He took the empty seat beside her without asking permission.

"Perhaps," Dev continued, "your amatory skills are not quite as sophisticated as you imagine and Fitz is already bored with you?" He shifted. "If you would allow me to give you some advice, yesterday in the carriage you did kiss rather like an amateur—"

"Pray keep your advice for someone who appreciates it," Susanna said. She knew he was trying to provoke her and he was succeeding effortlessly. It seemed that anything Dev said to her cut straight through her defenses and set a barb in her heart. She was hurting somewhere and she neither liked it nor understood it.

Dev smiled and shrugged. "Very well. We will change the subject. Fortune hunting can be so devilishly boring, do you not find?" He stretched out his long legs, casting her a sideways glance that was full of amusement. "You look blue-deviled. But then I am not surprised. I'm afraid that Fitz is not the sharpest blade. His conversation can lack sparkle."

"I am enjoying my evening," Susanna said shortly.

"Of course you are." Dev's mouth twisted into a grin. "You invest a great deal of time, energy and patience in cultivating Fitz's interest and then—" he snapped his fingers "—he throws you over for a courtesan."

"That does not trouble me," Susanna said, entirely truthful.

She felt Dev's cool blue gaze search her face and wondered what he saw there. "No," he said after a moment. There was a hint of a frown in his eyes. "I don't believe it does. How singular." His tone was pensive. "It can only mean that you do not care a rush for him."

Susanna gave a little shrug. She was not going to pretend to affection for Fitz that she did not feel. Dev would only call her on it. Annoyingly he seemed to understand her too well for her to dissemble.

"A woman is setting herself up for disappointment if she expects fidelity from any man," she said.

Dev's blue eyes were very bright, his expression impassive. "A somewhat negative philosophy," he murmured.

"A realistic one," Susanna flashed back bitterly before she could help herself.

"I am sorry you have found it so," Dev said. "I

had no idea that your late husband was a rake." He paused. "Or do you speak of other lovers?"

"I don't wish to speak of any lovers," Susanna snapped.

Dev's mouth twisted. "Well, at least you cannot reproach me," he murmured. "You never gave me the chance to be unfaithful to you. You were gone too quickly from our marriage bed."

"I am not talking about us," Susanna said. "Let us change the subject again. Did you enjoy the first half performance, Sir James?"

"Oh, the performance was masterly," Dev said. There was a hint of grimness in his tone now. "But I found little to enjoy in it." He turned in the chair so that he was looking at her more directly and she felt his gaze very keenly on her face. "Or were you referring to the play?"

"You are determined to quarrel with me tonight," Susanna said.

"Yes," Dev agreed. "I suppose I am." He laughed. "I thought your pretence of enthusiasm very well done when surely you must find the theater dull."

"I don't know why you would think that," Susanna said. She felt stung by his cynicism. "I love the theater. One can escape reality and lose oneself in a play—" She stopped abruptly, aware that she had given away more than she had intended and that Dev, always so sharp, had already spotted her slip.

"How interesting," he said slowly. "You have so

much, Lady Carew. Why would you wish to escape? What would you wish to escape?"

Their eyes met and held and once again, as at Tattersalls', Susanna felt the elusive pull of affinity between them. She forced herself to look away and gave a little careless shrug.

"Oh, I merely meant that I enjoy the playacting."

"Oh, well, I can see you would be drawn to that," Dev said cynically. He relaxed back in his seat. "Do you not prefer faster entertainments, though? The pursuit of young sprigs of the nobility, for a start?"

"I never pursue more than one young sprig at once," Susanna said. She felt relief that Dev had apparently been diverted from questioning her about her previous words at the same time as feeling a hollow sense of regret that she could not be honest with him. "Fitz is older than I am," she added. "You make me sound as though I am trying to snatch him from the cradle."

"He may be older in years, perhaps," Dev said, "but he is a lamb to the slaughter."

Susanna stifled a laugh. "How absurd you are. Fitz is no naive youth. He is a thorough-going, dangerous rake."

"Which evidently does not scare you."

Susanna shook her head. "I am far too old a hand to be frightened of a libertine," she said.

"Perhaps it is his bad reputation that attracts you? Oh, I forgot," Dev said, with studied insolence, "your own lack of morals and principles should surely be enough for two."

The atmosphere in the theater, stiflingly hot on this humid summer night, seemed to freeze.

"Do you have a point to make, Sir James?" Susanna asked frigidly.

"Yes," Dev said. "I find I have to be very plain with you." He paused. "You are aware, I am sure, that Fitz is to marry my sister, Francesca?"

His tone was even, with no trace of a threat, yet Susanna still shivered. She had known it would not take Dev long to warn her off openly and here it was, the moment she had been anticipating. She flicked him a look under her lashes.

"Forgive me," she said, "but you wish your sister to wed a philandering Marquis?"

The grim line to Dev's mouth deepened. "Fitz will not deceive Chessie once they are wed," he said with constraint. "I will make sure he understands that."

"You delude yourself," Susanna said. She waited, but Dev did not reply. His face was carved from stone. "You are torn," she said, after a moment. She was not certain that she should pursue this but the words spilled out anyway. "You want Fitz to marry Chessie in order to give her all the things you value," she said. "You want her to have a title, money and status, but the price is too high, isn't it, Devlin? The price of seeing your sister humiliated by her husband's infidelities is too great—"

Dev's hand came down hard on her wrist. "You

value those things, too, Lady Carew," he said through his teeth. "You seek more wealth and a better title, so do not seek to preach to me."

Susanna freed herself very deliberately, drawing in a deep breath to steady herself, grasping for the control she had very nearly lost. It was dangerous to speak freely. She knew she had touched a nerve with Devlin but in doing so she had also put her own motives under question. Dev thought she wanted to marry Fitz for his money and title. She had to remember that, had to remember that that was precisely the belief she wanted to foster. No one could suspect her true commission or she would be undone.

She smoothed the golden gauze of her skirts. "That's true," she said. "I do value material riches very much." She gave him a little taunting smile. "Miss Devlin and the Marquis are not formally betrothed, are they?"

A heavy frown came down on Dev's brow. "There had been an understanding between them," he said. His tone had hardened.

"An understanding," Susanna repeated. She sighed. "They are so often misunderstandings, don't you find, Sir James? A pretty girl thinks she has caught the interest of a handsome peer but then—" she shrugged "—someone prettier comes along to distract his attention."

"Someone dangerous and manipulative comes along," Dev said. He had abandoned any pretence of courtesy now. Dislike colored his voice. "Let us be plainer still, Lady Carew. I assume that you plan to cut Chessie out and wed Fitz yourself?"

"That is no business of yours," Susanna said.

"You mistake," Dev said. "It is very much my business. As your former husband—"

"I was under the impression," Susanna said, "that the word *former* implied that the marriage was over. Nor did I think that former husbands played a role in their wives' future choices. I repeat, it is no business of yours."

Dev had shifted away from her a little, allowing Susanna to breathe again. She pressed her hands together, willing Fitz to return so that Dev would be forced to abandon this inquisition. She closed her eyes tightly. Her prayers went unheard for when she reopened them Fitz was still missing and Dev was watching her thoughtfully.

"There is something...suspicious about this," Dev said slowly.

Susanna's heart bumped against her ribs. "About what?" she said.

"The Duke and Duchess of Alton introduced you to Fitz," Dev said. "Yet they are very high in the instep and surely would not welcome their son marrying the widow of an obscure baronet, no matter how rich." His gaze narrowed on her. "Fitz could make a dazzling alliance with anyone in the ton. You are a virtual nobody and yet the Duke and Duchess support your suit. I find myself wondering why."

Susanna could feel the hairs on the back of her

neck prickle a warning. There was no room for hesitation here. Dev would pounce on any uncertainty or anything she gave away.

"I imagine that the Duke and Duchess think a rich widow for Fitz is preferable to him eloping with a penniless Irish nobody," she said dryly.

Dev shook his head. "The Altons put more store on bloodlines than a bloodstock agent. They would never countenance you for their son, Susanna. So I find myself wondering just why the Duchess sponsors you." He smiled. "I thought I might make a few inquiries."

Fear gripped Susanna's throat. There was absolutely nothing to connect her directly to the Duke and Duchess. Dev could never guess, nor discover, that they were employing her. The Altons' family lawyer, Mr. Churchward, had hired her and it was he who paid her bills. She had only met the Duke and Duchess once. Even so it was astute of Dev to realize that their behavior in taking her up was out of character. He was suspicious of her and would seize upon any weakness. She would have to be very careful, especially as her marriage to the imaginary Sir Edwin Carew was no more than window dressing for the role of rich, sophisticated widow. On no account could she let Dev discover the shocking truth that she was actually being paid to come between Fitz and Francesca.

"By all means make any inquiries you wish," she said, affecting a yawn, "if you have so much spare time on your hands. There is no mystery, though. The Duke and Sir Edwin were old friends—"

"Of course," Dev said, with immaculate courtesy. "Your less than sainted husband, the one who taught you such a hard lesson about male fidelity. What a mystery he is! I must discover more about him."

"You have left it too late," Susanna said, "since he is dead."

"I am sure," Dev said, and now at last she could hear the undertone of threat in his voice, "that I shall be able to find out about him anyway."

Susanna took a deep breath. This was getting very dangerous. When she had invented Sir Edwin as her husband she had not thought that anyone would dig into her past. There had been no reason why anyone should do so. But that was before Dev had reappeared with his searching gaze and his damnably awkward questions.

"By all means," she said politely. "I would tell you about Sir Edwin myself but I have no desire to spoil your fun. You must have a very great deal of leisure—or be very bored." She looked up as Emma came back into the box on Freddie Walters's arm. Emma gave Dev a glance that smoldered so much, Susanna was afraid that the seats might catch fire. Dev looked supremely uncomfortable, caught her watching him and glared at her.

"Perhaps you should devote some of your spare time to your fiancée," Susanna said. "She appears most desirous of your company."

"I do not require romantic advice from you, thank you, Lady Carew," Dev snapped.

"I beg your pardon." Susanna gave him a glacial look. "Since you have spent so much of your time giving me advice I thought that I would return the compliment. It is the privilege of an old friend, after all."

She saw something dark flare in Dev's eyes, an expression that made her feel dizzy and weak.

"But we are not friends, are we?" Dev said. "We may be many things but we are not friends at all."

He stood up, sketched a bow and walked away, leaving Susanna feeling shaken. No, she and Devlin were not friends. They could never be friends. Nor were they old lovers whose mutual passion had burned out. Strong emotion still smoldered between them. There was something hot and dark and angry that might kindle to a blaze at any moment. And that was what she wanted. Susanna realized it with a pang of fear. Fitz aroused nothing in her but the deepest indifference. But Devlin… She had always felt too much for Devlin, too much love and too much guilt.

As the curtain rose on the second half of the play she turned her attention to the stage and concentrated fiercely. She could not let Dev get under her skin, not when there was so much to play for. Not when there was so much to lose.

CHAPTER NINE

EMMA HAD BEEN WAITING and waiting for Dev and now the dew upon the grass was soaking her slippers and she felt cold inside and out. The night was hot and still with the feeling of thunder in the air. She heard the clock on St. Michael's church chime at half past one. Dev was not coming. He did not want her.

She sat down on the little stone bench by the side of the ornamental pool and stared into its black depths. She was not sure if she felt relieved or disappointed. She was not even sure why she had attempted to seduce Dev. She was very bored, she supposed, and it would have been quite exciting. And she had been curious. Dev had such a reputation as a rake and yet in the entire two years they had been engaged he had behaved toward her with nothing but the most tedious propriety. It seemed very unfair that London was full of women who had all experienced Devlin's shockingly libertine attentions whereas she, his fiancée, had no notion what it would be like to be ravished by him. That was surely quite wrong.

When they had first become engaged everything had been so much more exciting. Dev had been lauded as a hero then, a daring explorer, famous for his courage, resourcefulness and charm. Emma had seen him, wanted him and bought him with the promise of her fortune. She had wanted to wed him immediately but then some tedious relative had died and the family had been plunged into mourning, and after that it was the grouse-shooting season and then a year had slipped by and now another and she was beginning to think the wedding might never happen.

She was beginning to wonder if she wanted it to happen.

She knew that her parents had opposed the match from the start and perhaps they had been right. She had wanted an adventurer and now she could not shake the conviction that she had bought a fake. So perhaps it was just as well that Devlin was not here. She had changed her mind about seduction. She was sure it was overrated.

She stood up to go back inside the house. Her wrap caught on a twig of the privet hedge and she paused to release it, a difficult maneuver in the dark. As she did so the shadows shifted in the corner of her eye, there was the scrape of gravel and someone moved. Emma spun around, tearing the delicate fabric of her scarf, her heart beating in her throat.

A man was standing before her on the path. Evidently he had jumped down from the high wall encircling the garden and now he stood dusting his palms and straightening his jacket. Emma's heart started to race even faster. So he had come after all.

Suddenly Emma felt small and frightened, as though she had released a genie from its bottle and did not know how to force it back inside. He was walking toward her now, his stride long and unhurried and yet somehow extremely purposeful. Emma gulped.

"I've changed my mind," she croaked as he drew closer to her. She pressed her damp palms to the silk of her skirts and felt herself trembling.

The man paused. "You've changed your mind about what?"

"About seducing you—" Emma's throat dried completely.

"How disappointing," the man said. He shrugged. "But since we have only just met it might be for the best. Take a little time to get to know me first..."

Emma could hear the amusement in his voice and, as he stepped into the moonlight, she could see she had made a mistake. This was not Devlin, though this man did bear a superficial resemblance to Dev in terms of his height and broad build. But where Dev was fair this stranger was very dark. He had a confident swagger that was curiously attractive. He was not young—older than Dev, to be sure—and he was smiling at her now in a way that made her want to smile back. How odd. How disturbing.

"I apologize," she said stiffly, although he was the one who was trespassing in her parents' garden. "I thought that you were my fiancé. He was supposed to meet me here."

"So that you could seduce him?" The man had

taken her hand and Emma found herself sitting next to him on the stone bench. She was not quite sure how that had happened. "What an ungracious cad," the man said, "to leave you here unattended. And an ungrateful one, too, to turn down such an offer," he added thoughtfully, his dark eyes appraising Emma in the moonlight. "Why did you want to seduce him?"

Emma blushed. "I was bored and I thought it might be fun," she said. "We have been betrothed for two years and he never lays a finger on me! And I don't know why I am telling you this," she added crossly. "Who are you?"

The man sketched a mocking bow. "Thomas Bradshaw, illegitimate son of the late Duke of Farne, entirely at your service, my lady."

Emma gaped. She had never met anyone's illegitimate son before. Illegitimate children were not the sort of people of whom her mother approved. And yet Thomas Bradshaw looked and spoke like a gentleman. Except that he did seem rather dangerous. Emma could not quite explain why but she knew it. She felt it. A frisson of excitement skittered down her spine.

"What are you doing in my parents' garden?" she demanded. She felt better, more in control, when she assumed the role of aristocratic lady. Bradshaw, however, demolished her grasp after confidence by the simple expedient of taking her hand again. His touch left her breathless. The worn leather of his glove against her bare palm was like a caress.

"I am working," he said, as though that explained everything.

"Work?" Emma frowned. She had never met anyone who worked for a living. Devlin had worked once, although a commission in the Navy was vastly different from a proper job and was quite acceptable for a gentleman.

"What sort of work?" she asked.

"You are full of questions." Bradshaw still sounded amused. "I…find things out about people. I hunt down criminals."

That sounded exciting to Emma, enough to give her another shiver down the spine were it not for the fact that Thomas Bradshaw himself felt more dangerous than any malefactor.

"I doubt you will find any criminals in our garden," she said primly.

She saw his teeth flash in a smile. "One never knows." His gaze turned serious, intense. "Your fiancé, perhaps. He seems like a fool if nothing worse. Who is he?"

Emma was betrayed into a little giggle. "His name is Sir James Devlin," she said, and saw Bradshaw's eyes widen.

"Well, he's enough of a rogue," he said.

"So people keep telling me," Emma said irritably, "but I see no evidence of it at all."

"And you thought you would if you asked him to take your virginity?"

Emma blushed again, very hotly this time. "That is not a very proper question!"

"This is not a very proper conversation." Bradshaw smiled. "Nor is boredom a particularly good reason to seduce a man. What else would you like to do to make your life more exciting?"

Emma's mind whirled through a procession of giddy images. There were so many things that she wanted to do, things that were forbidden to her.

"I want to drink in a coffeehouse," she began, "and go dancing in a tavern, not in a ton ballroom, and gamble for high stakes. I want to be in a carriage stopped by a highwayman or footpad, and I want to kiss a man who is not a gentleman—"

Bradshaw kissed her. She had wanted it, had spoken the words quite deliberately, as a provocation, and now she felt a huge flash of triumph. The excitement whipped through her like a lightning strike, leaving her quivering in his arms. The kiss was gentle, promising much but denying her the fulfillment that she grasped after. It left her wanting so much more that as his lips left hers she was breathless with frustration as well as desire.

Bradshaw smoothed the hair back from her flushed cheek. "You want all the things they wish to protect you from," he said. He cupped her head, drawing her closer. This kiss was more demanding and when he let her go Emma could not smother a gasp of longing.

He slid his hand down to take hers. "Come with me." Then, as she did not move, he tilted his head to one side, smiling. "What is stopping you, Emma?"

Emma was still trembling and now she trembled even more at the caressing way he said her name. She did not wonder how he knew it. She was too swept away by her feelings. Her skin felt damp and feverish, hotter than the sultry night, and her body was tight with anticipation and exhilaration. And yet she hesitated. This was wrong; Thomas Bradshaw was a stranger, and behind her desires was a small voice—did it belong to her mother or her governess or her chaperon?—that warned her about the dangers of allowing random men too much license. She had already given this stranger a great deal of latitude…

"I cannot," she said dully, and felt the all the excitement drain out of her.

Bradshaw smiled again, pressed a kiss on her palm and released her.

"Maybe next time," he said.

The shadows shifted and he was gone as quietly as he had come. Emma felt as though she was awakening from a trance. She grabbed her shawl, wrapping it about her with trembling hands, trying to draw comfort from its flimsy folds. Suddenly she felt shaken and a little frightened, yet beneath that the current of excitement still burned.

Next time, he had said. There would be a next

time. She did not believe it. She wanted to believe it. She shivered as she ran back to the house and let herself inside. And in the darkness of her bed she dreamed.

DEV WAS LATE, VERY LATE, and more than a little drunk. The clock struck two as he turned into Curzon Street. The pavements were empty except for a man disappearing around a street corner, a darker shade against the night. In the skipping moonlight Dev could not see his face although he had the oddest impression that it was someone he knew, someone he had met before. He also felt a trickle of warning down the spine, a premonition alerting his senses to danger. But the man was gone and the night was heavy and still.

Dev paused with his hand on the latch of the garden gate. He had never approached the house from this direction before. Truth was, he did not really want to approach it from any direction. He had spent the last two hours at his club searching for his ardor at the bottom of a brandy bottle. Alas his desire for Emma was no stronger now than it had been earlier in the evening, which was to say that it was nonexistent. And yet this was his chance and the key to his future. He had to take it. He had to seduce Emma and use the seduction to press for the wedding to go ahead with all speed. Then his fortune and his position in society would be secure.

He lifted the latch. The door opened and he stepped through.

He had never been in the garden at Emma's parents' town house before. In the fitful moonlight he could see that it was small and entirely enclosed by a high brick wall. Miniature topiary trees dotted the gravel paths and roses trailed their rich scent on the humid night air. There was a tiny ornamental summerhouse that looked designed for seduction. Dev looked at it and felt his spirits sink.

Emma was standing by the little pool, where a fountain in the form of a stone cherub spouted a sparkling stream of water in the moonlight. She was facing away from him, half in deep shadow, and she did not turn as he approached. He could see her gown, a pale silver shimmer in the moonlight.

Dev took two strides toward her, reached out and with a fervor borne of desperation rather than eagerness, pulled her into his arms and kissed her.

As soon as he touched her he knew with a rush of profound relief that it would be all right. She made a soft sound of shock deep in her throat as his lips took hers but within a second she was melting into his arms and she was hot and wanton and willing, and the light burst in his mind, drawing pleasure in its wake. He closed his eyes, twisting his hands in her hair—such soft, silken strands beneath his fingers—and held her still whilst he plundered her mouth with his own, tangling his tongue with hers, delving deep, ravishing her.

He moved his lips to the line of her neck and the sweet, vulnerable hollow of her throat. She tasted divine, of fresh air and cool summer skin, and she smelled of thyme and roses. The lust kicked him in the stomach with such force he groaned. How could he not have wanted her? She was so pliant and responsive in his arms.

Dev drew back reluctantly to take a breath and in that moment the moon peeked out from behind the rising bank of cloud and the light fell full on her face.

Susanna.

This was Susanna, her hair tumbling over her shoulders, her lashes a dark smudge against the shadow of her cheek, her lips parted, swollen and full from his kisses. The shock splintered Dev's mind followed by another jolt of lust so wicked and powerful that it stole his breath.

Afterward he was not sure how long he had hesitated for; less than a second, probably.

He knew exactly what he should have done. He was in the wrong garden and he should have apologized and walked away. That was what any gentleman would do. But he was a rake facing overwhelming temptation. He wanted Susanna—he had wanted her from the moment she stepped back into his life—and she was here, and she was willing in his arms, and he was going to take her. His desire for her was so acute it felt like physical pain.

"Devlin?" Susanna's voice was a whisper. She

sounded confused and adrift, utterly seduced by his kisses. "What—"

Dev kissed her again, softly, persuasively, mastering the need that drove him. He felt Susanna's body melt into acquiescence, felt her sigh against his lips as she returned the kiss. He pulled her down onto the stone bench in the shadow of the trees. He had meant to do this in the summerhouse, he remembered hazily, where no doubt there were soft cushions to lie upon and walls to guard their privacy from prying eyes. Except that here in the gardens it was hot and scented and he wanted Susanna here, now, on the damp grass with the moonlight dancing on the water and the wind in the trees and the night air caressing their skin.

He slid the gown from her shoulders—she was wearing a loose confection of the sheerest, silkiest gauze and no stays—and again she gasped as the air touched her nakedness. He could feel the way her skin puckered, her nipple tight and hard against his palm and then against his lips as he bent his head to take her in his mouth. He sucked; she cried out, a muted sound that made the desire roar through him. Her gown slid down to free her breasts completely. She looked exquisite in the dappled shade, her nakedness fully exposed to his gaze, her pale skin etched in silver, her nipples dark and pointing, begging for his touch as she arched toward him. He took her in his mouth again, cupping her breast, sliding his tongue over the taut peak in a caress that had her begging for more, her words soft and broken.

He ran a hand under those gauzy skirts—light, delicious, smooth—and up her leg to the ribbon at the top of her stockings. The skin of her inner thigh was even more soft and delicious than the silken skirts that fell back to uncover her to his touch. He could feel the heat of her and smell the scent of feminine arousal. He was burning up now with the need to possess her but again he mastered his impatience.

His knuckles grazed the core of her and the contact wrenched a groan from her throat.

"Oh, please..." She was a supplicant, utterly his to command, pleading for release. He would not give her what she craved. Not yet.

He kissed her, long and deep, and her lips clung to his eagerly, opening beneath him, offering everything, shockingly responsive. He remembered this passion in her and his heart surged to have found it again. He pressed openmouthed kisses against her breasts, running his tongue up to the peak in long, hot strokes until her whole body rose under the domination of his touch. He dropped his lips to her belly, pushing aside the gown, impatient now to explore every plane and curve.

She tasted impossibly sweet and silken. He flicked his tongue into her navel and felt her shiver. His fingers returned to the moist core of her, seeking, finding. Her thighs opened to him. He pressed down gently on the hot, hard little nub and she cried out as she came immediately. Her body tensed, racked by spasm after spasm in utter obedience to his touch, powerless to resist the seduction.

"Now..." Did he speak or did she? He picked her up and carried her to the summerhouse where he stripped the gauzy skirts from her and laid her down on the wide chaise. He was aware now of nothing but the need to have her. It clawed at him with the fiercest desire he had ever experienced. He had to be inside her, to possess her completely. In a frenzy of impatience now he tore open his pantaloons and followed her down onto the chaise, pushing apart her thighs as wide as he could. He felt her close about him, impossibly tight, the pressure enough to make his head spin and his control falter on the edge.

"Gently, sweetheart..." He eased back and felt her body give to accommodate his more deeply. He pressed a kiss to her trembling lips, felt her upper body lift and her nipples brush his chest. One thrust, two; long, slow strokes, exerting absolute control over his desires, feelings himself sliding toward the edge again and reining in his own needs yet again... He had not known that he possessed such patience when every instinct prompted him to plunder her body with ruthless intensity. Yet still he kept the pace slow, deepening the strokes now, hearing her gasp and feeling her move with him.

She ran her hands down his back and over his buttocks, pulling him into her more deeply and he was lost. She came again, her body clasping his. The light exploded in his head. Every muscle tensed. He felt the world slipping and sliding away from him in a whirlwind of sensation, splintering into the brightest and most dazzling pleasure. And behind the pleasure was something more profound; a lightness that flooded his whole being, a deep sense of connection, a feeling of peace that should have scared him witless but instead felt honest and true, a measure of pure, raw passion, as though he had regained the most valuable thing he had ever lost. He was still breathing as hard as if he had been in combat. His body felt supremely content and his mind was hovering on the edges of satisfied exhaustion. Then he felt Susanna move. She sat up and the panic he felt in her movements and the raw shock in her voice broke his state of bliss splintered into a thousand pieces.

"Devlin!"

She sounded horrified, as though she had only just come to a realization of what they had done. She rolled away from him, scrambled off the chaise, grabbed her gown and started to try to dress herself again. The slippery gauze slithered and slid through her hands. Dev heard her swear fiercely under her breath. He could see her slender fingers trembling in the moonlight as she tried to fasten the ribbons and he was shot through with regret and a strange tenderness. He stood up, took a step toward her and saw her recoil.

"Let me help you," he said.

The minute he touched her she froze, like a wary

creature measuring the danger. Her hair, that beautiful silky mass he had buried his hands in, was tumbled in wild profusion about her shoulders. He brushed it back from her face and felt her shiver. He wanted to draw her into his arms and hold her. The strength of the impulse shook him. But there was something in her that forbade it; he sensed her complete withdrawal from him and saw the dignity with which she belatedly tried to cloak herself.

She was frowning, at a loss. "I don't know…" Her voice sounded as hesitant as he had ever heard it.

"You don't know what you were doing?" he supplied. It was a common enough excuse from a woman who had allowed herself to get carried away and then wanted to pretend it was all a mistake. He'd heard it often enough from bored society wives and widows who wanted some fun but did not want to admit it openly.

"I can throw some light on that," he said pleasantly. "You were making love with me."

He saw the flash of irritation in her eyes. "I realize that," she said sharply. The edge went from her voice as quickly as it had come. "I don't know what happened…" she said. She sounded bewildered. "I don't understand how it happened."

"It happened because we wanted it to happen," Dev said. He had never seen the need to indulge in any pretense over sex. It had always been a pleasurable pastime to him but no more. Except that this time it had felt different, more profound, more important somehow. But that was nonsense. The simple truth was that he had wanted Susanna all evening, had wanted her in fact from the moment he had seen her again. And now he had taken her.

He waited for Susanna to deny it but she was silent. She was trying to tidy her hair now, a pointless process since the pins that had held it were probably scattered over half the garden. Her face was in shadow and her hands steady now as she smoothed her gown down over her hips. The movement only served to remind him of what lay beneath those gauzy skirts; the sleek smoothness of her belly and thighs, the heat of her body as it closed about his. He felt his cock stir again. The only problem with breaking two years of celibacy with astounding sex was awakening the need to do it again. And again.

He saw Susanna's gaze travel over him. He had not stopped to remove any of his clothes. His jacket hung open, his shirt was untucked and his cravat had disappeared somewhere. He had done up his pantaloons but they struggled to contain his renewed erection. He felt as callow and hot as a youth who had only just discovered sex.

"You are not looking your usual immaculate self," Susanna commented. Her voice was her own again, cool, composed.

"Well, forgive me," Dev said. "I am sure that if you give me the chance I could make love to you so delicately that neither of us need disarrange our clothing."

Once again she was silent. That was unusual. Most women he had known wanted to talk after sex, about him, about themselves, about their nonexistent future relationship. Susanna, in contrast, walked softly across to the summerhouse door and stood facing the garden, her back to him. The wind hushed through the birch tree and the moonlight painted its trunk in shades of black and silver.

"What the devil were you doing trespassing in my garden?" she said abruptly, after a moment.

It was so incongruous after what had happened between them that Dev almost laughed aloud.

"And what the devil," Susanna added, "were you doing behaving like that..." Her voice faded away and Dev knew that for all her apparent calm she was still shaken to the core, utterly shocked by what had happened between them.

"I was trespassing in more than your garden," Dev drawled. "If it comes to that, what were you doing responding to me?"

She turned. He saw confusion in her eyes and realized that she did not know the answer to that question. She did not know why she had wanted him, why she had responded to him so passionately, or why she had made love with him. He could see that it troubled her deeply.

The flickering silver moonlight seemed to accentuate her blush. "I thought—" She stopped.

"You thought that I was Fitz?" Dev suggested.

"No!" She almost snapped the words. "I knew it

was you…." Her voice trailed away into uncertainty again.

"You said my name," Dev pointed out helpfully.

"Yes…" She was frowning. "And I didn't… I haven't—"

"You haven't made love with Fitz?" Dev felt a blaze of triumph.

"That is none of your concern." She had regained her poise now, at least outwardly, although the agitated tap of her footsteps as she turned and walked away from him rather suggested otherwise. Her swishing skirts caught the rosemary edging the path and released a tumble of fragrance onto the hot night air. It smelled sweet and poignant.

Dev followed her for no better reason than that he wanted to.

She stopped, turned; looked exasperated. She raised a hand to halt him in a gesture that betrayed her nervousness.

"You didn't answer my question," she said. "What are you doing in my garden?"

"This is your garden?" Dev said. He could not help but laugh. Susanna looked disgusted at his facetiousness.

"In point of fact it's the Duke of Portsmouth's garden," she said. "I am renting his house for the rest of the Season."

"But this is number 25 Curzon Street?" Dev said.

"Number 21." She looked more closely at him. "I

think that your navigation may be at fault. You were looking for Lord Brooke's house?"

For some reason Dev did not want to admit it and it was not simply because he wanted to protect Emma's reputation. But Susanna had already worked everything out.

"You had an assignation with Lady Emma." Her tone was suddenly flat. "I see. Well, at least I suppose she is your fiancée." An odd shade came into her voice. "I did not think that you would have seduced her."

"You've thought about it, then?" Dev said politely. "Jealous?"

She gave him a look of searing contempt. "Naturally not."

"After what has just happened," Dev said, "I find it difficult to believe you."

"A case of mistaken identity." She snapped a twig from the privet and shredded it between agitated fingers. "You thought that you were seducing Emma and I—" She stopped again.

"I thought no such thing," Dev said. "I knew it was you."

She shot him a sharp look. "Then why did you do it if it was Emma you originally intended to seduce?"

"Because I wanted you more," Dev said.

He saw her eyes narrow. "You have even fewer morals than I had imagined," she said contemptuously.

"Very probably," Dev said. "But we are not talking about me, we are talking about you." He braced one hand against the trunk of a leaning apple tree, trapping her between him and the garden wall. "Perhaps you make love with all random strangers who wander into your garden at night," he said softly.

"Perhaps I do." Her green gaze was defiant. She made no move to escape him though he sensed the tension in her and the urgent need to get away. "I think you should leave," she added. She glanced across at the door in the wall. "And I will make sure to lock the door behind you."

Dev did not move. He wanted to kiss her again. He wanted to make love to her again. He wanted it with a ferocity and a need that was startling. He had never wanted to make love to a woman he did not like before. Fortunately that had left him plenty of choice since he liked women very much as a rule. But this woman… He despised her calculation and her utter lack of moral compass. Yet he desired her so much that the hunger raked at him fiercely. And now that he had taken her once his need was a hundred times more potent, a thousand. Perhaps the celibacy of the previous two years had sharpened his lust for her. Yet even though he would have liked to have dismissed it as something so simple he knew it was not so. The need he had for Susanna was as complicated as it was unquenchable. She felt it, too. He knew it. It was the reason she had responded to him, against all sense and all reason. Neither of them could explain it and right now he did not even want to try.

"Of course," he said. "I should go." He made no move at all.

Susanna looked at him with those troubled eyes. Somewhere in the distance a roll of thunder rumbled. The moonlight had almost vanished now and the night felt hot, the darkness heavy and the air still, as though it was waiting.

Dev raised a hand, gently brushing the strands of hair away from the pure line of Susanna's neck. Her skin felt cool and smooth beneath his fingertips. His hand slid to her nape and he exerted the tiniest pressure to bring her closer to him. She took a step forward. Her palms came up against the front of his jacket.

"Devlin…" There was a warning in her voice. He heard it but it was so at odds with the expression in her eyes that he discounted it. It was surely impossible that she, the adventuress, could look so innocent. Lost even. Yet he remembered the honesty of their lovemaking. Not even the finest actress could have simulated such sincerity. Some element of artifice would have given her away. No, there had been no pretence between them when they had been in that most intimate of embraces.

So… This was real. Neither of them understood it. Neither of them was comfortable with it. Both of them wanted it.

Dev bent his head and kissed her, very gently this

time. He felt her stiffen as though she was trying to put up barriers against him but after a second the rigidity in her melted away and her lips softened beneath his. Primal possessiveness roared through him, urging him to grab her and carry her inside, up to her bed. He mastered it and kissed her again, softly, sweetly, his lips brushing the line of her jaw and the corner of her mouth before returning fully to take her lips again in a deep, demanding kiss.

"What you said in the carriage is correct," she said when he let her go. She sounded slightly lost, as though she had drunk too much. "You are very good at this." She sighed. "You are a rake."

The thunder was rolling closer now. Dev felt the first drops of rain starting to fall, slow and heavy. He smiled and drew Susanna back into his arms. He could feel her breasts pressing against his chest, the beat of her heart slamming against his. The raindrops were running down her neck now. "Your point?" he murmured as he lowered his lips to the curve where her neck met her shoulder. He licked up the water and felt her quiver.

"God help me," she said, "I even know you are trying to seduce me again and yet—"

"And yet you don't want to stop me."

Her silence was eloquent.

"We cannot do it again," she said and he heard the longing in her voice and felt his desire sharpen. He dropped his lips to the hollow between her breasts, tasted her, and heard her breath catch.

"Yes, we can." His hand came up to her breast. The gown was plastered to her body now as the rain fell with a steady beat. One sly brush of his thumb over her nipple had her shaking and he exulted in his power to do that to her.

"In full knowledge rather than in the heat of the moment—" She sounded breathless.

"Why not? It is more honest."

She was silent again. He could hear her rapid breathing beneath the drum of the rain. He could also feel the conflict in her. Temptation coiled about them, thick and heady as wine, drugging the senses. She gave a tiny gasp and he felt the resistance ease from her.

"I don't know why I want you…" She sounded bemused. She had also capitulated. He sensed it.

He picked her up in his arms, strode up the steps onto the terrace and in at the doors, kicking them closed against the storm outside. The room beyond was lit by one candle. It was a drawing room, elegant but oddly characterless. There was a pile of fashionable magazines on the marble-topped table. A harp stood in a corner. The breeze drew a tiny shimmer of music from its strings.

"Your servants?" There was no sense in being indiscreet. Gossip would harm him as much as it would harm her. This was clandestine. It must remain a secret. The thought only intensified his lust.

"They are abed." She pressed her fingers to his

lips in a brief caress that he felt through every last muscle and sinew in his body.

The house was silent. He carried her up the stairs. He was already hard again now in expectation of what he knew would follow, the downright pleasure and decadence of lying with her, pleasuring each other, making love for hour after hot hour through the night. It was inordinately exciting. He almost stumbled in his haste and anticipation.

"Your room?" he whispered. He felt the soft strands of her hair against his lips as she turned her head.

"There." Her answering whisper was against his lips. She gestured to the door on the right.

He placed her on the bed and turned to secure the door with a stealthy click. The room was dark, lit only by the reflection of moonlight in the mirror. She moved to close the curtains but he caught her wrist, pulled her to him and started to strip the soaking golden gauze gown from her with sure hands this time, tossing it aside, discarding his own clothes so that at last he was completely naked, skin against skin. He felt her shake as they touched and caught her gasp of pleasure in his mouth, kissing her, his tongue plunging deep.

"Hush…" He murmured it against her lips. "Remember the servants. You are going to have to be very, very quiet…."

He felt her shudder in response to his wicked words. She reached for him, hungry and eager, but he flipped her over onto her stomach on the bed and straddled her. She tried to rise but he gently forced her down, bending to cover the satin skin of her shoulders with soft, biting kisses, to trail his tongue down the length of her spine, a lick here, a flick over the ribs there that had her squirming. She was hot and panting beneath his hands. He could tell that she wanted to turn over and face him but he held her still, his thighs pressing into her hips. When she felt his cock hard against her buttocks she gave a little stifled cry and he slipped lower, parting her, letting the tip rest against the core of her, pressing gently within. She tried to arch up to meet him. He withdrew and felt the frustration in her tighten like an overwound thread.

"Later." He leaned over to drop a kiss against the back of her neck. "Not yet."

She mumbled something that sounded like a curse and he laughed. Some impulse in him wanted to punish her for everything she had done to him and yet at the same time he did not want it, for his anger had already transmuted to pleasure and never had the punishment been sweeter nor the victim more willing.

He slid down the bed, driving her legs apart so that he could press his lips to the tender skin of her inner thighs. Again she tried to roll over and he held her down, his hand splayed in the hollow of her back. Inch by slow inch he explored every last curve of her with his lips and teeth and tongue, working back to the swell of her buttocks and down again to the smooth, vulnerable expanse of her thigh. He could feel how taut she was with frustration and longing. When he touched her with his tongue she bent upward, tense as the strings of the harp.

She tried to press her thighs together to gain surcease but he held them wide, running his tongue over her hot core back and forth in the most delicate and teasing caress, again and again, feeling the unendurable tension in her build tighter and faster until at last she came apart beneath his touch. Then he tumbled her over so that he could see her face, see the sweet agony and the bliss reflected there and feel her shaking uncontrollably in his arms, her skin hot and damp against his. He pressed kisses to her mouth and ran his hands soothingly over her trembling body until she quieted, and again he felt the most enormous sense of triumph and possession and other, more troubling emotions that stirred beneath the surface but which he chose to disregard. He was adept at ignoring any deep feelings stirred by the sexual act; in his experience they usually boiled down to gratitude and pleasure rather than anything more profound and certainly he had no wish for anything else with Susanna. They shared a past and now, unexpectedly, it seemed they shared the ability to give each other deep physical enjoyment. That was enough. It was more than enough. He would soon drive out any other emotion, drowning it in pure sensation.

"I like being able to do this to you." He propped

himself on one elbow, watching her as she lay there spent in her pleasure, her skin flushed, her lashes spiky dark against the curve of her cheek. "It gives me great satisfaction."

He ran a hand possessively over her breast, felt her instinctive response and lowered his head to take the nipple in his mouth.

"I like it, too." She sounded sated, confused. "I must be mad. I do not understand."

Dev did not understand, either. Nor did he care. He had been plunged into a maelstrom of physical delight tonight and once he had tasted it he was lost. His desire for Susanna was deep and dark and compulsive and it rode him like a devil.

He raised his head from her breast. "You owe me." He smiled at her wickedly and saw her eyes widen as she took his meaning. He held her gaze, challenged her, and after a moment she rolled over, all tangled black hair and sinuous limbs. She pushed him back on the bed. Her lips brushed his belly, his thigh, and then she had taken him into her mouth and his excitement was so extreme he almost shouted aloud.

Almost he let her take control. The sweep of her hair against his stomach, the caress of her tongue, the shimmering moonlight on the bed, the silken sheets against his back were part of a sensual enchantment that threatened to drive him beyond sanity. The first time, in the garden, had been for her. This was where she paid by meeting his price.

He watched her in the mirror; watched her mouth

on his shaft and thought of the utter bliss of demanding what he wanted from her and giving her absolute pleasure in return, sensual delight searing enough to bind them together in perfect union. The erotic image of her, etched in the black and white of moonlight and shadow, the soft touch of her lips and tongue, the dark whirling spiral of his lust threatened to drive him too far too fast.

"No more." He ground out the words and pulled away from her. "I want to come inside you."

He saw the flare of excitement in her eyes as he drew her up and pulled her on top of him so that she slid down to encompass him in her heat.

Outside, the rain fell with an insistent primitive beat in echo of their lust. The storm broke overhead, the thunder shaking the house. The night was so humid and dark one could get lost in it and Dev felt adrift, driven to the furthest shores of pleasure. Hotter and hotter the spiral burned. He felt Susanna push him to the very furthest extremes of bliss and realized with helpless abandonment that he, the perpetrator, the one who had wanted to make her pay, was the most willing, most helpless victim of all. Then she came in great rolling waves that carried him with her. Even as he felt the ecstasy wash through him and recede he felt something else, that elusive emotion he had felt before and sought to drive out, and now it was stronger than before and it wrapped around his heart like the tendrils of a vine. Even as he sought to dislodge it he had the most disturbing sensation that it was too late. He was caught, ensnared, the trap tightening even as he drew Susanna's exhausted body closer into his embrace and fell asleep.

Later he woke her and made love to her again whilst her body was still soft and drowsy with sleep. Her movements were slow and languorous, spinning out the delight they took in each other. He felt desperate to have her again, like a youth who had only just learned how much pleasure there was to be had in bedding a woman and grasped greedily after it. He felt Susanna smile against his lips and knew she was aware of his driving hunger but he was powerless to hide his need from her. It made him angry that his restraint was so wafer-thin. He took her with a controlled intensity that forced them both to a peak of ecstasy so sharp it was almost like pain.

"Open your eyes," he ordered her as he felt the first irresistible ripple of her climax close about him. "I want you to be sure who is making love to you. I want you to remember me."

She opened her eyes and they were slumberous and dark, full of sensual secrets and the smile in them made his body clench. He came then, feeling her clasp him as she, too, fell deep into pleasure.

Later still, as the first pale streaks of dawn were lighting the eastern sky and shining on the cool, rain-washed streets, he left her without waking her again.

CHAPTER TEN

SUSANNA WOKE VERY SLOWLY. The room was filled with light and the bed was empty. She, too, felt curiously light and empty. Her memory presented her with a succession of images of what had happened the night before. She knew that they were true. Yet she could not believe it.

She had made love with Dev, flagrantly, wantonly, deliciously and too thoroughly ever to be forgotten. Her entire body heated at the memories of that wicked night. And she was still no closer to understanding why she had done it.

She reached for her wrap. She felt slow and hollow, as though all feeling had been drained from her, all emotion spent during the long, hot hours of the night. And yet her feelings felt sharply alive. Devlin… Once before he had come into her life and he had lit it up with his danger and reckless intensity. She had paid a high price for that. Matters had never been the same again. She could not believe that she had made the same mistake twice.

Dev. Her husband, though he did not know it. It did not make it better, easier, that they were still wed. It made the layers of deceit and emotion all the more complex. When she had known him at seventeen she had been fathoms deep in love with him. Now she was no longer that naive girl, now she most certainly did not love him anymore and yet she had given herself to him, offering up body and soul.

She sat down before her pier glass and started to brush her hair, the long strokes setting up a rhythm that soothed. In the past nine years a score of men had tried to seduce her, more than a score probably. She had not been counting. But she had refused them all. There were times when she had been tempted, times when she had wanted to escape the poverty and the hardship and the loneliness for a few brief hours, yet when she thought about giving herself to a man it had felt tawdry, an empty bargain where once with Dev she had glimpsed paradise.

She had seen paradise again now. Perhaps that was why she had wanted him—because she had wondered if her youthful memories of their time together could possibly have been true. Yet it had not merely been curiosity that had prompted her to take Devlin to her bed. Her emotions were far more profound, complicated and confusing than that, so overwhelming, in fact, that they scared her. So it was an insult to both of them to try to dismiss her response to Dev as mere curiosity.

And then there was Emma. She did not like Emma and she knew Dev did not love his fiancée but she was damned if she was going to be the means for

Dev to betray the girl. She had done it once and it had been wrong. She did not imagine that Emma would be complaisant about Dev keeping a mistress. She was Dev's wife, not his mistress, but no one knew that. No one could know.

With a sigh she laid down the pearl-handled hairbrush and let her hand fall to rest on her stomach. She had been foolish but, she hoped, not dangerously so. She was blessed that her courses were extremely regular and always had been so she should at least be safe from pregnancy this time. She shivered as the memory of the past brushed her like dark wings. Loving and losing… Her family, her husband, her child… Loss was all she had ever known. She could not let it happen again. If it did it would destroy her.

Her mirror image gazed back at her, pale and wan this morning. She had known that she was vulnerable to Dev but she had not calculated the depth of her own susceptibility. Any man was resistible, no matter how arrogantly he believed the opposite, if one simply did not desire him. Her difficulty was that she had imagined herself immune to Dev and had discovered the opposite to be true. Well, it must not happen again. If anyone found out it would ruin her plans to entrap Fitz, ruin the job she was doing for the Duke and Duchess of Alton and with it her entire future and that of the twins, too. Once again the anxiety stirred in her and she forced the dangerous fears away. She could do this. All would be well. She must keep away from Devlin now, focus on bringing Fitz to the point as quickly as possible, take the money and run.

There was a tap at the door and Margery poked her head around. When she saw that Susanna was awake she looked relieved.

"My lady, I came in earlier—twice—but you were sleeping so deeply I did not want to disturb you. I hope I did the right thing."

Susanna had a sudden vision of the little maid stumbling on a scene of utter debauchery, herself asleep in Dev's arms, both of them stark naked, their clothes scattered about the room. But there was nothing on the maid's face to indicate she had received such a shock to her sensibilities.

"Thank you, Margery," she said. "Pray do not concern yourself about it."

The maid's expression eased. "I fear you have missed Lady Phillips's Breakfast, ma'am," she murmured. "And Mrs. Carson's recital."

Susanna glanced at the clock. It was well past three. "It is astonishing that I have not missed the Duchess of Alton's soiree, as well," she observed. "Pray fetch me a cup of tea, Margery, and lots of chocolate biscuits, and then come and help me choose my gown for this evening."

The maid withdrew and Susanna walked across to the wardrobe, riffling through the gowns hanging there. The golden gauze from the previous night had disappeared, she saw. No doubt Margery had retrieved it earlier. She hoped none of the ribbons had been torn. That would be difficult to explain.

At least Dev was unlikely to be present at the Duchess's soiree since it had been specifically arranged as a very select gathering to throw Susanna into Fitz's lap. Gloom settled in Susanna's stomach like a dull weight. Tonight she must make sure to flatter Fitz and hang on his every word. The sooner she could extract a declaration from him the sooner Francesca Devlin's hopes would be permanently destroyed and she could ring the curtain down on this sorry charade. She sorted through the gowns with increasing irritation, trying to choose something that was revealing but demure, a little bit racy but not enough to frighten the dowagers. She had to look tempting but irreproachably respectable. She shook her head. Last night had been deeply, delightfully unrespectable. Her skin prickled again at the memory, little shivers of pleasure racking her. This was no good, no good at all. How could she seduce a marriage proposal from Fitz when all she could think of was Devlin?

Her hands stilled. How could she not seduce Fitz? She had no choice. Once before she had ended in the poorhouse. The stench of sickness and desperation was in her nostrils still. She could never condemn Rory and Rose to such a life. She had saved them from that fate when they had been little more than babies and part of the pledge she had made with their mother was that they would never, ever go back. She could feel Flora's dry hand clutching her own, see the terror in her friend's dull, dark eyes.

"Promise me…" Flora had said and there, surrounded by the dead and the dying, she had given her word and watched as her friend slipped away, finally at peace. She, who had buried her own child, would never desert the children entrusted to her.

"The figured rose cream silk would look beautiful for tonight, my lady," Margery ventured and Susanna jumped, realizing that the maid had returned and she had been so lost in her thoughts that she had not even noticed.

"Yes," Susanna said. "Thank you, Margery."

It was time to become Caroline Carew again, to forget the past and certainly to forget that her night with James Devlin had ever happened. She had a marquis to entrap. She could not fail. She reached for the chocolate biscuits and ate four of them in quick succession. She felt comforted. A little. Washing the chocolate from her fingers, she started to dress.

"YE WERE SLEEPING LIKE A baby or a man with a clear conscience." Dev came awake to find Frazer shaking him none too gently. "Strange," the valet continued, "since you were out until first light and I'll wager ye were up to no good."

Dev stretched, yawned and lay back on his pillows. "I wouldn't say that," he said. He felt good; more than good, his temper mellow, his body satiated. He knew that he should not. Guilt at his betrayal of Emma, shock, remorse… Those were the emotions that should be troubling him now, coupled with a determination to put the hot, sensual night with Susanna behind him and ensure it never happened again. What he should not be feeling was physical satisfaction tempered with a strong urge to repeat the experience again, as soon as possible, as often as possible.

Frazer's mouth had turned down at the corners. "Your harlot must have been a cut above those Haymarket drabs," he said sourly.

"I don't want to talk about it," Dev said, ambushed by a sudden fierce protectiveness toward Susanna that took him by surprise. He threw back the covers and stood up.

"Aye well, ye be careful, laddie," Frazer said, handing him his robe. "Seventy thousand pounds Lady Emma has. Worth more than a quick fumble with a whore—"

"That in no way describes my experience last night," Dev bit out, holding on to his temper by a thread, "and I suggest you speak of it no more, Frazer."

It was the first time that he had ever spoken in such a way to Frazer and he saw the man's brows rise before a faint wintry smile touched his lips.

"Very good, sir," the valet said, and there was approval in his voice. "There's a gentleman to see you by the name of Hammond," Frazer continued.

"I wouldn't have woken you otherwise. Said you had consulted him on a business matter last night."

Dev stopped. He had completely forgotten that the previous night he had stopped off in a coffeehouse to speak to Hammond, the most illustrious inquiry agent in London. He had asked the man to find out all he could about Susanna—and her husband, the late lamented Sir Edwin. Hammond had looked at him with weary, cynical eyes and had said he would report back the following day.

"Changed your mind?" Frazer said, not unsympathetically, as Dev hesitated. "I can send him away."

"No," Dev said slowly. He was aware of a curious duality in his feelings, a need to know the truth and at the same time a feeling of reluctance. He might not like what Hammond had to tell him. Very likely he would not like it. Protectiveness toward Susanna stirred in him again and he shook his head impatiently. He had made wild and uninhibited love with Susanna but that should not mean anything to him other than that it had been deeply pleasurable and he wanted to do it again. It did not mean that he thought her any less of an adventuress. It certainly did not mean that he cared for her. Yet he could not quite erase the picture of her sleeping in his arms, her hair spread across his chest, her head resting on his shoulder, her body soft and sweet against his, vulnerable in sleep.

With a sigh he reached for his shirt, shrugged himself into his jacket whilst Frazer *tutted* at his impatience and lack of care, then went through to the drawing room. The late-afternoon sunshine lay across the floor in bars of gold. He had indeed slept late.

"Sir James." Hammond got to his feet and shook Dev's hand. He brought with him the smell of the alehouse, of old smoke and stale beer. It seemed ingrained into his skin. But his shrewd dark eyes were bright.

"An interesting case you gave me," he said, "that of Caroline Carew." He sounded, Dev thought, like a man who had solved a particularly complex and pleasing puzzle.

"I did not expect you to have an answer for me so soon," Dev said.

Hammond bared his teeth in something that just about passed as a smile. "I pride myself on the speed and efficiency of my work. Besides, I was already asking a few questions about the merry widow."

Dev felt a stir of disquiet.

"Why?" he said swiftly.

Hammond gave another of his vulpine smiles. "When a woman as rich, beautiful and mysterious as Lady Carew comes to Town I am…shall we say… naturally curious? I already had a man working on it. Just in case."

Dev grimaced. Even though he had commissioned Hammond to find some information on Sir Edwin Carew it disturbed him that others had already been digging into Susanna's secrets. Somehow it made him feel protective of her all over again, which was folly when Susanna was surely as vulnerable as a tigress.

He signaled to Hammond to take a seat and waited, aware of the same odd mix of anticipation and unease.

"Caroline Carew," Hammond said deliberately, "is not, strictly speaking, a widow."

For a moment Dev was rendered speechless. "Sir Edwin Carew is still alive?" he queried.

Hammond grinned. "Not at all, sir. Edwin Carew never existed."

Dev frowned. Evidently Hammond was not as accomplished an inquiry agent as he claimed to be. "Of course he does, man," he said. "I've met people who claim to have known him! The Duke and Duchess of Alton—" He stopped again. Hammond was looking very amused.

"It's a neat confidence trick, sir," the inquiry agent said. "I've seen it happen before. One person claims to know Sir Edwin and before you know it there will be people who remember meeting him, or discussing astronomy with him at a lecture or sharing a whisky with him in an Edinburgh inn. They will even give you a physical description of the man."

Dev sat down heavily. If Susanna had invented Sir Edwin Carew it could only be for one reason—to hide her real past. She had told him that she had left Balvenie for Edinburgh, to find a rich husband. Sir Edwin was supposed to have been that man. Sir

Edwin had not existed. She could only have invented him in order to bait the trap, the rich widow out to catch a marquis. Would that marquis find, when it was too late, that the prize he thought he had captured was no more than a penniless adventuress on the make? A cynical smile twisted Dev's lips. Susanna had been very clever. She had pulled the wool over everyone's eyes. But now the thread was starting to unravel and if he was cunning he might just be able to find a way to persuade Susanna to cease her pursuit of Fitz before it was too late for Chessie. It was unlikely, given the secrets she knew about him, but if there was a way he would find it.

"You are absolutely certain of this?" he questioned.

Hammond looked offended. "I am the best, sir."

"Very well," Dev said. "Thank you."

Hammond nodded, stood.

"I cannot really afford to commission you to find out more, Mr. Hammond," Dev said, "but if you were to take on this case, what would you do next?"

Hammond laughed. "You're asking for free advice, sir?"

"Yes," Dev said, "I suppose I am."

"I'd find out all about the lady, sir," Hammond said. "I'll wager Caroline Carew is not her real name, for a start."

"I could save you the trouble there," Dev said. "It is not."

Hammond laughed again. "Well then, sir," he said, "you don't really need an inquiry agent, do you?"

"I want to know what Lady Carew has been doing since we last met," Dev said.

"Then ask her," Hammond said. "My guess would be you will find a way to persuade her to tell you." He looked Dev straight in the eye. "Set a thief to catch a thief, eh, Sir James?"

Dev smiled ruefully. "Are you implying I am a scoundrel, Mr. Hammond?"

"No more than Lady Carew is an adventuress, Sir James," Hammond said. He raised his battered hat in a salute. "Diamonds cut diamonds, so they say."

"So they do," Dev agreed softly as the door closed behind the inquiry agent. He thought of Susanna, naked in his arms, her mouth open and eager beneath his, her body clasping his in the most intimate and abandoned of embraces. It was true that there was a bond between them, a passion as violent and consuming as their lovemaking had been. What the bond was and how it might be broken he had no idea.

He walked across to the mantel and picked up the sheaf of invitations there, flicking through them all. In two days' time he was supposed to be squiring Emma to Lady Bell's Midsummer Ball. He felt his heart drop like a stone at the thought. Then, like the purest temptation the thought crept in that Susanna might be attending and if so, he would contrive for them to be alone together. He would enjoy confronting her about her fictitious husband. And then he would take her home, bundling her into a carriage, taking her on the seat, her skirts up about her waist, her body warm and willing about his, and he would drown once again in that wickedly pure pleasure.

He already felt hot and hard at the thought of it. But it could not be. It must not be. He had to put Susanna from his mind and never think of seducing her again. He had to atone for the wrong he had done Emma by being the most attentive and faithful fiancé in the world. He had behaved without honor. Not only that, he had put all his future plans at risk.

Dissatisfaction stirred within him. For a moment he glimpsed an alternative future, one where he took up again his Naval commission and did something more useful with his life than fetch and carry for Emma. Once again he would have broad horizons and life-and-death challenges. He felt the excitement rise within him. Then he thought of his debts, sufficient to see him in the Fleet, and of Chessie ruined through his disgrace. Her hopes of marrying Fitz were almost lost already. He could not condemn her to suffer for his foolishness, too. He had looked after Chessie since the day his father, the most reckless, feckless gambler of them all, had shot himself, leaving their lives ripped apart when he was nine and his sister six years old. He had been stupid, following in his father's footsteps in profligacy, but for him it was not too late and he would never let his sister down the way that Sir Gerard Devlin had.

As for Susanna, he had to forget the wild passion that there was between them and concentrate on bringing her down. If she gave him the slightest advantage he would take it. If he could spill her secrets whilst keeping his own he should not hesitate. Susanna was ruthless in pursuing what she wanted. He had to be ruthless, too. This dangerous attraction he felt and the even more dangerous urge to protect her had to be denied. With a muttered curse Dev let the invitations scatter on the table and went out to find Frazer and a large bowl of ice-cold water to cure his ardor.

LADY BELL'S BALL WAS the most desperate crush, yet with an inevitability that seemed preordained, Susanna saw Dev the moment that she stepped into the ballroom. He was dancing with Emma; the two of them were halfway down the set of a country dance. Emma was looking about the room as though she was desperately searching for an acquaintance in the crowd whilst Dev was making desultory conversation to her and was being largely ignored.

It was two days since they had met, days that Susanna had spent almost exclusively with Fitz, driving in the park, dancing at a succession of balls, luring Fitz closer and closer to a proposal of marriage whilst he became increasingly possessive and almost equally sexually frustrated. She had flirted with him, teased him, provoked him and promised him access if not to her body then certainly to her huge, fictitious fortune. She was beginning to think that Fitz was almost as keen to get his hands on the money as he was to get them on her person, which was interesting since he was not a poor man but he was almost certainly a greedy one. The more time she spent with Fitz the less she liked him, recognizing that beneath his appearance of conviviality was a man who was inconsiderate and selfishly devoted to his own pleasures. If it had not been for hurting Francesca Devlin's future then she would have had no qualms about her role in distracting Fitz and then ultimately discarding him. He richly deserved something to go awry in his pampered life.

It was also two days in which Susanna had—almost—convinced herself that when she saw Devlin again it would cause her no emotion other than indifference. It was two days in which she had consistently deceived herself as well as others because now she looked at Dev and felt her awareness of him blaze into vivid life and she knew she could never, ever escape her feelings for him.

Her eyes locked with Dev's over the heads of the dancers. He kept his gaze on her for one long, long moment. The expression flared in his eyes and Susanna felt the impact of it wash through her, down to her toes, hot and turbulent. It almost wrenched a gasp from her. The events of the previous two days faded as though they had never been.

So they were not to pretend that it had never happened. Neither of them had the power to deny it.

"Cold?" Fitz asked heartily, seeing her shiver.

"Dash it, my dear, it is as hot as Hades in here." His handsome face was moody. He had suggested in the carriage that they might cut the ball and go somewhere more exciting, a party for just the two of them. Susanna, knowing that Fitz had partaken liberally of the brandy before they set off, and knowing also precisely where his thoughts were tending, had not been encouraging. Fitz had been in a sulk ever since.

A very pretty countess wafted up to them intent on claiming Fitz's attention. The room was indeed stiflingly hot, the music and chatter exceedingly loud. Susanna suppressed a sigh. Before she had come to London she had been assured that it was the most exciting place on earth. That might be so, but the Season was no more than the same people encountering each other over again in the same places pursuing the same pastimes: dancing, drinking, flirting. It was beginning to feel unconscionably boring.

She left Fitz flirting with the countess and wandered into the supper room. So much food… Her stomach growled but she forced herself to take only a meager amount. People were watching. She ate a bowl of strawberries and longed for a cream puff. Perhaps later…

"How charming you look, Lady Carew." The country dance had ended and Dev was standing slightly behind her. She had not seen him approach in the crowd and now she jumped. He spoke softly in her ear. "Cream silk—how virginal and inappropriate. For a widow," he added as she turned to look at him. "At least you did not push the fiction too far and wear white."

"Sir James." Susanna kept her voice very level, ignoring the flutter of sensation along her nerves. "I would like to say that it is a pleasure to see you again but—" she shrugged lightly "—I would not wish to lie."

"I should not worry about that," Dev said lazily. "Deception is a speciality of yours, is it not? You seemed pleased enough to see me last time we met," he continued, before she could respond. "I remember—"

"Sir James," Susanna cut in quickly. They were not overheard but even so this was no place of a private conversation. She knew Dev was only seeking to provoke her. And damn it, he was succeeding.

"You will oblige me by forgetting our last encounter," she said coldly. "And as a gentleman you most certainly would not remind me of it."

"Ah…" Dev sounded regretful. He had taken hold of her hand, his fingers moving gently against the pulse at her wrist.

"I am sure that a gentleman would accede to your wishes, Lady Carew," Dev said. "But you know that I am no such thing." His smile was brilliant, devastating. "So, alas, all I can say is that if you ever wish me to oblige your desires I am always yours to command."

Remembering those desires and where they had

led her, Susanna felt her pulse jump. Dev felt it, too. She saw the light in his eyes intensify.

"Susanna," he said, his voice even lower, no more than a rumble against her ear, "you do not regret it. I know you do not."

Susanna looked up and met his eyes and could not look away. She had expected to see nothing but challenge in his expression. Instead there was sincerity and tenderness that made her heart leap.

"I..." She hesitated on the edge of disclosure, tempted to admit her feelings honestly but at the same time afraid. Dev was so close in that moment, his lips but an inch from hers, the scent of his skin and the sandalwood cologne filling her senses, his hand warm on hers. His touch, his proximity, made her stomach drop with longing. She forgot everything, the ball, the crowds, even her mission to entrap Fitz. There was nothing but Devlin watching her with that dizzying gentleness in his eyes.

Her gaze fell and she felt his fingers tighten on hers.

"Susanna, answer me." There was urgency in Dev's voice. "You can trust me. I swear it." He took a breath, leaned even closer. "I know you are in trouble of some sort," he said quickly, in an undertone. "If you need help then tell me. I promise to do all I can to aid you."

Susanna's heart started to race. She thought of her debts, of the crushing fear of failing Rory and Rose, of the anonymous note, of the whole complicated deceit that was now close to spinning out of control. She felt Dev's touch, warm and reassuring, she remembered the intimacy they had shared, and in that moment she was so lonely she almost cried aloud.

"Trust me," Dev said again and she looked up into his eyes and for a split second saw the flash of calculation there that gave the lie to the sincerity of his words.

The illusion snapped.

You can trust me...

The truth was that Dev had enticed her right to the edge of revelation and she had almost fallen for it. He had seduced her, ruthlessly exploited her attraction to him and then used that weakness against her. He cared not a rush for her. Oh, she did not doubt that he had found physical pleasure in her arms. But that was all it was to him, whereas she had felt such terrifying emotional closeness. He had felt nothing. And now she was so vulnerable to him that she had almost done as he had asked and trusted him, spilling all her secrets. She shivered to see how close she had come to confession.

"Trust you?" she said. "I'd sooner trust a snake."

Dev's smile was so arrogant it made her want to drill the heel of her delicate evening slipper into his foot. "It was worth a try," he said.

"Bastard," Susanna said, with feeling. Her heart felt sore and cold.

Dev laughed. "I may be many things, but not that,

as far as I know." He cast her a sideways look. "You almost fell for it. Admit it."

"I do not want to talk to you," Susanna said.

He kissed her fingers. "You'll sleep with me but not talk to me?"

"I won't do that, either," Susanna said. "It was a mistake, Devlin. Forget it." She smiled at him, a little taunting smile that belied the cold hurt that was inside her. "Or can't you do that? Can't you forget me?"

Their gazes locked again in anger and awareness. Susanna wanted to walk away but the same compulsion held her as before. The emotion shimmered between them like a heat haze, bright, fierce and undeniable.

"At least," Dev said, "you do not need to worry about forgetting Sir Edwin Carew. Since he did not exist, you may invent whatever details suit your purpose."

Susanna could feel herself paling. For a second the floor seemed to swoop and plunge beneath her feet and it was Dev who caught her arm to steady her.

"It seems," he said, with grim satisfaction, his eyes riveted on her face, "that I was right. Sir Edwin is pure invention."

For one long, terrifying moment, Susanna's mind was a tangled mass of apprehension and doubt. She scanned Dev's face trying to ascertain just how much he knew, but his expression was impassive.

She would get no help there. In fact, he would be waiting for her to stumble, to give more away, to reveal those secrets he had tried to charm from her only a moment earlier. If one method failed then he would turn to another. Her only defense could be to stand up to him, to brazen it out.

She straightened her spine and looked him straight in the eye.

"Very well," she said lightly. "I confess it. I invented Sir Edwin. He was…an embellishment."

Dev grabbed her arm and pulled her behind a pillar, away from prying eyes. "What was he—a lie to give you respectability?" he said harshly. "The rich widow who was nothing of the sort?"

"Precisely that," Susanna said coolly. It was a lie—just another lie—but at all costs she had to prevent Dev from getting close to the truth that she was in league with the Duke and Duchess of Alton. Her whole future depended on preserving that facade. Far better that Dev should think her an unprincipled adventuress on the make.

"You understand how it is, Devlin," she said. "A fortune hunter has to give the appearance of wealth even if there is precious little to support it."

Dev's gaze traveled over her thoughtfully and lingered on the diamonds at her throat.

"Those are real," he murmured. "They must have been paid for somehow."

Marvelous. Now he thought her a whore plying her trade on the streets of Edinburgh, or perhaps a paid mistress, a courtesan. Susanna shrugged mentally. There was no way that she could refute it, not if she wanted to keep the name of her paymasters a secret.

"Oh, yes, they have been paid for," she said wearily, and saw the disillusion deepen in his eyes. "How did you find out about Sir Edwin?" she added.

"I asked around," Dev said vaguely. She could see he was not going to tell her. "A number of people claim to know him but it seems their imaginations are almost as vivid as yours."

Susanna shrugged. She brought her gaze up to his face. "And what are you going to do with the information?" she asked bluntly.

Dev's gaze warmed into amusement. "What would you like me to do?"

Damn him. Susanna mentally piled curses on his head. Dev knew full well that she could not afford for him to make trouble for her with Fitz. Even if he hinted to acquaintances that she was not the widow she seemed, awkward questions might be asked. And the only thing she could do to stop him was to threaten to spoil his future if he hurt hers.

She smiled. "I ask only that you think about your own situation before you try to change mine," she said sweetly, and saw his lips thin.

"Blackmail," he said. "That's not pretty, Susanna."

"Call it insurance then," Susanna said. "You do not want to lose your heiress, do you? Well then…"

A faint smile curled Dev's lips. "What a piece of work you are," he murmured. "I almost admire you."

"And you, Sir James," Susanna countered. "You are scarcely a lily-white innocent, are you?"

He laughed then, the devilry leaping in his eyes. "Oh, Susanna," he said under his breath, "I want to carry you out of this ballroom and make love to you until you are begging me for more—"

The sensual heat blazed through Susanna, making her catch her breath. Dev heard it and the wicked light in his eyes intensified. "Come with me," he murmured. "You know you want to. That at least is no lie."

Susanna's reticule fell from her shaking fingers and spilled open. With a muffled curse she dropped to her knees, trying to push the contents back inside before Dev saw them. But it was too late. As she tried to force the last cream puff back inside, her hands trembling, she realized that Dev had seen.

"What on earth—" His tone had changed completely. So had the expression in his eyes. He was looking at her with puzzlement and something Susanna feared might be pity.

"So now you are stealing food, as well?" he murmured. "Perhaps you really are in trouble."

"It's nothing," Susanna snapped.

"Susanna," Dev said, "your purse is full of cream and pastry."

The color flamed into Susanna's face. "I'm hungry," she said.

"That is the purpose of the supper room," Dev pointed out.

Susanna pulled the reticule drawstring tight. Some cream squished out.

"You need to lick that up," Dev said.

Susanna looked up at him. Suddenly, oddly, she felt like crying as though this one foolish thing was finally the last straw.

"You don't understand," she said, and heard the betraying quiver in her voice. "Don't you remember what it was like never to have enough to eat and to long for it with so deep a craving you could not resist?"

She saw the frown snap down in Devlin's eyes. "Yes," he said softly, after a moment, and there was a wealth of emotion in his voice. "I do remember that."

Their gazes locked. "Then—" Susanna started.

"This is a damned tedious crush." Fitz, sounding disagreeable, had shed the flirtatious countess and come looking for her. Susanna jumped, hiding the reticule behind her back. Dev straightened up and gave Fitz the most immaculate bow. The dark frown on Fitz's forehead deepened still further as he saw whom Susanna was with.

"How do you do, Devlin." Fitz was sounding churlish and Susanna thought what a spoiled little boy he was. "Your sister not here tonight?"

"Francesca attends with Lady Grant and her

party," Dev said. "If you wished to beg a dance from her—"

"Don't think I'll bother," Fitz said, rudely cutting him off. "Dashed slow, these debutante balls." He turned to Susanna. "Come, my dear, let us go to Vauxhall. Some music, a little dancing, a stroll down the Dark Walk..." He smiled meaningfully. "It is far more to my taste."

Susanna could feel Dev's gaze on her and feel even more acutely the tension emanating from him. She saw Fitz's flushed, determined face—she knew he must have drunk several glasses of champagne down as though they were water in the short time since their arrival, on top of the brandy he had already consumed—and felt her heart sink. This was the critical point. She had to reel Fitz in. If she turned him down now she might as well kiss her commission from the Duke and Duchess of Alton goodbye because Fitz could only be thwarted to a certain point. On the other hand, the thought of Fitz touching her made her skin crawl. A little while ago the idea of allowing him to steal a kiss or two had not seemed so bad. Now it felt impossible. And if he wanted to take further liberties... She repressed a shudder. Dev was still watching her, his blue eyes cold, awaiting her response as much as Fitz was. She realized that Dev's reaction mattered to her more, far more than Fitz's. Her heart was bumping against her ribs. She felt horribly trapped. She wanted to deny Fitz, hated the thought of conceding, and yet what choice did she have? This was what she had agreed to do when the Duke and Duchess had paid her to take Fitz away from Francesca Devlin. Tonight, if she was clever and played her cards aright, she could turn Fitz up very sweet indeed and seal the deal. But she felt sick at the thought. The idea of Fitz's kiss, when she remembered Devlin's, Fitz's hands on her, when all she could think of was that she ached for Dev's caress…

She raised her chin. In truth there was no reason to turn Fitz down for there was no future for herself and Devlin. Her senses had been bewitched by Dev's lovemaking and that was all. She had been captivated, seduced by no more than physical pleasure. If she denied Fitz now she would be sabotaging all that she had worked for. This was just a job, like the ones that had gone before.

She smiled. "Vauxhall?" she said. "That would be charming, my lord."

Fitz smiled, his good humor restored, and tucked her hand through his arm in an ostentatiously possessive gesture. Susanna risked a glance at Dev's face and wished she had not. The brief moment that had drawn them together over shared memories had vanished. Now the contempt she saw in Dev's eyes seared her to the soul. He thought her a whore, which was scarcely surprising. She should not care for Dev's opinion, of course; it should be a matter of complete unconcern to her. Besides, he was no better than she.

"Enjoy your evening," he said very politely.

"You, too, Sir James," Susanna said. "I am sure you will find someone to divert you."

Dev gave her an ironic smile, sketched a bow and turned away, and Fitz steered Susanna toward the doors, one hand on the small of her back to guide her, his palm sliding lower over the slippery silk to cup her bottom in a brief but telling gesture that indicated exactly where he was planning the evening to end. Susanna kept her smile pinned on her face whilst her mind spun frantically. She was not only going to have to be clever tonight but she was going to have to be extremely careful. For one brief but intense moment she wished with all her heart that she had never come to London and never taken this role. But it was too late. She was in far too deep.

CHAPTER ELEVEN

MISS FRANCESCA DEVLIN stood outside the house in Hemming Row and stared at the tiny sickle moon caught up in the branches of the cherry tree in the square opposite. She had been there for three hours, waiting for her lover. It was a warm summer night, a beautiful night, and a night made for romance. The scent of blossom was on the air. She almost expected a nightingale to start singing. No doubt there were many lovers plighting their troth under the midsummer moon but she had a feeling that there would be no happy ending for her. She had suspected it for a while, known how foolish she had been to risk all on the one throw of the dice and give herself to a man in the hope that it would make him love her. Love did not work that way. He had taken all that she had offered but he had given her nothing in return and the cold, creeping dread in her heart told her that he never would. She had gambled and lost.

She remembered her childhood again and how gambling and losing had always stalked her happiness. She thought of Devlin, who had always tried to protect her from the danger and despair that had threatened them. Dev would be so disappointed in her now.

Chessie swallowed a sob. Dev must never know what she had done, the risk she had taken, the gamble that had failed. She could not bear for him to look at her with horror and shame in his eyes.

Fitz was not coming back. She knew it. She had seen him leave the ball with Lady Carew and she had known this really was the end and that the beautiful, mysterious widow had snatched Fitz from under her nose once and for all. And she could not even blame Lady Carew. Not really. A few days ago she had been filled with hatred for the beautiful Caroline Carew. She had wanted to blame her for everything. But Chessie was fundamentally honest and she could not deceive herself. She knew no man could be snatched against his will. Fitz was weak. Chessie had always known it and yet she still loved him, stubbornly, stupidly, but loved him all the same.

She put up a hand to wipe the tears from her cheeks and in the same moment there was a clatter of hooves on the cobbles and Chessie shrank back into the enveloping shadows. A hackney carriage drew up outside the house and she saw Fitz jump down and give his hand to the lady inside to help her down. He put an arm about her waist and swept her up the steps to the door. Chessie could see his impatience and see, too, how the lady—if lady she was—laughingly protested at his haste. The moonlight fell on her golden ringlets as she paused to reach up and kiss him, a long, deep, passionate kiss.

"So this is how you celebrate your betrothal!" Chessie heard her say as they drew apart. "What a charming arrangement, Fitz darling!"

Not Lady Carew, this painted and pouting hussy. Chessie had never seen the woman before but she had no problem in identifying her for precisely what she was. She felt a huge sadness well up inside and a weariness that sank into her soul. She even felt a tiny, unexpected flicker of sympathy for Lady Carew. There had been something about Caroline Carew that she had wanted to like, despite knowing from the very first that she was dangerous to her. It was odd and inexplicable but she wished that matters had been different.

She squared her shoulders. Matters were not different. Both she and Caroline Carew had lost in their separate ways. Perhaps Lady Carew would not care that on the very night of her betrothal to Fitz he was betraying her with another woman. Chessie did not know. She only knew that she cared for all that she had lost and it hurt. It hurt like nothing she had known before.

IT WAS PAST THREE IN the morning when the carriage turned in to Curzon Street and stopped before number 21. Susanna was swaying with fatigue as she descended the steps and walked slowly to her front door. She wanted nothing more than to kick off her shoes, sink into her feather bed and sleep for as long as she needed, preferably forever. She was bone weary and she felt sick in her heart.

She was aware that she should feel satisfied—more than satisfied, triumphant—that all her plans were coming together now. She had achieved what she had set out to do. Fitz was caught. He had made a formal proposal and she had, naturally, been delighted to accept. The Duke and Duchess of Alton would be overjoyed. More importantly they would pay her and then she could start to disentangle herself from this web of deceit she had cast, pay off her debts, begin afresh, reclaim the twins and make a new life for them all somewhere a long way away from the taint of dishonesty and fraud. The thought made the tears sting her throat. It was so unusual for her to cry. She could only attributc it to tiredness.

Susanna dismissed the footman and sent Margery yawning to bed. She did not need the maid's help to undress and she had no intention of doing anything other than stripping off her clothes and letting sleep claim her. She ignored the letters that were waiting for her on the shiny walnut table—it would only be the usual invitations, another threatening letter from the moneylenders and possibly another anonymous note. Since the last one she had been waiting and waiting for her anonymous correspondent to write again. She knew he—or she—would demand something in return for her silence. Blackmailers always did.

For now she refused to think about it. Everything could wait until the morning. She made her way wearily up the stairs, carrying her evening slippers and allowing her feet to sink into the thick carpet. There were some aspects of this luxurious lifestyle that she was going to miss a great deal, she thought. It was delightful to live in such comfort. She was warm, dry and never without food. But the entire house, the entire life, was an illusion. Nothing belonged to her: the house, the clothes, even the name and the history of Caroline Carew. All lies. She was tired of it all.

She slipped into the bedroom. Margery had drawn the curtains and lit one candle and the room was all golden light and shadows. And in the center of the vast bed lay James Devlin, fully clothed, arms behind his head, watching her with a feral glitter in his blue eyes.

Susanna came awake with a jolt, feeling the excitement course through her body like lightning, banishing her tiredness and waking all her senses to sudden and vivid life. She closed the bedroom door very softly behind her and walked forward into the room. Dev did not move, nor did his eyes waver from her face. She felt naked beneath that cool blue gaze, vulnerable and stripped bare. Her pulse rate soared. She took a deep breath.

"What are you doing here?"

A foolish question when she knew the answer. She knew what he wanted; she wanted it, too. For the last two nights she had ached to hold him again, to feel the press of his body against hers, over hers, in hers. She wanted his kiss, his hands on her skin. For a moment she felt almost faint, light-headed, her heart hammering. She wanted Devlin and she could never, in truth, deny it. But she was never going to make the mistake of giving herself to him again.

"You knew I was here," Dev said. "You sent your maid away. Why would you do that unless you knew—hoped—that you would find me waiting?"

"I was tired," Susanna said. "I did not need her." She shook her head. "How arrogant you are, Devlin, to assume otherwise, especially when I told you earlier that I would never sleep with you again."

Dev smiled, stretched. Susanna tried not to watch the ripple of muscle beneath his shirt and tried not to think about ripping it off him. She wrenched her gaze back to Dev's face, saw he had read her thoughts and wanted to slap him for his conceit.

"How did you get in?" she said. "The servants—they do not know…"

Her voice trailed away as she saw him smile. "Of course not. I can be discreet. I climbed over the balcony." He nodded toward the long window that looked out across the garden. "The Duke of Portland should have greater care in securing his house."

"Clearly," Susanna said coldly. She put her hands on her hips. "I think you should leave. You tried to seduce my secrets out of me earlier, if you remember. And you failed." She turned a shoulder. "Go away,

Devlin. Stop playing games. I'm tired and I want to go to bed. Alone."

She slipped the cloak from her shoulders and let it pool at her feet in a velvet puddle. She saw Dev's gaze follow the movement and then return to her bare shoulders, exposed by the low neckline of the cream silk gown. She knew without looking in the mirror that her skin would be stung pink from the ardor of Fitz's kisses. She had had to allow Fitz some license that night in order to extract what she wanted. For a moment she felt cold and sick and used.

The wild glitter in Dev's eyes intensified as his gaze swept over her and lingered on the telltale marks on her skin. Still he did not move. Susanna stood still, too, trapped now, pinned by the light in his eyes.

"I was not sure," Dev said softly, after a moment, "if you would come back at all tonight."

"Or if Fitz might come back with me?" Susanna said. She drew in a deep, steadying breath. "I have told you before that it is none of your business, Devlin."

Dev's gaze did not falter from her face. Susanna could feel the violence in him, barely held in check. A muscle moved in his cheek. "Did you make love with him?" He sounded as though the words were bitten out against his will. Then, before she could reply, he rolled off the bed and caught her by the forearms, his hold as gentle as his tone was vicious.

"Goddamn it," he said, "it makes no odds to me.

I still want you, whatever you have done with him." His furious blue gaze raked her from the top of her head to her toes. "I cannot believe it, but it is true—" He cupped her face, brought his mouth down on hers. Again, the tenderness of his lips against hers was a terrifying counterpoint to the anger Susanna could feel seething in him. "I'd take you now even though your body still bears the marks of his."

He kissed her again, harder this time, his tongue plunging deep, demanding a response.

"Did you?" he said when he released her. "Did you have him?"

"The announcement of our betrothal will be in the papers tomorrow," Susanna whispered.

She saw Dev's face change; heard him release his breath on a long sigh. He drew her closer still, so she could feel the thunder of his heart against hers. "Susanna…" He sounded shaken. "Why are you doing this?"

The anger jetted up in Susanna, too. She pulled back. "I am securing my future, Devlin," she said. "Just as you are, through a rich marriage. That is why I am doing this." Suddenly she wanted to tell him everything. It felt so strange because he was the very last person she should confide in, but it was lonely living a false life and Dev was the only one who knew who she really was. "We both do what we have to do," she said. "Do we not, Devlin, you with Emma and me with Fitz?"

"This is nothing to do with Fitz or Emma," Dev said roughly.

He pulled her to him and kissed her ravenously as though his very life depended on it. Her tongue tangled with his and her head spun at his taste and she breathed in the scent of him.

"We agreed—" she started to say when he lifted his mouth from hers. "We should not—"

"You knew it would happen again," Dev said harshly. "How could it not?"

How could it not, Susanna thought hazily, when for all their fortune hunting it felt as though they were two halves of a whole, two people who needed each other, who should, against all the odds, be together? The thought terrified her. It was so much easier to pretend that it was simple lust that united them. Except that that would not be true. She felt more than that for Devlin. She always had, even if he did not feel the same.

Dev caught her face in his hands and kissed her again. There was still anger in him and a strange sort of anguish and reckless need. He ripped the gown from her. She heard the sound of seams splitting and protested.

"Get your friends the Duke and Duchess of Alton to buy you some more clothes since they seem so anxious for you to seduce their heir," Dev ground out. He turned her toward the candlelight so that the golden glow bathed her whole body. "Goddamn it—" Again his gaze searched her ruthlessly from head to foot and every inch of her skin heated beneath his gaze. "I cannot bear to think of it."

"We didn't—" Susanna began, but Dev shook his head.

"Spare me."

He pulled her down onto the bed, bracketing her wrists above her head, holding her still with one hand. Susanna struggled to free herself but he simply exerted more pressure, holding her down with ease. Her stomach tumbled over and over as she realized that there would be no waiting this time. A fierce gladness took her. She wanted this. Already she felt desperate, carnal.

His mouth closed warmly over one nipple and she felt a flare of pleasure race through her blood. He sucked. She writhed against the grip of his hands. He bit down. She gave a gasp that ended in a moan. So she had been wrong. He was going to make her wait after all.

"It seems," he said, his lips brushing the underside of her breast, "that your evening so far has not been as fulfilling as you might have hoped." His tongue flicked her nipple. "Has it, Susanna?"

"Devlin—" Susanna's mind spun with hot, dark images. "Please…"

"Tomorrow," Dev said, "you announce your betrothal to another man." He paused and she felt his breath feather across her skin sending tiny shivers skittering along her nerves. Again he sucked down on her nipple. Another flare of sensation blazed through her, setting her trembling, making her furious that he had such mastery of her body.

"What are you trying to prove?" she said, through her teeth.

She saw the flash of his teeth as he smiled. "Only that you respond to me in a way that you will never feel for Fitz."

"Male pride, then." She felt angry and contemptuous even as she felt hopelessly aroused. "In that case I admit it freely, Devlin. I will never respond to Fitz the way that I do to you. So you have nothing to prove and you can go."

Dev ran a hand down her body. "I don't think so."

Susanna was still angry even though the caress made her quiver with need. "You are a hypocrite demanding such things from me," she said bitterly. "It is not as though you are mine, are you, Devlin? You belong to someone else entirely."

"Ah..." With the astonishing tenderness that he could show he kissed her, gently this time, as though drawing the soul from her body. When he let her go they were both trembling. He brushed the hair back from her brow and his fingers were cool against her cheek. "Once we belonged to each other, Susanna," he said. "And for this one night we can do so again."

It was that thought that finally gave Susanna the strength to stop him. One night. Oh, yes, she could give herself to Devlin for one more night. It would be easy to plunge into that maelstrom of passion and forget everything in the bliss of Devlin's possession.

But in a few short hours he would be gone—she would have lost him again—and she would hate herself for weakening. The pleasure would be gone but the heartbreak would remain. She had told herself that never again would she risk loving and losing. She could not falter now or she would indeed have lost.

"No!" She tore herself away from him, grabbing the sheet to cover her nakedness, wrapping it about herself with shaking hands. "No," she said again. She backed away from the bed, feeling her legs tremble, fearing she might fall. "This is not right, Devlin. We have to stop."

Dev rolled over and sat up. For a moment he looked completely dazed, as lost in sensation as she herself had been but a second before. Then he shook his head as though to clear it. His gaze came up and focused on her and Susanna was astounded to see that there was amusement in it.

"You do have the most frustrating sense of timing," he murmured.

"I'm sorry," Susanna said. She caught the arm of a chair and sank down into it gratefully. "I did not mean deliberately to tease you—"

"I know." Dev bit out the words, his physical frustration all too visible. He caught her gaze, looked down ruefully and shook his head again. "You would be faithful to Fitz," he said, "when you want him only for his title and even now he is probably screwing some Covent Garden whore?"

The brutality of his words made Susanna wince. Dev thought that her engagement to Fitz was genuine, of course, when she knew it was a sham. But that did not change the principle that was at stake.

"I believe in fidelity," she said steadily.

She saw the incredulity in Dev's eyes. He pushed the hair back from his forehead in an impatient gesture. "Am I supposed to believe that?" he said.

It hurt that he did not but Susanna had expected no less. "What about you?" she challenged. "Could you say you have always been faithful to the woman you are with?"

Dev's expression went blank. "Until that night with you..." He stopped, spoke slowly. "I had never once been unfaithful to Emma in two years."

Now it was Susanna's turn to feel shock. Yet she did not. The James Devlin she had known, for all his rakish ways, had had an honor and an integrity that had always guided his actions. It was one of the reasons why she had loved him.

"Then you must see," she said quietly, "why this has to end, Devlin."

Dev did not answer immediately. Instead he came across to the chair and drew her gently to her feet. For a second his cheek rested against hers, his stubble rough against the smoothness of her skin.

"Goddamn it, Susanna..." he said. He sounded shaken, regretful.

Susanna placed a hand on his chest. "You know

it, Devlin. You are a better man than this. Prove it by finishing this now."

As soon as she touched him she felt Dev go still, all but the pounding of his heart beneath her hand. There was puzzlement and a dawning awareness in eyes. All provocation and pretense between them dropped away and nothing but the truth remained. The moment spun out between them as delicate as gossamer, then Dev put his hand over hers where it rested against his heart.

"Thank you," he said. He shook his head slightly. There was puzzlement and some other emotion in his eyes now. "You are a surprising woman, Susanna," he said slowly.

"You have no idea," Susanna said with feeling.

Dev gave her a smile that was for once devoid of all mockery, then he stepped back and Susanna felt as cold and alone as she had ever done before in her life.

Dev picked up his jacket and slung it over his shoulder. He walked toward the door.

"The balcony!" Susanna said. "You leave as you arrived."

Dev pulled a face. "I might damage myself."

Susanna blocked his path to the door. "You will have to take that risk," she said. "I'd rather you damaged your health than my reputation."

Dev gave her one final dazzling smile that set her pulse awry again. "Good night then, Lady Carew," he said. "Good luck."

Another second and he had vaulted over the balcony and was gone. Susanna caught her breath on a gasp of shock and horror. When she had suggested he leave the way he had arrived she had assumed he would climb down to the ground rather than leap recklessly from a first-floor window. She ran across to the balcony, peering over the balustrade. The first light of dawn was breaking across the sky in streaks of pink and gold, and by its light she could see Dev standing in the garden below, completely unhurt, dusting down his jacket. He glanced up and caught her watching. She saw his teeth gleam as he smiled.

"I knew you would have to make sure I was safe," he said.

"Damn you," Susanna said, furious at having proved him right.

He laughed. "Sweet dreams."

Susanna closed the doors quietly and drew the drapes, then went to sit down on the edge of her bed. She was still trembling a little. She knew she had done the right thing in sending Dev away. She knew he knew it, too. Yet now she felt more empty and alone than she had ever done in her life before.

She wrapped her arms about herself for comfort, even though the night was warm. Devlin. Her husband. There was so much more that he did not know, so much that he could never know. She shivered. If she could keep her secrets, keep the moneylenders away and keep everything safe then soon she could buy the annulment and run away, away to a new life. She only had to hold on a little longer. Then she would never see James Devlin again and that was the right thing, the only thing to do, because she had lost so much and she knew that to lose love again would utterly destroy her.

CHAPTER TWELVE

"YOU'RE EARLY," ALEX Grant said, putting aside his newspaper as the butler ushered Dev into the breakfast room at Bedford Street. He eyed his cousin's evening dress. "Or is it that you have not yet been to bed?"

"The latter," Dev agreed. He accepted gratefully the cup of coffee Alex poured and pushed in his direction. "No need for that look," he added dryly. "It was not that sort of a night."

Alex raised a brow. "I make no judgments," he said mildly.

Dev shrugged moodily. He could feel his cousin watching him and knew that in a moment Alex would put his finger on the precise problem that troubled him because his cousin had always been able to read him like a book. It had been damnably awkward when he had been young and Alex had been his guardian, as well. He had never been able to get away with anything. The nine years seniority Alex possessed had always given him the edge. Added to that, Alex had been a famous explorer, a hero, and Dev had wanted nothing more than to follow in his footsteps and please him. That sensation still lingered, even in adulthood.

"You look," Alex said after a moment, his dark eyes grave, "like a man who wishes he had spent the night in uninhibited dissipation, knows it would have been the wrong thing to do but still regrets that it did not happen."

Dev gave a reluctant crack of laughter. "I have to hand it to you, Alex, you know me far too well." He looked around to check that the door was tightly shut. "I take it that the ladies will not be joining us?"

Alex glanced at the clock on the mantel. "At seven-thirty? Do you know nothing of women after all?" A smile twisted his lips. "You are quite safe, Devlin. Though if you are about to talk scandal I imagine Joanna will be disappointed to have missed it."

Dev took a mouthful of the strong coffee and slid down more comfortably in his chair.

"There is a woman," he admitted. He did not know why he was telling Alex this. He had had no intention of talking about Susanna when he had come here.

Alex nodded. "I knew there would be, sooner or later." He raised a hand to stop Dev's instinctive protest. "I apologize. I did not mean to imply that I thought you would be unfaithful to your fiancée. Merely—" he stopped, toyed with his cup "—that when one chooses to marry without love there is a danger that one will then fall in love with someone else."

"I'm not in love," Dev said automatically. He did not love Susanna. He could not. He had been burned too harshly on that bright particular star before to fall again. But he could not deny the need he had for her nor the compelling tie that bound them so tightly. He felt his body stir, shifted uncomfortably and wondered if he would ever be free of the fierce desire she could arouse in him.

Alex smiled. "Then forgive me again," he said, "but whoever this woman is, you have feelings for her that are far stronger than any emotion you have ever felt for Lady Emma."

That, Dev thought ruefully, was true. He had admired Emma for her beauty and wanted her for her money and felt nothing more for her than that. It was an empty bargain he had offered her and it was unworthy of both of them.

He sat forward. "I didn't come here to discuss my romantic difficulties," he said. "I wanted to ask for your help." He paused. "I had a rather large favor to ask, actually."

"Ask then," Alex said mildly.

"I am going to petition the Admiralty to restore my Navy commission," Dev said. He looked up. "I was hoping that you would support my case, Alex."

Alex almost choked on his coffee. "Devlin," he said, "you sold your commission to finance a treasure-hunting trip to Mexico. I doubt that the Lords of the Admiralty will look kindly on you after that." He placed his cup gently back in its saucer.

"Then there was the chandelier on the mainmast, the pearl earring, the deflowering of the Admiral's daughter, and the incident where we boarded Hallows frigate in the Arctic…" He stopped and shook his head. "Are you mad to even consider it?"

"I was not the first with the Admiral's daughter," Dev said.

"That," Alex said dryly, "is precisely what the Admiral did not want to accept."

"They took you back after the incident with Hallows' frigate," Dev said. "And then they refused to court martial you after you helped Ethan Ryder escape capture."

"That was an accident," Alex said smoothly. "The Admiralty accepted that I had tripped and accidentally hindered the guard who was trying to shoot him."

Dev snorted. "Balderdash. And the incident with Hallows?"

"I argued that I was under the influence of extreme passion. I was trying to reclaim my wife."

"They bought that?" Dev asked derisively.

"It was true," Alex said. His voice changed. "I would have done anything to get Joanna back." He sighed sharply. "Why do you want to go back to sea, Devlin?"

Dev thought of what Susanna had said to him a few brief hours before. Her words had only confirmed the thoughts that had plagued him for weeks; that he was bored, that he was wasting his life; that he was a better man than this idle fortune hunter he had become. He knew Susanna had been talking about fidelity and honor but what she had said applied equally to his whole life. He could no longer sit around waiting upon Emma's whim simply because he wanted wealth and status. When he had first gone to sea he had earned his money and his fame. The sea had been a demanding mistress and he had answered her call. Now he knew he had to go back.

He had Susanna to thank for that revelation. It was Susanna who had challenged him to be a better man and made him face the truth. She had given him back his self-respect. She had shown him the way. For a moment he felt a profound gratitude and an equally powerful sense of loss. He would never have imagined that Susanna could give him something so precious. She had shown strength of character he would never have believed in, principle that seemed in stark contrast to her behavior. He tasted bitterness. He should try to stop thinking about Susanna. She would be Marchioness of Alton soon and the further away from her he was the better. A ship on the other side of the world would be as good a place as any.

He realized that Alex was still waiting.

"There are lots of reasons," he said. "I grow tired of playing the lapdog to Emma's demands. I am wasting my life."

A faint smile touched Alex's lips. "I thought that

you wanted money and a place in society," he murmured.

"I do," Dev said, "but the price is too high."

"Lady Emma may not wish to be wed to the oldest lieutenant in the Navy," Alex said dryly, "for you may be sure that in the unlikely event of them offering you another commission, Devlin, they will make you start from the bottom again in order to punish you."

"I'll still get to be an admiral one day," Dev said with a grin. "You know I can do it." His smile faded. "Besides, Emma will not like any of the things I am going to tell her. It is best that I accept our betrothal will be over."

Alex refilled his coffee cup and pushed the pot toward his cousin. "Once again I am tempted to ask if you are mad," he said. "Your debts must run in to thousands. If Lady Emma breaks off your engagement the moneylenders will foreclose and you will be ruined."

"I know," Dev said. He looked up and met his cousin's eyes very seriously. "I can make it work," he said, "if I get the commission, and have a regular income and win some prize money I will pay it all off—" He broke off. "I have to get my self-respect back, Alex," he said suddenly, fiercely. "I hate what I have become. The only way to redeem myself in my own eyes is to go back to sea."

Alex laughed suddenly. "Damn it, Devlin," he said, "it's madness to throw away all your advantages, but I admire you for it. For too long you've wasted your time and I have grieved to see you do it." He paused. "There is only one other matter that concerns me. Chessie."

"Yes," Dev said. He grimaced. "I am only too well aware that I am in your debt, Alex. You give Chessie a home and you have promised her a dowry and that should be my role—" He stopped as Alex raised a hand.

"I was Chessie's guardian as well as yours," Alex said, "and for too long I was absent from your lives and you had to fend for yourself. You did plenty then, Devlin, to protect your sister. Allow me to do something now to ease my guilt a little." A frown touched his brow. "For a while I thought Chessie might make a match of it with Fitzwilliam Alton," he added, "but it seems not?"

"No," Dev said. "Alton is to marry Lady Carew. The announcement of their betrothal will be made today." He put his coffee down abruptly. It was cold now and tasted too strong and bitter on the tongue.

"A pity," Alex said. "Chessie genuinely loves him. She seems very unhappy. Joanna commented on it to me only a few days ago."

"Fitz is not good enough for her," Dev said shortly. "I thought it would be a good match but I was mistaken."

"Money and status again," Alex said. He stretched, throwing down his napkin on the table. "Ah, well, so the mysterious widow catches the marquis. You know, when I saw her I had the oddest feeling we had met before."

"I doubt it," Dev said, even more shortly. "I do not believe she has visited London before." He did not understand why he was protecting Susanna but some stubborn impulse nevertheless prompted him to keep her secrets. He was not going to tell his cousin that Alex had known Susanna when she had been the Balvenie schoolmaster's niece.

"She is from Scotland, though, is she not?" Alex said. "I thought, perhaps—"

"Excuse me," Dev said, standing up. "I need to go to the Admiralty and then I must call on Emma and acquaint her with my plans. Thank you for the coffee, Alex. And the advice."

"My pleasure," Alex said. He stood up and shook Dev's hand. "Good luck, Devlin," he said. "I will write in support of your application. It takes courage to do what you are doing," Alex added, clapping Dev on the back. "You deserve it to go well for you."

"Thank you," Dev said. He went out into the summer sunlight. There was a fresh breeze and a bright blue sky overhead. It was the sort of day to be on the prow of a ship.

A newsboy pressed a sheet into his hand and Dev glanced down absentmindedly. There was a lurid cartoon of a half-naked woman with long black hair sitting astride a ducal coronet whilst in the background a man recognizable as Fitzwilliam Alton was counting out bags of money with an equally lascivious expression on his face. “Money sells itself for a title,” the caption read.

For a moment Dev felt such a blinding rage that he froze where he stood. To see Susanna displayed in such an appallingly blatant and disrespectful fashion was sickening and filled him with violence. Then, with a cold shudder, he remembered that this was what she had wanted, to catch a title, to secure her future. Until very recently it was what he had wanted, too. This, then, was the price one paid.

He crumpled the scandal sheet in his hand so tightly that the corners cut his palm. Then he tossed it back to the newsboy and walked off without a word.

LADY EMMA BROOKE WAS in a bad mood. She tilted her parasol to block out the dazzling sunlight sparkling on the water and drew her shawl closer about her to ward off the nonexistent chill of the breeze off the river. The fact that it was such a beautiful day made her feel sour. Her mother had forced her to rise early—at ten o’clock!—in order to attend a breakfast party at Crofton Cottage on the Thames. Emma had not wanted to go but unusually the Countess had overruled her. Now, two hours later, Emma was beyond bored and approaching utterly exasperated. She knew her parents wished her brother to marry the Duke and Duchess of Crofton’s daughter but she did not see why she had to put up with the witless girl, as well. Let Justin do his own wooing. She was fed up, and she was done with men anyway—who needed them? First Devlin had proved a massive disappointment to her and then Tom Bradshaw had been full of empty promises.

After the encounter in the garden at midnight she had burned for the moment that she would see Tom again. She did not understand why. He was everything that she had been brought up to ignore: illegitimate, poor, a man who worked for a living. Yet none of that mattered to her because he had brought into her life an element that had been missing before, something new and different and exhilarating, and now that she had tasted it she wanted more.

She had looked for Tom's tall figure everywhere, in the ballrooms of the ton, even though she knew he would never set foot there, in the shifting crowds in the Park where once she thought she had glimpsed him, on every street corner. Everyone had noticed her distraction. Her mother had commented that she had become withdrawn and had she taken a chill at the Cravens' fête champêtre? Her father had rustled his newspaper irritably and said that he hoped she was not going to be so foolish as to go into a decline. He had said that perhaps they should bring forward her marriage to Devlin and when Emma had squeaked out a negative her parents had exchanged a long and meaningful glance. Later her mother had come to her and said very gently that if she had been having second thoughts about her betrothal that was perfectly acceptable and Devlin would understand if she had changed her mind. He would release her from her promise like the gentleman he was not. But Emma was stubborn. She did not want to give up her property quite yet, not whilst she did not have something better to take its place. And it seemed she had made the right decision because for all his pledges to see her again, Tom had proved to be full of lies. He had simply been amusing himself at her expense. Emma felt a fool and she wished she could hate him for it yet oddly she could not, which made her even angrier.

Her mother was beckoning to her. It was time to leave. Thank goodness. The lemonade had been warm and the sandwiches were curling up in the sun and it was too ridiculously hot to sit outdoors. Emma trailed her mother, Lady Bell and the two Misses Bell down to the river, past flower beds full of rioting roses whose scent hung on the hot, heavy air. She could feel the sweat prickling the back of her neck and running down her spine. It was most unpleasant. And why they had to take one of those silly little riverboats rather than bringing the carriage was anyone's guess.

There were two boatmen. One had come forward to assist the ladies into the skiff. The other was checking that the mooring ropes were secure. Miss Bell and Miss Annie Bell were giggling as they climbed into the boat. Silly girls. Emma scowled.

"A beautiful day, my lady."

Emma jumped and dropped her parasol. She knew

that voice. Normally she did not look at servants, which was why she had completely failed to notice that the man tying the boat to the bank was Tom Bradshaw. He straightened up, strong and lithe, and handed the parasol to her with a little mocking bow. When she took it from him he covered her fingers with his own. Emma's throat dried and her heart started to bang against her ribs.

"What are you doing here?" she gasped. She glanced around to see if her mother had noticed but Lady Brooke was talking to Lady Bell and had her back turned.

Tom was laughing at her. She could see it in his eyes. The expression in them made her stomach melt. "I come and go as I please," Tom said, "and today it pleased me to find you."

"I've looked for you—" Emma began, then clamped her lips tight shut.

"I know," Tom said. He was standing very close to her. The sleeves of his shirt were rolled up and Emma could see the fine hairs on his forearms and the play of his muscles under the skin. His arm brushed hers and Emma felt the warmth of it through the thin cotton of her sleeve. She felt a little dizzy, too hot, her blood hammering in her veins.

Lady Bell was settling herself in the boat now, making a great fuss and taking up at least three seats as she smoothed out her skirts. Emma held her breath but still Lady Brooke did not turn around.

"I'll come to you tomorrow night," Tom whispered, his lips brushing Emma's ear. "Be waiting for me."

A shiver took Emma, raising the goose bumps all over her body. Tom was smiling, his eyes so dark, his expression so wicked that Emma felt as though the ground had fallen away beneath her feet and she was stepping into empty air. She felt Tom slide an arm about her on the pretext of guiding her down to the jetty. She felt the press of his hand at her waist; his fingers brushed the underside of her breast and she gasped aloud.

Her mother had noticed nothing and was waiting for Emma to join her in the boat. Tom held out his hand to her to help her aboard. Emma hesitated before touching him and felt her senses jolt as his hand closed about hers. It was as though someone had dropped hot wax on her naked skin. The heat enveloped her whole body. She was burning up yet she felt chilled to the bone at the same time.

Emma took her seat on the cushion beside her mother and watched in a trance as Tom cast off and seated himself in the bow. He was facing directly toward her and she watched him pull on the oars, watched the muscles in his thighs tighten as he rowed and the way the wind flattened his shirt against the contours of his chest. She felt transfixed, her mother's conversation rolling over her like a soundless reel, whilst her ears were full of the splashing of the water and the sun beat down on her parasol and in her belly was a hot, demanding ache she had never imagined before. She did not understand why no one else seemed to notice her discomfort when it was so acute. Yet everyone was behaving perfectly as normal. Only she was caught up in a painful spiral of lust and wanting. Only Tom knew.

They were drawing up at Westminster Quay. Tom jumped ashore. Gravely he helped the ladies up onto dry land and to their carriages. He was all that was proper and deferential. Emma saw her mother graciously hand him a tip and felt obscurely ashamed. Once again she hung back and felt his touch on her wrist and his lips brush the corner of her mouth in the briefest of caresses.

"I'll take payment from you tomorrow, Lady Emma."

She was in the carriage and she felt limp and boneless with the tension and the tight desire inside her.

"You look done up, my love," Lady Brooke said, viewing her flushed face with some concern. "Too much sun, I suppose. It was unconscionably hot."

"Yes," Emma said. Her skin felt feverish and sticky. "When we get home I think I might lie down for a little."

She had promised herself that she would not look back to see if Tom was watching but she could not help herself. As the carriage turned the corner and headed away from the river she craned her neck to catch one last glimpse of him but he was nowhere to be seen.

SUSANNA WOKE LATE, HAVING slept deeply through sheer exhaustion. She only awoke when Margery came in, flustered, with a cup of tea and a copy of the *Gazette*. The hall, Margery said, was full of flowers. The Duke and Duchess of Alton had sent a footman with a note that they would be hosting an engagement party for Susanna and Fitz that very evening. Margery had taken the liberty of sending for the hairdresser. Several modistes had called to offer their services in the design of the wedding gown. They had left gifts, samples…

Susanna resisted the urge to pull the bedcovers over her head. After Margery had gone out to draw her a bath she got out of bed and went across to the balcony, opening the long doors, remembering with a lurch of her heart how she had closed them the previous night after Devlin had gone. It was a beautiful morning. The sky was a clean bright blue and the sun was high and the air was fresh. Susanna rested a hand on the stone balcony and looked down into the street below where another flower cart had arrived and John, the footman, was struggling under the burden of a huge arrangement of lilies that looked more appropriate to a funeral than a wedding. No doubt they were from Fitz, Susanna thought. He was given to the grand gesture when he knew that people would be watching. Poor Francesca Devlin. People would be watching her, too. Today, with the announcement of Fitz's engagement, her humiliation would be complete.

With a sigh Susanna closed the doors shutting out the shiny new day. She felt hollow and lonely. The prospect of going to the Altons' party, of accepting the congratulations of the ton, of acting the role of Fitz's fiancée was almost intolerable. She missed Devlin acutely, as though she were seventeen and had lost him all over again. She had wanted to avoid this pain. Instead, for the first time in years, the hard carapace that she had built about her heart to protect her felt as though it was breaking. She did not know why it hurt so much. She knew that she had no future with Devlin, knew, too, that at the end of this charade she would slip away, pay for the annulment and be gone. In a month she could very courteously end the betrothal—she did not flatter herself that Fitz's feelings would be touched: only his pride and his wallet—pocket her payoff from the Duke and Duchess and slip away. She would never see any of them again. A month seemed an unconscionably long time.

She took her bath in the rose-scented water that Margery had so thoughtfully provided, dressed listlessly and wandered downstairs. Underneath all the notes of congratulation that had already accumulated on the hall table were the letters that she had dreaded finding the night before. Her heart did a small, uncomfortable flip. She took them out of the pile and went into the drawing room, closing the door behind her.

Her hand shook as she opened the first one. The

moneylenders were not so polite this time, which was not surprising since she had ignored their previous missive. Susanna thought of the possibility of them going to Fitz and telling him that she was in debt and was not the rich widow he thought her. The delicate structure of her charade shivered a little. One word out of place, one false step and the delicate pretense she had built would be ruined and she would tumble back to the poorhouse, and take Rory and Rose with her. He heart swooped. How she hated this tangled web. She was so desperate to be free of it all.

There was another anonymous note. She recognized the bold black capitals and the arrogant strokes that said her mysterious correspondent had a hold over her and was determined to use it.

"If you wish me to keep your secrets meet me in the Bell Tavern in Seven Dials on Saturday night."

Susanna stood up, crushing the letters fiercely and throwing them into the grate. She had no intention of keeping so dangerous an assignation. Yet if she did not there was no telling what her blackmailer might do. She thought of Devlin. Her heart was full of doubt and uncertainty. Surely it was not possible for Dev to make love to her with such passion and such tenderness, and then to pen a letter threatening to hurt her. They were locked in conflict equally as much as desire and yet she could not, she would not, believe Dev so dishonorable that he would threaten her like this. But if not Devlin then whom? Had he told his sister her secret? Could Chessie be blackmailing her out of jealousy and revenge because she had stolen Fitz from her?

Whoever the blackmailer proved to be, Susanna knew she could not ignore them, for they held her future in their hands. They could destroy her, plunge her back into the nightmare of poverty and ruin. She felt the flutter of panic spread through her, setting her shaking. She had nowhere to turn and no one to help her.

Then she paused. There was one other person who knew who she was and perhaps—just perhaps—he might be able to aid her. Ignoring Margery's protests that she could not possibly go out when there was so much to be done, she asked John to call a hackney carriage and set out for Holborn.

She stepped down outside the discreet door of Churchward and Churchward, lawyers to the noble and discerning. The Duke and Duchess of Alton, naturally enough, had no desire to pay her directly and so she had been instructed to submit her bills to Mr. Churchward and also to go to him should she have any financial or other matters that required attention. Susanna hesitated for a moment then set her hand to the knocker. She did not want to trouble Mr. Churchward. She was accustomed to dealing with her own problems, had done so all her life. But she needed assistance urgently. There was no alternative. Squaring her shoulders, she knocked decisively on the door. It seemed an inordinate amount of time before the door swung open and a man Susanna assumed to be a clerk stood in the doorway.

"I would like to see Mr. Churchward, if you please," Susanna said in a rush.

The clerk looked down his nose. "Do you have an appointment, madam?"

"No," Susanna said, "but it is very important." She could hear the desperation in her own voice. "My name is Lady Carew. Please tell Mr. Churchward that it is extremely urgent that I see him."

For a moment she thought that the clerk would refuse but then he stepped back reluctantly to allow her inside. She followed him up a polished wooden stair and was shown into a neat waiting room. She found she could not sit. She was too agitated. Fortunately Mr. Churchward did not keep her waiting long.

"Good morning, Lady Carew."

Mr. Churchward was all that was civil. Not by a flicker of intonation did he suggest that he knew she was not all she pretended to be, least of all Caroline, Lady Carew, relict of a scholarly recluse. Mr. Churchward placed a chair for her before resuming his seat on the other side of the desk. There was a copy of the *Gazette,* neatly folded, in front of him. Susanna realized that he must have read about her engagement to Fitz. The whole of London would have read about the engagement. She felt a little sick.

Mr. Churchward moved the paper aside and leaned forward, steepling his fingers. His eyes were piercingly shrewd behind the thick spectacles. He waited politely for Susanna to state her business. Despite the physical warmth of the room, though, and the courtesy of his manner, Susanna was sharply aware that Mr. Churchward disapproved of her. No doubt he undertook whatever business his noble clients required of him but that did not mean, she thought, that he agreed with it. And in the matter of entrapping Fitzwilliam Alton into a false betrothal and ruining Francesca Devlin's hopes, Mr. Churchward most certainly did not approve.

She opened her reticule and took out the letters that she had retrieved from the grate. Her hands shook a little. She knew that Mr. Churchward had noticed.

"I am in a certain amount of difficulty, Mr. Churchward," she said, "and I am not at all sure where to turn. I wondered if you might help me."

"I will, of course, do my best, madam," the lawyer said austerely.

Silence fell. Susanna reread the letters although she knew the wording exactly. She looked up and met Mr. Churchward's gaze.

"I am sure that you must disapprove of me," she said in a rush. "Indeed, who could not if they knew the truth? But despite that I must throw myself on your mercy because I have nowhere else to turn."

Mr. Churchward was silent. Susanna felt his gaze on her face, thoughtful, noncommittal, and felt her heart sink like a stone.

She stood up. “Excuse me,” she said rapidly. “I made a mistake in coming here. I am sorry to have troubled you.”

Mr. Churchward did not try to stop her. He stood, too, and came forward to open the door for her. Susanna felt a large fat tear drop on the paper and furiously bundled the letter back into her reticule. She turned her face aside so that the lawyer would not see her distress. Another tear fell, thwarting her. She made a sound of combined exasperation and misery and scrabbled for a handkerchief.

Mr. Churchward pressed his own large, white handkerchief into her hand. He shut the door.

“Dear me,” he said. “I have never seen a lady make such strenuous efforts not to cry.”

“I’m not a lady,” Susanna sniffed, burying her nose in the handkerchief, “so no doubt I do not have the requisite self-control.”

“My dear... Miss Burney,” Mr. Churchward said. “If Miss Burney is your real name—”

“Actually,” Susanna said, “my real name is Lady Devlin. And that, Mr. Churchward, is part of the problem.”

To her astonishment she saw a gleam of amusement come into Mr. Churchward’s eyes. “If you are the wife of James Devlin and have just become betrothed to Fitzwilliam Alton, then I can see that you do have a problem,” he agreed. He paused. “Does Sir James know?”

Susanna gave a snort that was somewhere between a laugh and a sob. "Yes… No. That is, he thinks our marriage was annulled years ago…"

This time Mr. Churchward actually smiled. "I see." He gestured her to resume her seat. "Was that what you wished to consult me about?"

"No," Susanna said. She felt panic rise as she thought about the letters. "There is something else. Actually there are two things…" She stopped.

"Well," Mr. Churchward said, "all in good time. I have some very fine sherry for emergencies only," he added, opening the lower drawer in his desk and retrieving a bottle and two dusty glasses. "I think that this might qualify. Would you care to join me in a glass, Lady Devlin, and tell me all about it?"

CHAPTER THIRTEEN

DEV STOOD IN THE RECEIVING line at the impromptu ball the Duke and Duchess of Alton were throwing to celebrate Fitz and Susanna's engagement. Emma was not present and Dev had not seen her in two days owing to a migraine headache she had apparently developed after Lady Crofton's Breakfast the previous morning. Thwarted in his plan to tell Emma of his intention to resume his Naval commission, Dev had finally written her a letter and left it with the Brookes's grim-faced butler who had assured him that it would be delivered to Emma once she was restored to health. Dev thought it would very probably send Emma off into another migraine as he had bitten the bullet and added a coda.

"I also have to tell you that I have betrayed your trust with another lady. I deeply regret having behaved so dishonorably and fully deserve your condemnation…"

It was in fact a barefaced lie. He did not regret one second of his lovemaking with Susanna but he did regret having fallen short of his own honor in betraying Emma when she did not deserve it. Dev knew what the outcome must be: he knew Emma would not tolerate his infidelity and yet he also knew he could not lie to her further. He had had to wipe the slate clean.

The receiving line shuffled forward and Dev suppressed a sigh. He had attended some excruciating social events in his time, the inauguration of the witless governor of an obscure island in the West Indies being one and the debutante ball of a girl who had got drunk and declared passionate love for her brother-in-law in front of the entire ballroom being another, but nothing he had ever attended before had been as personally painful as the celebration of Susanna's engagement to Fitzwilliam Alton. Not content with throwing one party, to which he had thankfully declined the invitation, the Duke and Duchess were hosting this ball for the entire ton. Dev was only there to support Chessie who had declared that of course she would attend, and damn the gossip. Dev wished she had not. Chessie stood pale and blank-eyed beside Joanna Grant and her sister Tess Darent, confronting her humiliation and the ruin of her dreams with the eyes of all of society on her. Dev was so angry that he wanted to take Fitz by the throat and throttle him using his own neck cloth. Everyone knew that Fitz had encouraged Chessie's hopes yet he had been clever enough not to commit himself in any way. Fitz had been calculating and utterly careless of Chessie's feelings and her reputation, Dev thought. That in itself should have shown his sister how little he deserved her regard. Except that love did not always work like that…

Dev's gaze moved from Fitz, as swollen with conceit as a bladder, to the woman standing by his side. Susanna. She looked entrancing in scarlet silk with diamonds in her hair. He wanted to hate her for accepting Fitz's offer, for the sheer avarice of her behavior in selling herself for a title, for making such achingly sweet love to him and then accepting this hollow sham of a marriage. Except he could not hate her, not when he felt bound to her by such dark and complex bonds.

Fitz touched the back of Susanna's hand to claim her attention and she bent obediently closer to him to listen to whatever it was he was saying. Dev saw her smile and felt the anger and the lust close inside him like a tight fist. It was, he thought viciously, the perfect society match: good looks, money and charm, without a single shred of love or even genuine respect on either side, unless it was a healthy mutual regard for the advantages of the match.

"I'm sorry," Chessie said suddenly. She was so pale Dev was afraid she might faint. She swayed a little and he put an arm about her. "I do not feel very well," she whispered. "It is so hot in here and there is no air…"

Over her head, Dev's gaze met the concerned one of Joanna Grant. "I'll take her home," Joanna said. "Chessie, darling…" She had taken Chessie's icy cold hands in her own. "Come along. You are not well."

Together they supported Chessie back down the stairs and into the hall. A few latecomers were still arriving, joining the crowds who thronged the reception rooms. Dev went first, his broad shoulders shielding his sister from the curious stares and the whispers and titters of the guests. He felt furious and protective, knowing everyone was talking of Chessie's humiliation, feeling her misery and grief. Joanna and Tess, who both looked fragile but were a great deal tougher than they appeared, swept along with their heads high.

"Just a little farther, darling," Tess coaxed Chessie, as Joanna rustled off to find a footman to fetch their cloaks. "Soon you will be home."

Dev asked the footman to call their carriage for them.

"Don't come with us," Joanna whispered as he helped them inside. She squeezed his hands to soften the words. "Chessie may want to talk and she is so anxious for you not to disapprove of her that she won't do it if you are with us." She reached up to kiss Dev's cheek. "I'll send you word."

Dev nodded reluctantly. "Nothing Chessie could say or do would make me love her the less," he said gruffly. "None of this is her fault."

"I know," Joanna said. She smiled at him. "Thank you, Devlin."

The carriage rumbled away and Dev stood on the steps and watched it go. He had no desire to spend the evening watching Susanna waltzing with Fitz, reveling in her triumph. He felt tired and bitter and angry. It was not often these days that he chose to drown his sorrows in wine but tonight the idea had definite appeal.

"Leaving already, Devlin?" A tall fair man grabbed him by the arm and drew him back within the entrance of the Alton town house. "Come and share a glass of champagne with me first."

"Purchase!" Dev said. "You're back in Town!"

Owen Purchase shook him by the hand. "Just arrived," he said. "I've been visiting my estates." He laughed. "I never thought to hear myself say those words."

"The title is yours then?" Dev said.

"Hence the champagne." Purchase paused. "Though I would appreciate you keeping that quiet for now," he added. "The legalities are complex and I have no desire to be identified as Viscount Rothbury quite yet."

"Good luck in keeping that from the matchmaking mamas," Dev said dryly. "As soon as they hear you have come into a title you will be chased all over Town."

"Ah well, I'll cope," Purchase said, smiling broadly. "Though I prefer to do my own chasing."

"So you have come to pay your respects to the future Duke and Duchess of Alton," Dev said.

"The Alton estates run with mine in Somerset," Purchase said, grimacing. "It seemed politic as we shall be near neighbors. Cannot stand Fitzwilliam

Alton, all the same—" He broke off, looking dumbstruck, as Susanna came down the stairs and into the hall to greet one of her acquaintances who had just arrived.

"You are staring at the bride," Dev said. "Not, perhaps, the best way to ingratiate yourself with your future neighbors. Not," he added, "that she is not worth staring at."

"An exceptionally beautiful woman," Purchase agreed. "And difficult to confuse with anyone else."

Dev looked at him, his attention arrested by Purchase's tone.

"That is Alton's future wife?" Purchase persisted.

"That's what I just told you," Dev said. "Lady Carew, from Edinburgh."

"Is that what she calls herself these days?" There was a broad smile on Purchase's face now as his gaze rested on Susanna.

Dev felt an odd sliding feeling in his stomach. "What do you mean?" he said.

"When I last saw Lady Carew," Purchase said, "she was known as Miss Ives and she was being courted by a certain John Denham who was the richest young man in Bristol. His father made a fortune in trade."

Dev shrugged. He could taste bitterness on his tongue and it owed nothing to the quality of the Duke and Duchess of Alton's champagne. So Susanna was an adventuress who had already tried to catch herself a rich husband. That was barely news. The only thing that did surprise him was that she had failed to entrap her previous prey. But perhaps she valued herself too highly. Perhaps she had thrown Denham over because she wanted a title as well, not merely a fortune made in trade.

"When was this?" he asked.

Purchase slanted a look at him. "A year or more ago," he said. "Denham had only just come into his majority, and a vast fortune with it. He was still practically in leading reins. They say he fell hard for her…made a fool of himself." He pulled a face. "I'm guessing he wasn't the first to do so." He took a long pull on the champagne. "She's a remarkable woman. Being a fellow…soldier of fortune, shall we say, I recognized her for what she was when we first met. And admired her for it. It is not easy living by one's wits and looks alone. You should know that, Devlin."

"I do," Dev said, with feeling.

"I even tried my luck with her," Purchase said, "seeing that we were two of a kind."

Dev was aware of a sudden urge he had never experienced before: the desire to plant Owen Purchase, one of his oldest friends, a facer.

"Any success?" he inquired tightly.

Purchase shook his head. "For all that she looks so luscious, she is as cold as driven snow," he said. His mouth twisted. "Turned me down flat."

"Bad luck," Dev said. He rubbed the back of his neck, feeling the tension in the muscles there ease. He watched as Susanna slipped across to Fitz, placed a gentle hand on his arm and stood on tiptoe to whisper something in his ear. Cold as driven snow, Purchase had said. She looked like a flame in the scarlet dress and she had been sweet and eager in his arms, not cold at all.

Dev cleared his throat. That was no way to think about a woman whose ambitions far outstripped his own, who was a fortune hunter and an adventuress, who had succeeded in catching a marquis and would one day be a duchess.

"I felt sorry for Denham," Purchase was saying. "He was heartbroken when she ended the betrothal. He'd already lost one fiancée because of the affair and then he lost a second—"

Dev's attention snapped back to him. "I beg your pardon?"

Purchase cocked a quizzical brow as he took in the expression on Dev's face. "I said that Denham had already lost one fiancée. When he took up with Miss Ives his childhood sweetheart jilted him."

Dev felt a prickle of something like premonition tiptoe down his spine. "This childhood sweetheart," he said slowly, "did she have any money?"

"Not a feather to fly," Purchase said cheerfully. "Cassie Jennings was her name. Pretty little thing, but she had no fortune and no connections. She'd known Denham before his father made his pile. The lad's trustees didn't approve of the match. Nor did his mama."

Dev took a deep breath. He thought of Fitz paying

court to Chessie and the Duke and Duchess of Alton disapproving of a girl with no money and precious few connections. He thought of Susanna jilting the richest young man in Bristol, a man who, before he had met her, had been about to make a match with his impoverished childhood sweetheart. His fingers tightened on the delicate stem of his glass until the crystal shivered.

"Just one other thing, Purchase," he said casually. "Do you know how Miss Ives met Mr. Denham?"

"Damned if I can remember," Purchase said. "No…" His face cleared. "Actually I do remember. Denham's mother introduced her to him. She was the daughter of an old friend, apparently."

The daughter of an old friend… The widow of a family friend… The story changed a little, Dev thought, but not very much. He had always wondered why the Duke and Duchess of Alton had claimed acquaintance with Sir Edwin Carew, a man he knew had never existed. He had wondered why they had been prepared to accept Susanna as a candidate for Fitz's hand in marriage when they were so high in the instep and she was nobody.

Well, he knew now. He knew he had underestimated Susanna. She had not even been an honest adventuress. She had never wanted Fitz for herself. She had destroyed Chessie's hopes of a future with Fitz for money alone, on the commission of his parents, because that was what she did. She broke hearts and she ruined lives. Dev felt a fury fill him that was greater than ever before, an overpowering anger that grabbed him by the throat and made him want to break something, preferably Susanna's neck.

"You're sure about this, Purchase," he said urgently, although he knew the answer.

"Oh, yes," Purchase said, draining his glass. "Don't think I'll pay my respects after all," he added. "Don't want to embarrass the bride."

"You are all goodness," Dev said grimly. He had every intention now of doing far more than merely embarrassing Susanna. She deserved worse than that. He had seldom come across such a cold, ruthless and conniving woman.

"She must have known that one day someone she knew would appear and ruin her chances," he said.

Purchase shrugged. "She was on pretty safe ground," he said. "The Denhams of the world do not move in these exalted circles and nor do their acquaintances. If I had not seen her—"

"Yes," Dev said. "She would have been safe."

He thought of Chessie's dashed hopes and her damaged reputation. Susanna had done that willfully, cruelly. She was paid to ruin people's lives, their expectations. He was sure that he was right. Susanna had wrecked Miss Cassandra Jennings' plans for a future with John Denham and then she had done exactly the same thing to Chessie. It had to be more than a coincidence.

"Poor Denham," he said as Susanna slid past his view and disappeared into the ballroom, beautiful, ethereal, captivating, enough to turn any man's head. "He didn't stand a chance."

He felt the cold, hard anger sweep through him again. Now, at last, he knew the truth. And now he and Susanna would have a reckoning.

LADY EMMA BROOKE LAY in her wide canopied bed and watched the drapes at the open window move in the breeze. It was late but she could not sleep. She had waited and waited, all through the previous day and night, and all through this one. As the time had crept closer to her assignation with Tom she had felt a mixture of terror and wicked wanton excitement possess her, but as the hours had ticked by and Tom had not come, the pleasure had drained away, leaving her feeling angry and thwarted. It was exactly as before: Tom came and went as he pleased and it pleased him to keep her dangling at his whim. Emma rolled over and thumped her fists into the soft feather mattress but nothing could ease the frustration inside her. Damn Tom Bradshaw and his seductive ways. She wished him in hell.

With a groan Emma rolled over again, then froze as she heard the stealthy click of the door closing. She opened her eyes and at first could see nothing in the darkened bedchamber. Then the shadows shifted; she heard the soft footfall and turned to see that he had come to stand over her in her bed.

Emma shot upright.

"You can't come in here," she said, grabbing the

sheets to her chin in the time-honored gesture of the outraged lady. She had waited for him earlier in the garden. She had had no idea that he would be so audacious as to actually seek her out in her room. Her heart beat a mad tattoo at the thought.

Bradshaw spread his hands wide. "I am here."

"I'll scream," Emma said, although she had absolutely no intention of doing so.

Bradshaw laughed. "Do it then."

There was a moment that seemed to Emma to spin out for the longest time and then he grabbed her and kissed her and he tasted as wicked and as tempting as he had done the first night in the garden, and Emma thought she would explode with the sheer excitement of it. She forgot her anger and outrage and reached for him in near desperation. The kiss deepened and Emma's head whirled and then Tom was touching her, pushing aside her night rail and taking the most shocking intimacies with her body. It felt wonderful and Emma knew with a mixture of astonishment and exhilaration that whatever Tom was doing was not enough and that she wanted more of it, and she wanted it right now. The taut ache inside her was tightening like a vise until she was almost crying aloud. And then he was beside her in the bed and he was inside her, and she would have screamed her pleasure had he not covered her mouth with his again even as he took her virginity.

Afterward Emma lay still in the hot dark, her mind swirling with exultation and disbelief that she could have been so lost to the dictates of proper behavior that she had given herself to a man she barely knew. It seemed impossible and yet it was so thrilling she felt lit up inside. What was more, her feverish hunger for Tom had not been banished by such outrageously wanton conduct. If anything, her desire for him burned all the more fiercely now. She wanted to do it again, straight away, and probably another time after that, as well.

She rolled over, trying to see Tom's face in the darkness. She could feel him, his strong, muscular body lying beside hers. The unfamiliarity of being intimate with a man was vastly stimulating but even so she felt the first tiny frisson of fear cut through her lust.

"What happens now?" she said, and strove to keep the anxiety from her voice.

Tom laughed. His hand came up to stroke her breast and she shivered.

"One of the many things that I like about you, Emma," he said lazily, bending his head to her nipple, "is that you go straight to the heart of the matter."

"I want to marry you," Emma said, squirming beneath his hands and his tongue. "I'm a good catch, Tom. I'm pretty and I'm very rich—" She broke off on a gasp as Tom bit down lightly and the sensation streaked from her breast to her belly and made it clench.

"I know," Tom said. He sounded as though he was

laughing. He licked her nipple. "You are also delicious." He raised his head for a second. The tone of his voice changed.

"What would you do if I said I did not want to marry you?"

The cold fear in Emma intensified, driving away the hot pleasure for a moment. "I would marry James Devlin straight away," she said, "and tell you to go to hell."

Tom laughed. "Another thing I like about you, Emma," he said, "is how very practical you are." He ran his hands over her and she shivered like a bow beneath his touch. "You don't love Devlin," he said, and it was not a question.

"No." Emma reached for him but he held back, his hands still moving over her bare skin in the most insidiously tempting caresses she could imagine. "I never did."

"Do you love me?" Tom asked. His voice was very quiet. He slid his hand over the soft skin of her inner thigh and her legs parted helplessly to his touch. Emma tried to concentrate on the question. She sensed it mattered. But it was almost impossible with Tom's fingers circling closer and closer to the very core of her.

"I don't know you well enough to love you," she gasped, "but—"

"Yes?" Tom's tone was very serious but his fingers had now slipped inside her and were doing the most shocking and tantalizing things to her. Emma thought she might simply come apart with ecstasy.

"But I love what you do to me..." Her broken whisper begged him for more.

Tom paused. Emma writhed in an agony of impatience.

"That," Tom continued, his fingers starting to stroke her again in smooth, stealthy circles, "is a very honest answer. So why do you want to marry me?" He paused in his caresses and Emma almost groaned.

"I want you because..." She hung on the edge of rapture, feeling her body gather and the pleasure build. "Because you're like me."

She realized it was true although she had no idea how she knew. Like had called to like and she had recognized him from the very first.

Tom laughed aloud. "I'm selfish and I'm greedy and I care for no one and nothing but myself."

"People say I am spoiled," Emma said, "and it's true. I always get what I want."

Tom eased himself above her, over her and then inside her, giving her exactly what she wanted.

"What happens next," he said as he started to move, "is that you run away with me tonight. We'll go to Gretna." He drew back and touched her cheek. "Is that what you want?"

"Oh, yes," Emma said, feeling so happy and excited that she wanted to cry. "But not yet—"

"No, not yet," Tom agreed. He slid inside her again and she arched to meet him. "There are still several hours before the dawn."

CHAPTER FOURTEEN

SUSANNA HAD BEEN GLAD when Fitz had brought her home, kissed her hand with the greatest propriety and had left her on the doorstep without any attempt whatsoever to inveigle himself into her bed. It felt, she thought, as though now he secured her and her fictitious fortune he was no longer particularly interested in her; either that or he found courting her too much effort and was still enjoying his liaison with the lovely Cyprian Miss Kingston. There was something in Fitz's attitude toward her now, something of self-satisfaction and possessiveness, which suggested that as Susanna was to be his wife she should accept his authority and wait her turn in his bed. It was a reflection of Fitz's utter arrogance, Susanna thought. She would richly enjoy jilting him.

She was fairly sure now that she would be able to see this masquerade through to its conclusion. Mr. Churchward had been most helpful once she had confided in him. He had agreed to advance a sum to stave off the demands of the moneylenders and he had also undertaken to try to discover the identity of her blackmailer. In return she had had to promise to tell Devlin the entire truth of her charade. On that Mr. Churchward had been most insistent. Honesty, he had said, his eyes gleaming behind his dusty lenses, could be her only policy toward her husband.

But, Susanna thought, she would not do it tonight. Tonight she was too drained even to think of it. She had seen Chessie at the ball, so pale and sad, and her heart had cracked a little to see how bravely Dev's sister had tried to face down the gossips. She had wanted to go to Chessie and help her because the girl's plight reminded her of herself, a young woman who had once been very much in love and very unhappy. She had ruined Chessie's future and she could not live with herself for it. She had seen Devlin, too, seen his contempt and his anger, and had felt shriveled inside.

Margery helped her out of the flame-red gown and went to draw her bath whilst Susanna wandered around the room feeling oddly restless. She tried not to look at the vast and empty expanse of the bed for every time she did she thought of Devlin and of those hours when he had made love to her so exquisitely that he had somehow imprinted himself on her soul as well as her body. With a sigh she went through to the dressing room and slid into the bath, lying there for a long time, trying to slough off her feelings of guilt and unhappiness along with her tiredness. When she finally came out Margery objected that she would be as pink and wrinkled as a baby but Susanna did not care. She picked up a copy of

Maria Edgeworth's novel *Leonora* and tried to concentrate on reading instead and finally lost herself amongst the pages. An hour later she was on the point of blowing out the candle when she heard a peremptory knock at the door, voices raised in the hall and then her bedroom door slammed open with a crash that reverberated through the entire house.

Dev stood there. He paused in the doorway, looking at her. There was something in his eyes, a mixture of controlled anger and contempt that made Susanna's heart lurch.

"Devlin," she said. "This is becoming a bad habit."

Dev ignored her words. She was not even sure he had heard them. Behind the carefully blank look on his face she glimpsed a coldness that chilled her to the bone.

"Get up, please," he said, though it was scarcely a request. "Put some clothes on. We're going out somewhere no one can overhear us. I want to talk to you."

The icy chill in Susanna's blood intensified. She stared at him. She did not move, could not. Dev came across to the bed. She could see turbulent fury in his eyes now and something else so scorching and fierce she felt scalded by it. It held her still for a second.

"Get up!" He had dropped the pretense at courtesy now. He was standing over her and she had no doubts that if she did not do as he asked—as he commanded—he would drag her bodily from the bed.

"Very well." She put her book aside. Her hands

were trembling a little. "You will have to wait for me outside the room." She tried to sound confident but her voice was thin. "I am not dressing in front of you."

The flare of dislike in his eyes seared her. "Oh, please—" his tone flayed "—tell me how I could possibly embarrass so shameless an adventuress as you?" His insolent glance swept over her. "Have you forgotten that I have seen every last inch of you?"

Susanna could see Margery's fascinated face peering around the door. She straightened her spine, sitting bolt upright in the bed.

"Either you wait outside, Devlin," she said, "or I stay here. Your choice."

Dev turned his back with a quick sigh of irritation as she slid from the bed.

Her hands were shaking so much now that it seemed to take hours to find her clothes, let alone dress in them.

Her mind spun like a rat in a trap. What did Dev want to talk about? What had he discovered? Did he know everything? She knew now that Mr. Churchward's advice on honesty had come too late, for Dev evidently knew some if not all of the truth. She could not guess at what he had found out. There were so many secrets. Did he know about the annulment? She shuddered. Not the child. Please, not the child…

"Devlin, what is this all about?" She still sounded woefully anxious when most she wanted to sound brave.

"Not here. Not yet." His voice was tight and furious. "Unless you wish your servants to know your business."

"I don't mind." Margery had come forward to help Susanna dress. "You know you can trust me, my lady." She turned to Dev. "My lady asked you to wait outside," she added sharply.

Looking from the maid's defiant little figure to the surprise on Dev's face, Susanna could have hugged her. Dev shrugged—but he did as he was told.

"Two minutes," he said from the doorway.

"Handsome," Margery said as he went out, "but he knows it. These gentlemen..." She shook her head as though she had seen a vast number of opinionated noblemen come and go.

"Devlin is no more a gentleman than I am a lady, Margery," Susanna said.

"Then you are well-matched, ma'am." The maid's hands were deft with the ribbons and hooks. "Which I had guessed," she added, "seeing as he passed that night in your bed."

"Margery!" Susanna was scandalized. "You knew!"

The maid gave her the sort of look that did not require words to accompany it. Susanna felt suitably castigated.

"Do you love him, ma'am?" The maid handed her the cloak.

Susanna hesitated—and wondered why she had

not simply denied it immediately. "I don't know," she said after a moment.

"I've seen the way you look at him," Margery said. "And he at you," she added. "As though he wants to—"

"Margery!" Susanna interrupted. "That is not love," she added.

"No, ma'am," the maid said. Her voice changed. "You sound sad," she said.

"I'm scared," Susanna said frankly. "I don't know what he knows."

The door opened. "Susanna," Dev said. "Must I fetch you bodily?"

Margery and Susanna exchanged a look. Margery gave a sniff. "My lady is ready to accompany you now."

Dev bowed ironically. "Thank you."

"See you treat her with courtesy, sir," Margery continued.

A hint of laughter broke through the black frown on Dev's brow. "My good girl, your loyalty to your mistress is admirable but entirely misplaced." He took Susanna's arm as they descended the stairs, not to guide her, Susanna thought, more to prevent her from running away. It was a sensible precaution. Had she had somewhere to run, she would not have hesitated.

Dev opened the front door for her and she stepped out into the street. Although it was another hot night Susanna shivered and drew the cloak more tightly about her. "What is this about, Devlin?" she asked again.

Dev looked at her for a long moment. "You must have known," he said, "that sooner or later someone would recognize you."

For the life of her, Susanna could not prevent the ripple of apprehension that ran through her. He felt it. She saw him smile in the moonlight. It was a smile without warmth. She doubted he would ever look on her with warmth again now, now that the thread was starting to unravel; now that he was learning all her secrets.

"Too late to pretend, Susanna?" There was derision in his voice.

"Who was it?" Susanna said. "Who gave me away?"

"Ah…" She heard the satisfaction in his tone. "So you admit it?"

"I am not sure what I am admitting to yet," Susanna said dryly. "Who told you…about me?"

"That does not matter," Dev said.

Susanna thought of the anonymous letter writer. This informant of Devlin's must surely be different from the man—or woman—who threatened her. No blackmailer gave their information away for free, which meant that there were several people in London who knew her true identity. She could feel the trap closing very slowly. There was nowhere to turn. There was no one she could trust.

"It matters to me," she said.

"It was Owen Purchase," Dev said. "He saw you at the betrothal ball tonight. I believe he was an acquaintance of yours in Bristol."

Susanna smiled. She could not help herself. It was an irony that Owen Purchase, the American sea captain who was as much a survivor, as much an opportunist as she, should have been the one to give her away. She had liked Purchase. Women did; not only was he ruggedly handsome but he had an indefinable charm that seduced them all. He had not seduced her, though. She had easily withstood his appeal. She would have preferred him as a friend. It was a pity he had seen fit to betray her.

Dev was looking at her. "You like Purchase," he said. There was an odd note in his voice.

"I do," Susanna said.

"He admires you, too."

"Not enough to keep my secrets."

They had been walking all the while, taking a route that Dev had set and that Susanna did not recognize, and now Dev held open the door of a tavern for her. It was not a place frequented by the gentry. The walls were roughly plastered and the floor bare. The air was thick with the fug of ale and smoke. There were, Susanna reckoned, a dozen men there who would slide their blade between your ribs first and ask questions later. It was still a great deal more salubrious than some of the inns she had worked when she had been in Edinburgh. As a tavern wench she had worked in places she doubted Dev would even set foot in, at least not unarmed, the sort of places where one would certainly get knifed in the alley outside if one said the wrong thing to the wrong man.

"A favorite haunt of yours?" she asked disdainfully, looking around the crowded and noisy taproom.

Dev grinned. "Scared?" he mocked.

Susanna raised her chin. "You'll have to do better than this if you wish to frighten me."

Dev's gaze was steady on her. "I will."

Susanna knew it and she shivered. There was one small table tucked in a corner and Dev held the chair for her, signaling to the servant. He ordered brandy and raised a brow at Susanna.

"What would you like?"

None of the genteel ladies' drinks seemed appropriate. "I'll have brandy, too," Susanna said. "Thank you."

"Dutch courage?" Dev said.

"Oblivion does appeal," Susanna agreed.

Dev laughed. She felt his blue gaze on her and it felt as though there was still that connection between them, defying enmity, defying everything, because they were bound together closer than close and there was no undoing it. But then Dev's expression turned cold and Susanna knew any affinity she felt was no more than an illusion.

"Tell me about John Denham," Dev said.

The brandy arrived. Dev poured her a generous

measure. "Denham," he repeated. "Must I remind you?" His tone was heavy with sarcasm. "Your most recent fiancé—before Fitz, of course." He touched his glass to hers in ironic toast. "You are quite a collector, Susanna."

"I don't keep them," Susanna said. She tasted the brandy. It was surprisingly good for such a villainously rough inn.

"No," Dev agreed. "That is the interesting bit. You are not a fortune hunter after all. I misread you completely." He rested his elbows on the table and looked at her. "The Susanna Burney I used to know would never have deliberately set out to break the heart of an impressionable young man solely for money," he said. "She would never have ruined the future hopes of his childhood sweetheart simply because she was paid to do so." He looked down at the brandy swirling in his glass and then up, directly into her eyes. Susanna's heart jerked. "What happened to you, Susanna?" Dev said softly. "What could have made you become like this?"

She almost told him. *I lost your child, Devlin. I was alone, I was sick and in the poorhouse... I would have done almost anything I had to do in order to survive.* She thought of the tiny body wrapped in the shawl, buried in the pauper's grave. The pain ripped through her, dark, excruciating. She grabbed the brandy glass with an unsteady hand and took a gulp.

"Susanna?" Dev's eyes had narrowed. He was too

quick, too perceptive. She had to be careful. She had to protect herself because to speak of Maura's death would destroy her.

She shrugged, turning her face away from the light of the candle, which suddenly seemed far too bright.

"Nothing happened to me," she said lightly. "I discovered something that I was good at. It was lucrative. That is all."

She saw Dev's mouth turn down at the corners. Disapproval, dislike, disdain... She was accustomed to all those emotions. She had seen them on the faces of those she had jilted—and those who had paid her.

"John Denham will find another lady to wed," she said. "One frequently imagines one's life ruined at one and twenty when it is no such thing." She tried, and almost succeeded, in keeping the bitterness from her voice. Life carried on after it was ruined; she had learned that. It did not end. One had to fashion something new out of the ashes.

"Perhaps," Dev said. His mouth twisted. "But that is not really the point, is it, Susanna? The point is surely the cruelty of deliberately toying with Denham's affections."

"I don't think that I can be blamed for John Denham's fickleness," Susanna said with a flash of feeling. "If he had truly been in love with his childhood sweetheart then no power on earth should have been able to separate them. I merely demonstrated to them both that Denham was young and unreliable. No great catch, in fact."

"Just as you demonstrated to Chessie that Fitz was not worthy of her by taking him away from her and destroying all her hopes for the future?" Dev queried, his tone soft but lethal. "You think that you were doing her a kindness?"

The candle flame quivered in the draught from the open window. Looking up, Susanna saw it reflected in Dev's eyes. Saw, too, his loathing for what she had done to his sister. His face was taut with distaste.

"No," Susanna admitted. "I do not claim to have been doing Miss Devlin a kindness. That would be taking too much credit."

She saw a tiny amount of the tension seep from Dev's shoulders. "I am glad that you see it that way," he said, an edge to his voice. "Perhaps you do have some scruples left after all."

"But Fitz is not good enough for her," Susanna continued. "He is a bad catch for any woman. He is spoiled and arrogant and thinks to please no one but himself."

"I agree with you," Dev said. "But that does not justify what you have done."

"I know!" Susanna burst out. "Do you think I do not know that, Devlin?" She thought of Chessie looking pale and sick at heart. "I hurt her," she said, more quietly, "and I am ashamed of that."

Dev shook his head as though he had not heard her words and certainly had not given them any credence. "I would have stood by and watched my sister marry an unworthy man," he said roughly, "no matter how much it pained me, because I want her to be happy." He looked up suddenly and Susanna's heart lurched at the expression in his eyes. "I am not sure I can forgive you for what you have done to her, Susanna."

"Add it to the list of all the things you blame me for," Susanna said bitterly. She stood up abruptly. "If that is all you wanted to say to me—"

Dev caught her wrist, pulling her back down onto the rickety wooden chair, which squeaked in protest. "We have not even started," he said pleasantly. "I want to know everything, Susanna. I do not believe that Denham was your first victim. Where else have you worked?"

"Why should I tell you?" Susanna countered.

"Why should you not?" Dev said. "I already know half the tale anyway. Consider it a confessional."

He did not know half the tale. He barely knew a quarter. Yet Susanna found herself dangerously tempted. No one knew the history of Susanna Burney and the trail of broken hearts she had left across Britain. It would almost be a relief to tell someone.

She sat down again. The rowdy hum of the alehouse conversation rose in her ears. "I worked in Edinburgh first," she said, "then in Manchester and Leeds and Birmingham..."

Dev laughed shortly. "How fortunate for you that

there are so many other towns and cities still unexploited."

"This was to be the last time," Susanna said.

"Of course." Dev sounded courteous and entirely disbelieving. "Don't criminals always claim that?"

"I have done nothing illegal," Susanna said.

"No," Dev said. "Only deeply immoral."

"Fine words," Susanna flashed, "coming from a fortune hunter, a pirate and a thief!"

There was a hairsbreadth of hesitation. "In what way am I a thief?" Dev inquired mildly.

"You did not come by your original fame and fortune honestly," Susanna said.

"I think the piracy covers that," Dev said. He put a hand out and touched her lightly on the wrist.

"All right," he said, "I concede. We are neither of us saints, Susanna." He smiled, his wicked pirate's smile, and Susanna's treacherous heart missed a beat.

"Tell me about Edinburgh—and Manchester and Leeds and Birmingham," Dev said softly.

Susanna hesitated. She was very conscious of his touch on her wrist, light and insistent, like a brand.

"You've got nothing to lose," Dev added. "Whatever you decide, I shall go to Fitz and tell him that his loving parents are paying you to dupe him."

"Would that be revenge for Chessie," Susanna said, "or for yourself?"

Dev gave her a lopsided grin. "A little of both, perhaps," he said. He released her, picked up the bottle and refilled their glasses.

"When I took the commission," Susanna said slowly, watching the swirl of the dark amber liquid, "I had no notion that Chessie was your sister. The Duke and Duchess barely mentioned her by name."

"That does not surprise me," Dev said. "They consider her beneath their notice, a problem to be swept away." He looked at her. "They pay others to do the dirty work, whether it is to sweep their chimneys or seduce their son. It is all the same to them." He placed his glass gently on the table. "How did it all start?"

For a moment Susanna stared blindly into her brandy. It had started out of desperation and despair and the need to keep her inherited family together.

"It started by accident," she said.

"You did not choose to break men's hearts as a career?" Dev sounded cynically amused. "Do you expect credit for that?"

"You wanted to know, Devlin," Susanna snapped. The anger flared within her. "I thought that we had agreed that you are hardly on the moral high ground yourself!"

A rueful smile tilted Dev's lips. "Touché," he murmured.

"I was working in a gown shop in Edinburgh," Susanna said. She looked at him defiantly. "I told you I had worked for a living when I had failed to secure myself a rich and titled husband."

"I thought—" Dev said. He stopped.

"You thought I had become a whore," Susanna

said. “Well, I imagine you consider this to be little different.” She shrugged. “It is true that there were gentlemen who came into the shop, quite a number of them, and that some of the girls—” She could feel herself blushing under Dev’s steady gaze. Many shopgirls did supplement their earnings with wages of another sort but she had never succumbed. Sometimes, hungry and exhausted, with food to find for herself and for Rose and Rory, she had wondered at her own pride and folly. Yet somehow she had never wanted to sell herself so cheap.

“I get the picture,” Dev said dryly.

“One young man was most persistent,” Susanna said. “He wished me to be his mistress but I would not agree.” She raised her chin. She could not change the opinion Dev had of her but she was damned if she would let it go unchallenged. “I had no wish to be a whore,” she said, “and I never was.”

Dev said nothing. She waited, knowing she wanted him to say that he believed her, knowing that it mattered to her more than it should, knowing, too, that he would not give her that approval she craved. When he did not, she resumed.

“A few days later an older gentleman came into the shop asking for me by name. He turned out to be the father of my admirer. He was a cloth manufacturer, a rich and influential Edinburgh citizen. He was also in high good humor. He placed a bag of guineas on the counter and told me they were mine.” She took a deep breath, remembering. It had felt like a miracle. It was the only thing that had stood between her and another night without food.

"His son had been betrothed to a girl he had met before the father had made his fortune," she said. "The family had gone up in the world and wanted the son to marry into the gentry but the engagement stood in the way. When the son met me and—" she hesitated "—lost his head a little, I suppose, he boasted all over town that he would set me up as his mistress. His fiancée heard of it and broke off the engagement leaving the youth free to marry well, as the father desired."

"You took the money," Dev said.

"Of course," Susanna said. She thought of the feast they had had that night—Rose's little face greedy and excited in the candlelight, Rory stuffing bread into his mouth like a young wolf. New shoes, winter clothes…

"I had not thought of what might happen next," she said, "but within a few weeks another gentleman contacted me, a business associate of the first, who had heard the story. He was in a very similar situation—he had made money and was socially ambitious. His daughter was betrothed to a poor apprentice and was most stubborn in her affections. He wanted me to…distract…the fiancé, take him away from the girl. So I did."

"That was Manchester," Dev said.

"There are a great many newly rich and ambitious families in the industrial north," Susanna said.

"Leeds?" Dev asked.

"Another young man who had developed an affection for an unsuitable woman. His parents were most grateful to me."

"And no doubt showed their gratitude financially," Dev said.

"Of course."

"Birmingham?"

"Oh..." Susanna's voice flattened. She had not enjoyed Birmingham. Most of the time she had been able to console herself with the fact that the young men she tempted were spoiled and unsteady in their affections, and that the girls had been better off without them. It was not an excuse but it had softened the guilt of taking money for breaking hearts. Birmingham, though... Birmingham had been very different.

"That was more difficult," she said. "There was a nabob's daughter betrothed to a young gentleman of good family, a Mr. Jackson. Her parents should have been satisfied with the match but then Lord Downing came to visit and they decided that a mere gentleman was no longer good enough. They wanted to buy a title for her instead."

"Could she not simply have broken off the betrothal?" Dev asked. "Young ladies have that privilege where gentlemen do not."

Susanna shook her head. "Miss Price was very loyal. Like the young lady in Manchester, once her affections were fixed she did not waver in them. She refused to break the engagement so her parents called upon me to help."

"And what form did your help take?" Dev inquired, a hard edge now to his voice.

"I..." Susanna hesitated. "I led Mr. Jackson astray."

She saw Dev's mouth twist. "Dear me," he said. "All the way into your bed?"

Susanna's heart was pounding. "It had to appear so, certainly."

She had hated that. In order to persuade Miss Price that the object of her affections was utterly unworthy, she had lured Jackson into her bed and arranged that they should be caught in the act. It had been easy; the man was a rake and eager enough to bed her. Her difficulty had been to hold him off long enough for Miss Price and her parents to burst in. She had barely escaped with her virtue that time, if she could still be considered to have any virtue left after so notorious a career. That, she supposed, was a moot point.

"The girl must have been heartbroken." Dev's voice was soft.

"She was." Susanna's throat closed. It had been horrible. Miss Price had not cried or screamed. She had uttered no words of reproach. Her face had turned parchment-white and she had looked so stricken that Susanna had felt sick with pity.

"But he was a rake," she added. "He really was unworthy of her."

"So that makes it perfectly acceptable to break her heart," Dev said sarcastically. "I suppose you charged more for that one," he added. "For the extra work of taking him to your bed."

Susanna's lips set in a tight line. "I told you," she said. "I was never a whore."

"No, of course not." Dev sounded contemptuous. "To the edge, Susanna, but not over it? I congratulate you on your moral fortitude."

There was no answer to that one.

"And then you came to Bristol?" Dev said. "John Denham."

Susanna shrugged. "There were a few others. One failure…"

Dev laughed. "Someone resisted you? How piquant!"

"I'm not irresistible," Susanna said. "No more than you are, Devlin. I simply prepare my ground well. I talk to the parents and guardians, learn all my assignment's likes and dislikcs and plan my approach."

"You are the consummate professional, I am sure." Dev was smooth. "So why did you fail?"

"Because," Susanna said, "one young gentleman was steadfast and absolutely loyal in his affections. Nothing and no one could separate him from the woman he loved. So…" She shrugged lightly. "I failed."

"How gratifying that you proved him worthy," Dev said, the sarcastic edge back in his voice. "You must have been congratulating yourself on your role in showing the world what a faithful lover he was!" His voice changed. "Onward and upward. After Denham you progressed to the aristocracy. The ultimate challenge—Fitzwilliam Alton—the son of a Duke."

"Yes," Susanna said.

"His parents knew he was about to make Chessie an offer," Dev said. "So they paid you to distract him."

"Yes." There was no point in denials. "They suspected Fitz was on the point of proposing to Miss Devlin," Susanna said. "They were anxious to prevent it."

She saw Dev clench his fists so the knuckles showed white. "Because she was poor and had few eligible connections."

"I imagine so," Susanna agreed woodenly.

"And now you have ruined Chessie's hopes for the future," Dev said, his tone hot with anger, "what next? Do you progress to the Royal Family? There are plenty of unsuitable alliances there for you to work upon. You might even catch a Royal Duke for yourself. They do have an eye for a pretty face."

"Very amusing," Susanna said. She toyed with her glass before looking at him very directly. "I suspect that your plan is for my career to reach an abrupt halt now, is it not, Devlin?"

Dev did not answer immediately and for a second her hopes soared dizzily that he would not betray her.

But she could see his expression, determination and an odd sort of regret, as though despite everything it pained him to hurt her, and she felt those same hopes crash like a stone. Panic rose in her throat, choking her. She had come so close to success, to completing the job, claiming the fee, paying off the moneylenders and having enough spare to make a new life with Rory and Rose. If Dev gave her away now all would be lost. For a moment the candlelight wavered like tears and she felt the pain in her chest and the press of all those dark nameless fears.

The poorhouse, the stench of death, the lost child…

"Yes," Dev said, and his voice was very quiet, "I shall expose you for the fraud you are, Susanna. You might have ruined Chessie's future but at least I can prevent you from wrecking the hopes of anyone else."

This was the moment then. Susanna knew she had to stop him but she had so few cards left to play.

"You cannot give me away," she said. She could hear the desperation in her own voice. "We agreed at the start, remember? You know my secrets and I know yours. We both benefit from keeping silent. If you tell—" She fell silent again as Dev shook his head slightly.

"Mutual blackmail," he said, his mouth twisting. "It's not pretty, is it? Well, I have had enough of it, Susanna. It ends now."

Susanna's stomach dropped. She stared at him, disbelieving. "But Lady Emma—" she began.

She saw Dev smile. "I have been trying to see Emma for the past three days to tell her that I have reapplied for my Navy commission," he said. "I've written to her." He met her eyes. "I told her about us, Susanna. I told her I had been unfaithful. I fully expect her to break the engagement. So…" His smile deepened. "I fear you have no grounds left for blackmail."

Susanna could feel everything slipping away. The fear grabbed her by the throat. "I don't understand," she said. "You have huge debts… And there is your sister to consider—"

Dev gave her a contemptuous look. "You did not have the slightest concern for Chessie before so do not pretend to any now."

Susanna stared at him. There was something about his stillness and his quiet determination that told her that argument was useless. Dev had made his decision and he would not waver. There had always been a core of steel in him, she thought. It was not always apparent behind that careless exterior and the fortune hunter's casual charm, but it was there. She had underestimated him and now she had no leverage, nothing. Dev would go to Fitz and tell him the truth and she would not be paid and she would not be able to provide for Rose and Rory and the whole terrible cycle of debt and despair would start all over again. She felt so terrified that for a moment she could not breathe.

"Joanna and Alex will take care of Chessie," Dev said. "Alex is not a rich man but he has always done his best for us. He will make sure Chessie is safe if I cannot." For a moment Susanna could hear the self-loathing in his tone and knew how deeply Dev felt he had failed. "Meanwhile," he added, "I shall do my best to regain some honor."

His words were very final and she knew he meant them. The terror blocked Susanna's throat and deprived her of words and she looked at him in silent horror and Dev looked steadily back at her and she knew she had lost.

"Devlin," she said, and heard the despair in her own voice. "Please—"

Dev raised his glass of brandy. "Are you going to beg me not to give you away?" he asked. "That would be piquant, but I will save you the humiliation by telling you now that it would do no good. For too long I have done the expedient thing. I was in danger of losing my principles."

Susanna closed her eyes, thinking of the twins, of the entire desperate fight for survival. Dev had no idea, she thought, what it was like to be alone and destitute. His childhood had been hard but he had risen above it. He was a man and men had always had the best chances. He thought that he was poor because he only had a knighthood and a ruined castle and no money. He had absolutely no idea what it had been like to live cheek by jowl with eighteen others in a tenement with no food and no clothes and no bedding and no privacy and no money even to pay for a proper burial for her baby… He condemned her for the choices she had made and now he was going to send her straight back into that poverty, all for the sake of his honor and his principles. She felt sick and afraid and alone.

"Since you are clearly so desperate for the money," Dev said suddenly, "you could always try to buy my silence with your body."

Susanna caught her breath as his wicked glance raked her, lingering on the line of her mouth, dropping with explicit consideration to the curve of her breasts beneath the light muslin gown she wore. His eyes came up to meet hers and there was suddenly something so carnal in them that she thought she made a slight sound. He heard it, and smiled.

"I thought—" Susanna forced the words out "—that you were speaking of principle just now?"

Could she do it? she wondered as her mind spun, and hope and fear warred within her. Could she give herself to Devlin again to buy his silence, to seal their agreement? She was shaking at the mere thought. It was madness and yet the flare of heat under her skin, the warmth in the pit of her stomach, told her that she wanted it. She wanted him. She desired him shamelessly, without reservation and if it would buy her the future she so desperately needed then surely that could not be so wrong. Nevertheless she was shaking at the thought.

Dev took her chin in his hand and turned her face toward the candlelight and she felt naked.

"It seems that my principles are very flexible when it comes to you," he murmured. "I wish it were not so and yet..." he paused "...a part of me cannot regret it because I want you so."

He kissed her and he tasted of heat and brandy and himself, a taste that was becoming so shockingly familiar and exciting to Susanna that it was like a drug. His tongue danced with hers, delving deep, searching and commanding a response from her. The lights swam and the room tilted as Susanna closed her eyes and abandoned herself to sensation.

"Well?" Dev said as he released her. His eyes were a very bright, very intense blue.

"Yes," Susanna whispered. "I'll do it."

Dev paused and for a second Susanna wondered if she had surprised him, whether he had in fact had a higher regard for her than she had imagined and that he thought she would refuse to offer herself for his silence. The knowledge that he now thought her so venal was a bitter one, but there was nothing she could do. One night with Devlin to ensure he kept her secrets and ensure that she kept her future safe...

"I thought that you said you believed in fidelity?" Dev said. A sardonic smile tilted his lips. "Perhaps you believe in money more?"

It was just another betrayal but she nodded. She could not trust herself to speak.

"You'll do it because the Altons are paying you a lot of money," Dev repeated, "and you don't want to lose it." There was an ugly set to his mouth now. He stood up abruptly, his chair crashing back. "Come with me then."

For a moment Susanna did not understand and then she realized the truth. He meant to take her here, now, upstairs in an inn chamber. A wave of heat and shame washed through her. Dev was holding out his hand to her. There was anger and amusement in his eyes and after a moment he said mockingly, "Have you changed your mind, Susanna? Is the price too high?"

Susanna stood up and put her hand into his. Her legs felt so shaky she thought she might fall. She felt sick. She hated herself. Sometimes she thought she could not bear the person she had become, compromising her morals and her principles simply because life had taught her the bitter truth that in order to survive she had to lie, steal and now even barter herself. But she had failed her own child. That grief never left her. She could never ever fail Rose and Rory, whom she had sworn to protect.

She forced the words out despite the tight fear in her chest. "No," she whispered. "I haven't changed my mind."

CHAPTER FIFTEEN

DEV HAD NEVER INTENDED to do it. It had been a dare, a challenge, because he had been interested to see just how far Susanna would go. He had been furious with her for the callous way in which she had ruined Chessie's hopes and the casual cruelty she had meted out to the other couples whose lives she had torn apart. But he was curious, too; he had seen the fear in her and the desperation, so at odds with her blatant claims that it was all for the money. She had tried to hide her fears from him but he knew her very well. So he had thought to push her as far as he could and force her to tell him the whole truth. Instead she had agreed to sleep with him in return for his silence so perhaps he had been mistaken after all and she was corrupt through and through, an empty soul within that luscious, tempting body, a woman willing to give herself in return for a fortune. Either way Dev was not really sure he cared, not if he could possess her again and make love to her with the same ravishing intensity he had experienced before and had ached for ever since.

"First room up the stairs on the left, sir," the landlord said in response to Dev's urgent query. He had Susanna tightly by the hand; he was not going to let her run out on him now, not when his body felt so tight and primed and his need for her was so excruciating that he could barely see straight.

"Best make sure it's empty first if you don't want an audience or three or more in the bed," the man added, with a leer.

Dev saw the color fade from Susanna's face and her lips tighten. He could sense the hesitation in her; feel, too, the way that her fingers trembled in his as he drew her after him up the stairs. Her foot slipped on one of the steps. He swept her up and into his arms to prevent her from falling. She was light in his arms and her hair, scented with the honey and verbena that had haunted his dreams, brushed his cheek in the gentlest caress. The ache inside Devlin intensified, tightening like a vise.

On the small landing at the turn of the stair he put her down, turned her back against the peeling plaster wall and kissed her again. Her lips were very soft against his and her mouth opened readily to him and the taste and the essence of her swamped his senses. He wanted to take her right there, against the wall, pulling up her dainty muslin skirts and plunging into her and the fierce feral nature of his desire shocked him and warned him to rein himself in. He was almost out of control and he did not want that. If he were to have Susanna for one more night then he wanted to take pleasure in every moment.

Someone pushed past them, lumbering downstairs, and Dev thrust open the first door on the left and pulled Susanna inside. Here the roar from the taproom was muted and the only light came from a ridiculously romantic sickle moon that shone through the window and dappled the boards of the floor. The room, he was pleased to find, was a little less rank than might have been expected. The scent of lavender polish mingled with the dry smell of wood.

In the faint light he saw the shine of Susanna's eyes—eyes, wide and dark, as she took in the small, sagging bed.

"I don't trust you." She sounded a little dazed as though she were as punch-drunk from the kiss as he. "How do I know that if I give myself to you, you will keep your word?"

"You don't," Dev said. He started to undress her; halfway through he lost interest and simply pulled the clothes off her regardless, dropping them on the floor, until she was standing naked in the moonlight. She made no move either to help him or hinder him but stood like a statue, her hands by her sides, her nakedness challenging him to touch her. He could hear her quick breathing and see the rapid rise and fall of her breast, more evidence that she was a great deal less confident than she had pretended to be. She must want the Altons' money very, very much, Dev thought.

He started to kiss her. She pushed him away for a moment. "Promise me," she said, and there was the tiniest betraying quiver in her voice. "Promise me you will keep your word."

"I promise," Dev said. He would have promised her just about anything in that moment, feeling the warmth of her body pressed with such sinful seduction against his. The hunger roared through him again and he kissed her and felt her hesitant response, and kissed her again, softly, tenderly, running his tongue over her lower lip, courting a response from her. He thought for a moment that she might pull away from him and this would be when she lost her nerve, but then she gave a little broken gasp, and her need rose up to meet his and she twined her arms about his neck and gave him back kiss for feverish kiss. The triumph blazed through him. Whether it was for money or for pure lust, she was his this night. What did it matter if she was corrupt and dishonest through and through? She had a body made for sin and he would take it and tomorrow he would send her back to Fitz knowing that she bore the marks of his possession on her and that in truth she was his and his alone, because they were two of a kind and had always been meant to be together. The knowledge that Susanna was his—had always been his—sank into Dev's soul and for a moment it felt as though his heart turned inside out. Then the thought was lost in the sleek heat and softness of Susanna's body and he gave himself up to sensation alone.

SUSANNA HAD LEARNED with a shock that it was not so difficult after all to give in to blackmail—not when the man she was with was James Devlin and he was making the most delicious love to her and her body was singing with the pleasure of it and she thought for one moment that she might dissolve with pure bliss where she stood. It was appalling, wicked, to learn that she could do this when throughout her time as a heartbreaker she had prided herself on having some moral principles, chief amongst them the fact that she would never ever actually sleep with the man she was leading astray. But now, with Dev's kisses on her throat, his mouth at her breast, she was a different creature entirely, her senses woken once more to Dev's touch, entirely at his mercy.

Dev picked her up and put her down on the bed—the mattress seemed to sink a very long way, and she did, briefly, worry about fleas—but then Dev started to caress her with long, slow strokes that drove all thought from her mind. The insistent thrumming of her blood blotted out the sounds from the taproom below. She forgot the squalor of their situation as Dev's touch became more purposeful, insistent, demanding her absolute surrender. He had long ago shed his clothes and the rub of his skin against hers was a torment and a delight. His mouth toyed with her breast, teasing her to a peak of need. Her body became flushed and heated, crying out for the fulfillment that he was denying her.

"What do you want, Susanna?" His whisper was low, carnal. "Tell me."

Susanna hesitated. Was he going to make her beg

again—for his possession this time? She thought he probably was, and hated him for it even as she wanted to cry out to him to take her. He would like that, she thought, a streak of rebellion flaring briefly within her. He wanted to master her, to make her face the fact that he could command her body. Yet his hands were tender on her and his kiss drew out the pleasure between them to endless depths.

"What do you want?" She felt his breath against her lips, tasted the brandy again on his tongue as it flicked hers.

"I want to come." The words were forced from her, reluctant words, words she wanted to deny him, hating herself now as well as him for admitting the hunger she had for him. She knew he would not give her what she craved.

"In good time." His caress eased to the most light and teasing of touches, stroking up from the underneath of her breast to the very tip. The ache between her thighs intensified. She tried to think, tried to breathe, but all her attention was focused on the glorious need that coiled within her.

"I don't want to wait." Now she knew she was pleading and did not care. "Please. Devlin. I want to come—"

"You will." His lips traced a path down between her breasts to the hot skin of her belly. His tongue curled into her navel then licked down over the curve of her stomach. "You can come as many times as you like for me." His whispered words were like a heated incitement. He slid a finger inside her, stroking her, stretching her. "Twice, three times, as often as you wish until you are sated." He drew himself up until the tip of his penis replaced his fingers inside her. She reached for him but still he held back.

Susanna's body shuddered, clenching tight. The low, lust-filled words had stirred her mind, the images rampaging through her head in erotic display.

"Would you like that, Susanna?" Dev's voice was a low murmur. He moved inside her a tiny amount and she felt a hot rush of sensation. She was so close now and yet fulfillment shimmered frustratingly just out of her reach. She arched, trying to draw Dev in deeper, and in response he drew back and she felt angry and thwarted and almost driven insane with lust. She had never known that it could be like this—that she could be so utterly abandoned, wanton, so lascivious that she shocked even herself.

For a long moment they stared at one another and then he seemed to swoop down on her, kissing her deeply, and the fire rose in her again, burning up the last of her inhibitions. She felt him draw away a little and felt bereft.

In the dappled moonlight she saw him reach for his coat and take a small box out of the pocket. Dev flicked it open to reveal a huge pearl on a golden chain.

"Did you know—" his words were again a hot incitement "—that the touch of a pearl can be as soft as satin and yet as rough as sand?" He rolled it over her nipples. They hardened to tiny tight nubs, the blissful friction making Susanna want to cry aloud.

"This was part of an Eastern prince's treasure," Dev continued in the same quiet voice. He drew the pearl on its golden chain over the curve of her breasts again and another cascade of pleasure rolled over her. The rasping smoothness licked across her skin like flame. Dev's head was bent, his expression concentrated as he stroked the pearl down over her ribs, dipping it in an erotic circle into her belly button.

"I am told," he said, "that it gives the greatest pleasure." He paused, and the pearl rolled gently on its golden links across Susanna's belly. "What do you think, Susanna?" he said. "Tell me."

Susanna was incapable of forming even a single coherent thought. The pearl was tracing a low arc across her stomach now, rolling back and forth on its gold string. She knew that any moment Dev would take it lower, to find her most sensitive flesh. Her mind splintered at the thought.

"Do you like that?" Dev whispered as the pearl grazed her folds and she almost came off the bed in response.

"I… Ah…" Lush delight blocked Susanna's throat. She felt the pearl against her nub, rubbing back and forth, and could not help raising her hips in involuntary plea. She heard Dev make a harsh sound of satisfaction and then he slipped the pearl deep into her sheath and drew it out slowly on the long chain.

The sensation was indescribable. Susanna shuddered at the sheer voluptuous torment of it, feeling the pearl slip once again inside her and be drawn endlessly out, again and again, spinning her pleasure into something new and dark and sweet as it pressed down once more on the core of her. She arched up in ecstasy and Dev caught her as she came, his mouth plundering hers as the orgasm flowered through her, blazing in its intensity. He plunged into her, taking her with short, sharp thrusts that sent the wooden headboard of the bed crashing against the wall. She heard him shout, felt him tense and then she felt him drive deep into her one final time, spilling his hot seed inside her.

For a moment Susanna lay in utter bliss but all too quickly the raucous sounds of the alehouse penetrated her mind and wrenched her from her sensual cocoon, and then the shame and the humiliation rushed in on her. Everyone in the taproom would surely have heard the creaking of the bedsprings and the thud of the wood against the wall. Susanna's body turned into one burning blush. How could she have been so lost to everything that she had responded to Devlin with such wanton abandon? Suddenly she felt tawdry and empty. The pearl… She shuddered with remembered passion, tainted now with an edge of mortification.

She had to get away. Away from this place, away from her shame, away from the powerful grasp Devlin held over her emotions. She sat up, searching for her clothes, throwing them on, dressing haphazardly and feeling the panic rise as she could not find her shoes for a moment.

"Susanna?" Dev sounded lazy, drowsy with pleasure. "Come back to bed."

"Goodbye, Devlin," Susanna said, reaching for the door handle, fumbling in the dark, desperate now to be away.

"Susanna!" Dev shot out of bed. Susanna had never seen a man move so fast. She certainly had not known a man could dress so fast. Navy training, she supposed; so very useful for a rake to be able to get in and out of his clothes so quickly. Damn him. She slammed the bedchamber door behind her and started down the stairs, stumbling a little in her haste. A second later the door slammed open and Dev was coming after her, fastening his pantaloons as he did so.

"Wait!" he said. "I wanted you for the whole night—"

"You did not say," Susanna snapped. "You should be more specific in your blackmail in future." She reached the bottom of the stairs and burst into the taproom. "You've had what you wanted," she said, well aware that they now had a very large and very curious audience but so furious with both herself and with him that she was powerless to stop the words flooding out. "You've had me. Now I'm going."

Several people whistled and catcalled.

"Looks like your technique needs more practice

mate!" someone shouted from the back of the room. Dev shot him a filthy look and caught Susanna's arm.

"Susanna, wait—" he said.

"No," Susanna said. She had reached the end of her endurance. The self-loathing washed through her, the hatred of all the lies and the deception and where they had brought her. She was afraid that she might cry. She could feel the burning tears sting her eyes. "You had better keep your promise, Devlin," she said.

She saw the wicked light leap into his face. He released her, folded his arms.

"And if I don't?" he said.

It was the final straw. Susanna picked up a tankard of ale and hurled it at him. Dev ducked and it hit the wall. He had excellent reflexes.

"You promised!" she said. She had never felt so angry or so out of control in her life before. It was terrifying yet oddly liberating at the same time. "You utter, utter bastard!"

"Never trust a man when he's driven by his cock, love," one of the tavern wenches said sympathetically. She pushed another tankard toward Susanna. "Need another one?"

"Good advice," Dev said, smiling at the girl, who smiled straight back into his eyes.

Susanna picked up the tankard and took a long draught. The alcohol went to her head like an infusion of giddy euphoria. The room swam before her view. She took a deep breath. She had a feeling she was about to make a monumental mistake but it was already too late because she had been pushed too far and too hard and she could not stop. She did not want to stop.

"You had better keep your word, Devlin," she said, "because if you do not I will tell everyone that we are married and have been for nine years and then there will be the most appalling scandal that will damage you all, Chessie and Emma as well as you. None of you will ever recover from it. You will all be ruined."

DEV LOOKED AT SUSANNA, met her gaze, which was a mixture of defiance and terror, and knew without a shadow of a doubt that she was speaking the truth.

The inn had erupted into rowdy debate. "You're in trouble now, mate, and no mistake," one man opined, shaking his head.

"So I think," Dev said grimly.

"Never thought she was your wife," the man said.

"Neither did I," Dev said, even more grimly.

He took Susanna's hand and felt that she was shaking. Her gaze was blank, shocked. Dev realized that she had not meant to say it; only the extreme of her desperation had forced the words out.

"Come along then, Lady Devlin," he said, and saw the shock leap again in her eyes. "You've got some explaining to do," he said roughly. "Not before an audience, though, this time."

He dragged her with him out of the inn door,

almost forgetting to pay the shot on the way out and fumbling in his pocket for change, which he slapped down onto the counter. Out in the street he took several deep breaths of night air. It was cooler tonight with a cutting breeze off the river. Dev needed it; his head was spinning. First there had been his anger over Susanna's blatant demeaning of herself to buy his silence. He had thought—no, he had hoped—that she was better than that. Then their exquisite lovemaking had washed away all his anger and frustrations, replacing them with the pure sweet sensation of rightness he had always found with her. But now this… He could barely believe it. Except that he knew, deep in his gut with a wrenching feeling of shock that this time Susanna did not lie.

"I did intend to get an annulment—" Susanna began.

Dev turned on her. He felt livid, almost beyond reason, and had to exert absolute control over his temper. "Hell and the devil, Susanna," he said, "one does not simply forget a small matter like marriage! I might forget to attend a ball. I would not forget that I had failed to apply for an annulment!"

Susanna stopped and pulled her hand from his, stepping back. She raised her chin and faced him bravely. "Did you never wonder why there were no papers to sign, Devlin? Did you just assume that the annulment had gone through and that you need do nothing?"

The guilt shook Dev because that was precisely

what he had assumed. As with many other things in his life he had been rash and thoughtless and irresponsible, pushing away the memories of his one night of marriage, swearing to wipe it from his mind and his life, ignoring it for the mistake it had been. Now he was richly rewarded for that carelessness.

"Don't try to blame me!" He wanted to shake her in his anger and frustration, and once again clamped down on his fury. "You wrote to me! You said you had already applied!"

He saw Susanna make a hopeless gesture of despair. "I intended to do so—" Her voice faltered. Dev saw panic in her eyes and felt a sudden, unexpected pang of remorse. She looked as though she needed protection rather than blame, Susanna, who had always been so strong and so unashamed of all she had done.

"It was more difficult to obtain an annulment than I had originally thought." She made a pathetic attempt at dignity, drawing her cloak around her, holding it tight at the throat between clenched fingers. Her shoulders were hunched, thin. "It was complicated and I could not afford it and..." She gave a little, helpless shrug.

"You could not afford it?" Dev reached out and touched the rich velvet of the crimson cloak. "What about all the money you made betraying people's trust, breaking their hearts? Could you have not spared a little to get rid of me finally, once and for all?" He did not wait for a reply. He took a couple of sharp steps away, running a hand through his hair, turning back fiercely. "Devil take it, Susanna, I could have been married by now! You would have made me a bigamist. That is what really angers me!"

"Yes." Susanna's voice was still hesitant. "But you are not."

"No thanks to you." Dev smoothed his hair down. He was baffled, furious, but puzzled, as well. Something here did not feel quite right. There was the fear and the pain in her eyes—and the gaps in her story. They were little enough to garner his sympathy when she had treated him so badly yet they were sufficient to plant the doubts in his mind which, when taken with her desperate desire to buy his silence, her need for money and her shame and anxiety, told him there was a great deal here that he did not know.

"You said earlier that you were working in a gown shop in Edinburgh," he said, "when your plan to catch a rich husband did not succeed."

"I was." He could feel her tension easing. She sounded relieved. He wondered at it. Was he asking the wrong questions? She was hiding something, he was sure of it.

"So you were poor," he said.

"Very."

"And you could not afford the annulment."

"That's right." She sounded tired now, defeated. His anger and resentment bubbled up again to see her white, strained face. He did not know why he pitied her, did not know why he wanted to protect her, when she had done this to him. Yet his feelings were irrefutable and they made no sense to him. Susanna had proved over and over that she was materialistic and corrupt, that she would stoop to blackmail, that she had no thought but for herself. So why this impulse to draw her close and defend her? He was bewildered to feel it.

"Bloody hell, Susanna—" He turned away. "All the women I've had…" he said. He felt odd about breaking his wedding vows, all unknowing. He could not explain why he felt so disillusioned, so disappointed in himself, when he had not known he was still wed. He owed Susanna nothing, no loyalty, no fidelity, when she had misled him. Yet still he felt tarnished in some way.

He felt her hand on his arm. "You were not to know," she said. "It was not your fault, Devlin."

"I know that." He shook her off savagely, rejecting her comfort and the unspoken apology. "Thank God I did not wed," he said. "And that I never touched Emma." He caught her shoulders again. "If I had…"

"I know." Her eyes were closed. He saw a single tear trickle down her cheek, silver in the moonlight. "I'm sorry," she whispered.

It was the first time that she had apologized for anything in the entire evening. He let her go, disturbed at the sudden impulse to pull her into his arms and offer comfort to her when he was so furious with her.

"I need to think." He looked at her. "Don't believe

that I will keep quiet about this just to save Emma's reputation," he warned, "or to protect Chessie. There has to be a way around this without hurting either of them. This ends here."

Susanna was silent. She did not try to persuade him.

Dev took her hand again. "Come on."

She held back. "Where are we going?"

"To Curzon Street," Dev said. "I am coming back with you."

He saw her expression pucker in the moonlight. "But—"

"I do not trust you an inch," Dev said brutally. "I want you within sight at all times until I decide what to do about this."

The little maid was sitting on a chair in the hall when they returned, swaying with tiredness, stifling her yawns. The front door swung closed behind them and she leaped to her feet. "Will that be all, my lady?" she asked.

"Yes," Dev said, "thank you."

The maid waited pointedly.

"Thank you, Margery," Susanna said, giving her a faint smile. "Go and get some sleep."

The maid dropped a curtsy and went out. Dev looked at Susanna. There were smudges of tears beneath her eyes and he smoothed them away with his thumb, feeling the impossible softness of her skin. Anger and tenderness, frustration and gentleness warred within him. He could not understand it, still less explain. She had told him a story that made perfect sense; it all hung together—the failure of her plans for a rich marriage, her subsequent poverty, her desire for money. Yet something troubled him, something that still did not quite add up. He shook his head impatiently. What really mattered here was Susanna's failure to sue for the annulment of their marriage. He must make that good at the first possible opportunity. Alex would lend him the money. It would be yet another debt but it would finally set him free to start afresh. Susanna, too—he would see that she was provided for because that was his duty as her husband. He would go back to sea and Susanna could also forge a new life, the one she had always wanted, perhaps, with a rich man. The thought did not please him.

Susanna. His wife. It felt different, now he knew. He felt different. The possessiveness he had experienced when he had imagined her with another man had eased into something more profound, more disturbing, now that he knew she truly was his. His future life would have no place for a wife. Once he was back at sea the Navy would become his mistress once again. But for now Susanna was here and until they sued for annulment they were still wed…

"Lady Devlin," he said quietly. "That was what I wanted you to be nine years ago. But you did not want that, did you, Susanna? You never wanted to be my wife."

For a second some emotion shimmered in her eyes

that he could not understand. He tugged the ribbon that fastened her cloak. It came loose and the cloak, rich and red in the candlelight, slid from her shoulders to fall at her feet. He heard her breath catch. Her eyes were very wide and dark, full of shadows.

Dev bent and brushed his lips against hers in the lightest possible caress. Her breathing quickened, her eyelashes fluttered down. Her lips were soft and yielding beneath his. He wanted her then with a hunger so acute it felt like pain. He knew that he ought to despise her for all her duplicity and yet he seemed powerless to resist her even when he had made love to her less than two hours before. And now, of course, he could do it again because she was his wife. The thought slid into his head like the snake in Eden, impossibly tempting.

"Come to bed," he said.

Her eyes snapped open. There was confusion as well as desire in them. He was reminded of the night in the garden when she had said that she could not resist him but she did not understand why. He felt the same. All he knew was that there was some powerful bond that compelled them together and that until their need was sated neither would be free.

He saw Susanna bite her lower lip and felt his body jerk in response. "We agreed just the once," she said, and he could hear the conflict in her voice, the longing mixed with denial, and knew with another surge of excitement that she wanted him. They were impossibly drawn to one another, trapped in their mutual desire.

"That," Dev said, "was before I knew you were still my wife." He kissed the hollow of her throat and felt the hunger coil all the tighter inside him. "Now what was a pleasure has become a right."

"You are insisting on your marital rights?" There was shock in her voice. "But I thought we were to obtain the annulment?"

"We will," Dev said. "But until then we are still married." He trailed a path of kisses to Susanna's collarbone, running his tongue over the sweet, vulnerable curves, flicking over the pulse he found there.

She pushed him away. "You are so damnably arrogant, aren't you, Devlin? Has no one ever refused you?"

"Only the Duchess of Farne," Dev said. "And you, on that night you turned me away." He stood back, put his hands up in a gesture of surrender. "Do you want to do that again? If you can tell me you do not want me, I'll sleep alone."

The sensuality thickened about them like a spun web. He saw Susanna swallow hard. "Damn you, Devlin." Her voice was strained. "I don't understand what you do to me...."

"The sentiment is mutual, sweetheart." Dev pulled her back into his arms. "I'm sorry about earlier at the inn," he whispered as his lips brushed hers. "That was not good enough for you but I was angry with you for bartering your body to me."

He felt her shudder in his arms. "I've never done that before," she said. Her face was hidden against his shoulder. "I know you will not believe me, but it's true."

"I do believe you," Dev said. He thought of her untutored response to his kiss in the carriage and the innocence he had sensed in her when first they had made love. He ran a hand over her hair, soothing her trembling. She felt so vulnerable in his arms. Dev thought of her telling him how poor she had been, too poor to be able to afford the annulment. He thought of her forcing cream cakes into her reticule because she was still haunted by the need to steal food whenever she could find it. The compassion and pity swept through him. He could remember that sort of poverty, the sort where there was no food and the world went dark because you were so cold and hungry and exhausted. He had known that as a child and he had never forgotten. It had been the driving force in making him seek his fortune. So he could hardly blame Susanna for wanting to escape a similar plight. He could not condone her choices and a part of him was still furious with her, but equally he could not condemn her for fighting for her survival.

"Thank you." She sounded dazed. She kissed him, her mouth open to his, and his mind fractured and Dev forgot everything, almost forgot his own name in the hot carnal pleasure that swept through him. Susanna pulled away from him and took his hand, turning toward the stairs, but instead Dev drew her through the door into the sitting room. It was in darkness but for the moonlight that dappled the floor from the uncurtained windows.

"Let me undress you properly this time," he said. "Step into the moonlight."

Again he sensed the shock she could not hide and knew she had never played such dangerous games before as she played with him. She hesitated and he thought she might refuse, but after a moment she stepped deliberately into the shaft of moonlight and stood quivering beneath his hands as he slowly peeled off her clothes. She raised her arms, graceful as a dancer, to allow him easier access to buttons and hooks and the movement was so erotic he almost groaned aloud.

He put up a hand and pulled on the ribbon in her hair and it tumbled loose, blue-black in the moonlight. He ran his fingers into the silky mass and kissed her like a starving man, until she was shaking and he was, too.

He picked her up and carried her across to the window. She gasped as her naked back touched the cold panes. He spread her, his hands beneath her thighs and found her core and the heat that was a counterpoint to that cold. She writhed.

"The window—" She sounded dazed.

"Your garden is not overlooked," Dev said. He kissed her again, dropping his mouth to the hollow of her throat and the slope of her breast. He kissed her until he felt her body tighten and heard her moan against his mouth. Her head was tilted back, her hair like a black waterfall against the darkness of the glass. Her upper body was arched toward him in mute plea, her legs tightly clasped about him. The lust drove him to take her but he mastered it, waiting until it felt as though she was wound so tight she would come apart in his arms. Only then did he loose the band of his pantaloons and thrust up and into her. The relief, the pleasure, was intense. She cried out, hot and sleek and tight about him. He drove into her until she came, her palms flat against the glass. She was like a wild thing in his arms, a creature of heat and passion, so sweet he wanted to devour her.

He lifted her down gently onto the chaise so that he could slide into her once again, feeling the ripple of her orgasm still echoing through her body, feeling her body capture him, spinning out his own pleasure now and hers, too, with long, slow strokes until he felt her body quicken again. She reached up to kiss him, cupping his face in her hands. The spiral tightened, climbing higher and higher, and then he came and she arched up against him, crying her pleasure.

He took her up to her bed then and held her as she slept. Dev found he did not want to sleep. Watching Susanna was all he wanted to do. He remembered when they had wed and he had hurried her back to the inn, so anxious to make love to her in his youthful passion. He hoped he had had the finesse to do it well but he rather suspected he had not. For a brief moment he wondered if he had frightened her and if that was why she had never made love with another. He felt a clutch of guilt. He had thought himself so much a man at eighteen and yet he had had so much to learn.

Susanna moved a little, her hand coming to rest against his bare chest. Dev felt a huge swell of tenderness catch him utterly unawares, taking his heart and squeezing it tight. In that moment he felt acutely vulnerable. He did not like the feeling. Even so, he reached out and touched Susanna's hair lightly, feeling it curl around his fingers as it had once before, as soft and confiding as Susanna had once been.

She opened her eyes and smiled at him and the tenderness hit him again like a blow. Dev bent and kissed her, wanting to drive out that weakness, waiting for the lust to take him and make everything straightforward again. But this time, though he made love to her with a violent desire, the emotion ran ahead of him, ambushing him at every turn, so that what he wanted to be a simple physical act became so much more. Each touch, each whispered word seemed to drive him closer into a sweet intimacy he could not escape. And at the last, when fierceness and gentleness combined in the most astonishing pleasure he had ever taken, he knew that somehow he had lost the fight.

CHAPTER SIXTEEN

SUSANNA AWOKE TO FIND HERSELF asleep in Devlin's arms. Her head was on his shoulder and one arm was draped low across her belly in casual possession. Her body felt blissfully pleasured and content and for a few short moments her mind, too, was full of the same sweetness as she remembered his whispered endearments to her through the night.

He did not stir as she drew away and reached for her wrap. She had been very self-indulgent, she thought, to take what Devlin had offered and not to send him away again. Knowing that there was no future with him, knowing that this time they really would seek the annulment, she had wanted some memories to hold against her heart. She knew she would lose Devlin again and thinking on it she felt the happiness drain out of her like water slipping through the fingers. She had let herself feel too much. She had fallen in love again. She had not wanted to do it; she had thought that she was so much more experienced now, older, wiser, too careful and cynical to fall. She had been wrong. The combination of wild spirit and strong principle that had drawn her to Devlin in the first place was still there and she had tumbled into love with him all over again, as heedless as she had been at seventeen.

There was a tap at the door; Margery, looking utterly unsurprised to see Devlin in Susanna's bed.

"I am sorry to disturb you, my lady," she whispered, "but there is an urgent visitor." She nodded toward Dev. "She says she is Sir James's sister. She seems to be in some distress."

"Chessie?" Susanna said, startled.

"Miss Francesca Devlin," Margery agreed.

"I'll wake Sir James," Susanna said, stretching out a hand. She wondered how on earth Chessie had known Dev would be with her.

Margery stopped her. "Pardon me, my lady, but it is you Miss Devlin wishes to see. She was most particular."

Susanna frowned. She had no notion why Chessie would want to see her so urgently and in such distress, unless it was to beg her to give up Fitz. Her heart contracted with pity at the thought of Chessie caring for Fitz so much that she would forget pride and come and plead with her rival.

She eased herself from the bed. "Don't wake Sir James," she said. "I'll dress in the blue room, Margery. Thank you."

As Susanna came down the stairs she saw Chessie sitting on one of the mahogany chairs in the hall, her slender body upright and rigid with tension. When she heard Susanna's step Chessie turned toward her and Susanna caught her breath to see her face; she looked haggard and despairing, her eyes red from crying, all her youth and vivacity and prettiness fled.

Susanna hurried toward her and caught both her hands in her own. Chessie was ice-cold.

"Miss Devlin," she said. "Chessie—"

Chessie burst into fresh tears. Susanna put an arm about her and steered her into the drawing room. "Tea please, Margery," she said, over her shoulder to the maid. "Strong. As quick as you can."

She guided Chessie over to the sofa and sat down beside her. The girl moved stiffly as though every part of her hurt.

"What is this about?" Susanna asked, keeping a hold of her hands. "What can I do to help you?"

Chessie looked up. Her blue eyes, so like Devlin's, were drowned in tears. "I don't know where else to go or who to talk to," she said. "I don't know what to do. I'm pregnant with Fitz's child and he..." Her voice caught on a sob. "I told him and he...he said there was nothing that he would do, that he did not care, that there are rumors circulating that I am not chaste, so how did he know the child was his anyway? I am ruined...." Her words disintegrated into an explosion of tears.

Susanna drew her close, holding Chessie's shaking body until her storm of tears faded a little and she drew back, sniffing and reaching for her handkerchief. It was already sodden, shredded into little strips by Chessie's restless fingers. Susanna pressed a clean one into her hand.

"Thank you," Chessie said. She blew her nose hard then looked up frowning a little, as though she had only just recollected herself. "I'm not sure why I came to you," she said slowly. "I am so sorry—"

Susanna placed a hand over her clasped ones to prevent her from rising to her feet. "You came to me because you couldn't talk to anyone else," she said, "and you thought I might understand. And I do. Now—" She waited whilst Margery brought the tea in then poured. "Take this and drink it down. Forget brandy—it is tea that is best when you are suffering from shock."

Chessie obeyed, holding the cup in both hands as though greedily feeling its heat. "I couldn't tell Lady Grant," she said after a moment. "Or Devlin—" Her voice wavered. "They would be so disappointed in me. Dev has always cared for me and wanted what is best for me."

"I know," Susanna said, with feeling.

"He would have done anything for me," Chessie said. "He did do everything for me—he begged and stole on the street so that I could go to school, he made Alex take responsibility for us, he sent me back his Navy pay. And Lord and Lady Grant…" Chessie gave a hiccup. "They have so little money, you know Alex—Lord Grant—ploughs everything back into his Scottish estate to try to make it work, and yet they were prepared to give me a home and a dowry when I wed—" Her face crumpled. "Well, that will not happen now." She closed her eyes briefly. "So I could not tell them. I dare not. I have let them down so badly."

"It's not your fault," Susanna said fiercely. The grief and pity closed her throat. "Fitz has behaved very badly." She stopped as Chessie gave a little shake of the head.

"Yes, it was my fault," she said simply. "It's true that Fitz seduced me, but I could have refused him. He did not force himself on me. Far from it." A tiny frown marred her forehead. "It started with a game of cards, two months ago, just before you came to London." She smiled faintly. "Fitz taught me to play faro and it was such fun. Gambling is in my blood, I am afraid." She held her teacup tighter, spreading her fingers against the warmth. "Then I started to lose and I owed Fitz a lot of money, so he suggested…" She stopped. "It was not his fault," she said again. "I liked what we did."

Susanna pressed her lips tightly together to prevent herself from contradicting Chessie. If Fitz had extracted sexual favors in return for Chessie's gambling debts then he was the lowest of the low and she did not think that the blame could be laid anywhere else.

"I thought he would come to love me." Chessie's voice was very quiet. She sounded defeated. "I loved him from the start and I wanted to please him." She gave Susanna a painful smile. "Even now I still love him." Her shoulders slumped. "I can see all his faults but I…I would still marry him if he would have me."

Susanna looked at her stubborn little face, miserable but determined. It was not many women, she thought, who had the clarity to know all a man's faults, who did not delude themselves at all about his virtues, and yet still had the courage—or the folly—to love him.

"Are you sure that you really want Fitz?" she said. "You deserve so much better, you know."

Chessie gave a little hiccup of laughter that caught on another sob. "I did not expect to hear you say that, Lady Carew."

Susanna hesitated. This was scarcely the time to tell Chessie the truth about her identity and her own plans for Fitz. The only important thing was to help Chessie now.

"I can't help it," Chessie was saying. "I love him. That was the reason I gave myself to him. I loved him and I thought he loved me, too. Besides—" She made a little gesture. "It's too late now. No one else would want me, pregnant with another man's child."

"A good man who really loves you—" Susanna began. Then she stopped. She was not even sure if she believed the words herself. There were a number of good men in the world. Despite all she had been through she was not cynical enough to believe otherwise. But there were a number of cads like Fitz and an equal number of pompous fools who demanded virginity in their wives whilst sowing their own wild oats far and wide.

Chessie gave a little sniff. "I know you mean to be kind but we both know that I am ruined, pregnant and unwed."

"You must tell your brother," Susanna said. "He will help you—"

"No!" Chessie grabbed her hands convulsively. "Devlin—" Her voice cracked. "He will be so disappointed in me! I dare not tell him. He warned me not to become Fitz's mistress, little knowing I already was." She scrubbed viciously at her eyes. "He would hate me."

Susanna could hear the sound of voices in the hall outside and felt a clutch of anxiety.

"Your brother is here," she said quickly then she realized that Chessie had recognized Dev's voice, too.

"Did you send for him?" Chessie gasped, accusation in her eyes.

"Devlin was already here," Susanna said. "He has been here all night. I should have told you but I thought it was more important to find out what was wrong and try to help you."

Chessie's eyes opened very wide. "You and Devlin…" she said slowly. "But I asked him weeks ago to seduce you away from Fitz and he refused…" She stopped.

"Well," Susanna said, "maybe he changed his mind." She felt a little sick, her heart hurting. Chessie's words had pained her but they had not surprised her. She had known that Dev was fiercely attracted to her but that he had no deeper feelings for her. It simply hurt to have it confirmed in so brutal a fashion.

"I'm sorry," Chessie said suddenly. "That was unconscionably rude of me."

"Pray do not worry," Susanna said, pushing aside her misery, summoning a smile. "Your brother and I know exactly where we stand."

"Where do we stand, Susanna?" Dev had overheard her words as he strolled into the room, smiling, debonair. He stopped dead when he saw his sister.

"Chessie?" he said.

Chessie burst into tears again as soon as she saw him. Dev cast Susanna one horrified glance and went down on one knee beside her chair. Chessie was talking, the words spilling out, all jumbled, but the meaning was clear enough—and utterly devastating. Susanna watched Dev's face as he listened to his sister's words. He was very pale and his expression was set in hard lines, his blue eyes blazing.

"Chessie," he said again when his sister had finally fallen into exhausted silence. He gathered her into his arms. "Listen to me." He put his arms about her unyielding little body and hugged her tightly. "I'm your brother and I will always love you."

Susanna bit her lip at the raw emotion in his voice. She heard Chessie give a little broken sob.

"I'm going to go to Fitz," Dev said. "He has to answer to me for this."

Fear clutched at Susanna's heart. "Devlin—" she said.

Dev gave her a fierce look. "Don't try to stop me, Susanna," he said. "You knew the truth had to come out anyway."

"I didn't mean that," Susanna began, but Chessie had grabbed her brother's forearms and was shaking him. "Dev, no!" She sounded scared. "You cannot challenge Fitz!"

Dev freed himself with a quietness that terrified Susanna because it was both so gentle and yet so determined. "Chessie," he said, "I cannot simply let this pass—"

"But you must," Chessie wailed. "If you kill Fitz he will never be able to marry me!"

Susanna's eyes met Dev's again over the top of Chessie's head. She saw pity there and compassion that Chessie was still hoping against hope that Fitz would change his mind and wed her and that all would be well. They both knew it would not be... that it could not be. Fitz had already rejected Chessie. She had nothing to offer him. He had discarded her.

"Susanna," Dev said, very politely, "would you please take care of Chessie for me? I will be back as soon as I can."

"Yes," Susanna said. "Yes, of course. But Devlin—" She stopped as he looked at her. There was such protective fury and love in his eyes that she flinched. This then was how Devlin responded when those he loved were hurt. She would never see such emotion in him for her but to see it for his sister humbled her and for a moment she felt empty and desolate.

The door slammed behind him. "He will kill him, won't he," Chessie said, in a small voice.

"Either that, or Fitz will kill Devlin," Susanna agreed. She did not think there was any point in pretending otherwise.

"There is no way to stop him," Chessie whispered, sinking back down onto the sofa, a small, crumpled, defeated ball of misery.

Susanna looked at her. She thought of Chessie facing scandal and ruin. She thought of the ignominy that would be heaped on her, the loss of her good name, her future, her peace, her privacy and her very life. She thought of a young girl, pregnant and alone, bringing up a child out of wedlock. Chessie's case would not be like hers—she would not be abandoned, for her family would never forsake her—but it would still be a disaster and an utter devastation.

She knew what she had to do.

She went down on her knees before Chessie's chair. "Are you sure," she said urgently, "that you really want to wed Fitz? Think about it hard now—" But she stopped because a tiny flame of hope had already sprung into Chessie's eyes.

"Will you persuade him?" she whispered. The

flame flickered and died. "I do not think you can. I do not think anyone can."

"I can," Susanna said. She stood up. "And if you want me to, I will."

SUSANNA HEARD THEIR VOICES as soon as she stepped inside the Duke and Duchess of Alton's town house. The butler was looking frightened and unsure, and when he saw Susanna he looked even more fearful. She was not surprised. If the servants had overheard any of the conversation between Dev and Fitz they would deem this the worst possible moment for Fitz's fiancée to arrive.

"The Duke and Duchess are still abed, madam," the butler started to say.

"Well, thank goodness for that," Susanna said. "Though I doubt they will be able to sleep through all this noise. Don't trouble to announce me, Hopperton, I'll go straight in."

She opened the door of the breakfast room an inch. She could see Fitz, the remains of his meal spread about him, a newspaper tossed to one side. He had his feet up on the table and he was looking both bored and disdainful.

"Well, of course you won't do anything about it, Devlin, old man." Fitz's light patrician drawl was very pronounced. "You're completely hamstrung, aren't you? Impotent." Susanna could hear the contempt behind his words. "You hang on my coattails and on the promise of Emma's fortune and if we were both to drop you, you would be nothing. So go away, old fellow, and don't trouble me further with talk of honor and duels and such nonsense. Your little strumpet of a sister will just have to fend for herself. She was very sweet—" Fitz pensively selected a peach from the fruit bowl and bit into it "—but nowhere near good enough to tempt me into marriage—"

It was at that moment that Dev lifted him from his chair and hit him, cleanly, scientifically, peach and all. It seemed to Susanna that the blow drove Fitz into the air and carried him across the room to slump against one of the carved marble pillars at the east end of the room.

"Get up," Dev said through his teeth. His fists were clenched. "You'll answer to me for the dishonor you've done to my sister. I demand satisfaction—"

"No!" Susanna ran forward and caught his arm. "This isn't the way, Devlin."

Dev turned. His gaze was so blank with fury and there was so much violence in his eyes that Susanna was not even sure he had heard her. She tightened her grip on him.

"This is not the way to help Chessie," she said. "The scandal will come out and if one of you were to be killed—" She looked at Fitz who was wiping peach juice off his face and stumbling to his feet, leaning heavily on the back of one of the rosewood chairs. "Well, if Fitz were to be killed that would be no great loss," she said, "but still it would not help Chessie."

"He is a scoundrel." Dev's voice was fierce. "Chessie deserves so much better but the tragedy is that the only way to save her is through marriage and if I cannot compel Fitz to wed her then I have to call him out—"

Susanna heard the break in his voice then and saw, alongside the fury, the utter devastation in his eyes. She remembered Chessie's whispered words: "He would have done anything for me. He did do everything for me—he begged and stole on the street so that I could go to school, he made Alex take responsibility for us, he sent me back his Navy pay..."

And now, when his sister was ruined, there was finally nothing that Dev could do to help her. Susanna could see how much he hated that. For a man of honor, a man who put his family ahead of all else, it was intolerable. Her heart gave a pang and she felt as though the ground was dropping away beneath her feet and she recognized in that second just how much she loved him.

"No," she said. "You cannot compel Fitz to marry Chessie, Devlin. But I can." She turned to look at Fitz.

"Fitzwilliam Alton," she said. "You are a cad and a scoundrel."

"Not now, my dear," Fitz said, fingering his jaw. "This is just a little misunderstanding. Happened before we met. The girl threw herself at me. Well, you know her. Frightfully pushy little strumpet—"

Susanna felt Dev make an involuntary movement and grabbed his arm before he could hit Fitz again.

"Fitz," she said sharply. "You're not listening to me. Now, you are going to marry Miss Devlin, and you are going to do it with a good grace. I never want to hear you utter another word against her." She felt the shock go through Dev like lightning but with great force of will she kept her concentration focused on Fitz and did not look at him. "You are going to go and get a special license, Fitz," she said, "and you will wed Miss Devlin next week."

"Don't know what you are talking about, my dear," Fitz spluttered. "Wed Miss Devlin? But you and I are to marry—"

"Not anymore," Susanna said. "In point of fact, we never were. I was going to jilt you in a few weeks' time." She saw Fitz's mouth gape open. "Your parents paid me to engage your attention," she said, "because they were afraid that you were becoming too fond of Miss Devlin and might make her an offer. Little did they know—" her voice hardened "—that you had already debauched her and were enough of a scoundrel to ruin her reputation and abandon her."

Fitz's jaw practically hit the floor. "You were going to jilt me? Me?" He boggled at her. "You were paid by my parents?"

"That's right," Susanna said. "And that is the point. If you do not marry Miss Devlin with all haste and every sign of pleasure, I shall make public in the scandal sheets every last one of the things that your parents told me in order to help me capture your interest. Everything, Fitz," she repeated. "From the amount you owe to your tailor to the fact that your parents had to buy off the Marquis of Portside when you stole from his son whilst at Eton. From the fact that you need padding to fill out your pantaloons to the effect that figs have on your digestion. I may not be able to ruin you the way that you have ruined Miss Devlin but I can and will make you a laughingstock in the ton."

Fitz took several unsteady steps toward her, his face suddenly suffused with color. "You bitch," he said. "I'll see you damned for this."

Dev straightened, stepping between them. "Don't speak to my wife like that, Alton," he said, very coldly, and for a moment there was the same protective fury in his voice and in his eyes that there had been for Chessie.

"Your wife?" Fitz recoiled. "You're in this together?"

"Not at all," Dev said. "I absolutely deplore my wife's recent behavior but—" he shot Susanna a look in which there was, astonishingly, a hint of a smile "—I have to admire the ruthlessness of her methods."

"Think about it, Fitz," Susanna said. She glanced at the clock. "You have until one o'clock to present yourself at Lord and Lady Grant's house, with a special license, to make your proposal to Miss Devlin. If you choose not to do so—"

"I'll see you drummed out of London for this," Fitz said viciously.

"Too late," Susanna said wryly. "I am already going. But not before I lodge a certain letter with my lawyer. If you step out of line once, Fitz—" she smiled at him "—the papers will publish. You have my word."

DEV CAUGHT UP WITH SUSANNA as she was climbing back into the hackney carriage. Before she could give the driver the word to set off he swung up beside her and closed the door after them. He knew Susanna was trying to run away from him. The haste with which she had run out of the Altons' town house and the rigid set of her shoulders now that they were forced to share this small space told him that his company was unwelcome to her. He knew she did not want to speak to him because there was only one question that he could ask her now and that was the question why. Why had she obliged Fitz to marry Chessie when it went directly against everything that she had been working for? Dev could not fathom it. It made absolutely no sense at all that Susanna would not take advantage of Chessie's ruin and claim the victory—and the money—for herself.

"Did I miss something?" he said very politely. "Did you just compel Fitz to marry Chessie, when your entire purpose from the start has been to separate them?" He raised his brows. "Have you become matchmaker rather than heartbreaker?"

Susanna shrugged. It was impossible to read anything in her face or her demeanor other than that she was wishing him in Hades. She turned away from him and concentrated rather intensely on the passing streets. It was, Dev thought, a tactic of hers when she wanted to avoid his gaze and evade awkward questions. Well, she was going to need to do a great deal better than that now because he had every intention of asking some very difficult questions indeed.

"It was too late for me to take advantage." Susanna spoke lightly, her gaze still averted from his. "You said yourself that the truth would come out."

"Rubbish," Dev said. His prime emotion was deep puzzlement—and frustration that she was trying to thwart him. "You could have capitalized on Fitz's rejection of Chessie and taken the credit for it," he said. "You could have gone directly to the Duke and Duchess now, taken the money and run. Instead you have forced Fitz to make Chessie an offer—and in the process you have thrown away everything you had worked for." He shook his head. "Surely you can see that?"

Susanna shot him a brief look. Her cheeks were pink, her expression stormy.

"Of course I can see it," she said. "I am not stupid." She rubbed her forehead. She looked weary all of a sudden and Dev wanted to put a hand out to her and draw her close. Astonishingly Chessie had turned to Susanna when she was most in need and Susanna had responded. He felt stunned by that, and hugely grateful to Susanna for her compassion. But he was not sure that he would ever understand women.

"Why?" he said. He leaned forward. "Why did you do it, Susanna?"

He saw a shudder ripple through her body. Her face was white and strained as though tears of emotion, of exhaustion, were not far away. Yet still she fought them and fought him, too. As the hackney drew up in Curzon Street it was clear that she was not going to give him any answer at all.

"Don't come in, Devlin," Susanna said, setting her hand on the door of the carriage. "I must pack my portmanteau and leave. This house belongs to the Duke and Duchess and I doubt I am welcome here anymore."

"Of course I am coming in," Dev said. "We finish this conversation."

Susanna shot him a deeply irritated look from her glorious green eyes. "It is already finished, Devlin," she said. "Everything is finished." She was fumbling in her purse for change for the driver. Dev stepped forward, offered the man a coin big enough to make him tip his hat with respect and took Susanna's arm. She shook him off. He could feel tension in her and something more; a very deep distress that she was trying desperately to hide. She wanted to be rid of him. She wanted it very much. He sensed it and he was not going to oblige her because he knew now that there was some connection between what had happened to Chessie and something that had happened to Susanna herself. It was the only explanation that made sense. And he knew, too, that whatever Susanna was hiding from him was the last piece of the puzzle, the part she had not yet told him.

He felt the urgency seize him. He had to know the truth.

"I sent John to escort Chessie home," Susanna said. "You should go to her, Devlin. She needs you."

"Thank you for taking care of her," Dev said. "I will go to Bedford Street presently, when we have finished this conversation." He smiled at her. "I fear your diversionary tactics have not worked, Susanna. I still want to know why you made Fitz marry her."

He saw Susanna's mouth purse as tightly as a drawn string at the realization that he was not going to be deflected. She avoided his gaze and fidgeted with her reticule.

"I won't deny you the annulment," she said suddenly, "if you are afraid to leave me in case I run off. There is no need to keep me under your gaze."

"Just at the moment," Dev said, keeping a tight hold on his patience, "the annulment of our marriage is the last matter on my mind." Exasperation gripped him. He gestured to the door. "Are we going in or are we to discuss this in the street, Susanna?"

Susanna made a huffing sound. "You are monstrous persistent."

"And you are shockingly evasive," Dev said. He took her arm, steering her into the house and toward the drawing room. He closed the door behind them and stood with his palms resting against the panels.

"So," he said. "Why did you do it, Susanna? Why did you save Chessie?"

Susanna had gone across to the chaise and had thrown her bonnet and gloves down onto it. Now she turned and the look in her eyes made Dev's heart lurch. He had thought that she might still try to stall him, try to pass the matter off as nothing when it was everything. Now he saw that he was wrong. The distress in her, the pain occasioned by Chessie's situation, was clearly so fresh and so close to the surface that she could no longer deny it. He saw her grip her slender fingers together so tightly that they turned white. She looked brittle, as though she might snap in two under the strain of her emotion.

Dev instinctively started to move toward her. "Susanna—" he said.

"I know what it is like to be pregnant and alone," Susanna said abruptly. She spoke so softly that Dev could barely hear her. Her head was bent and though he sought her eyes she did not look up. "I know how it feels to be as afraid and as lonely as Chessie is now," she said. Her voice shook a little. "It is terrifying to feel so lost and to have nowhere to turn. I did not want that for your sister."

Now at last she met his eyes and Dev almost flinched at the vivid pain he could see in hers. "I lost your child, Devlin," she said. He saw the tears gather in her eyes but they did not fall. "So now you know," she said. "Now you know everything."

CHAPTER SEVENTEEN

SUSANNA WAITED FOR DEVLIN'S anger. She waited for him to demand an explanation. She waited for him to walk away. He did none of those things. He came across to her and took her frozen hands in his and urged her gently toward the chaise.

"You should sit down." He spoke very softly. His grip on her hands was warm and reassuring. It seemed to cut through the cold grief that was seeping through her and comforted her a little. Dev gave her hands a squeeze and then left her briefly; she heard him asking Margery, very politely, for a pot of tea. Then he was back at her side. And all the time Susanna sat dumb, her mind shrinking from the truth, fearful of the pain she had now raked up and the fact that Devlin would surely hate her for failing him and failing their child, too. She closed her eyes and took a convulsive breath and felt with huge relief Devlin place his hand on hers again, entwining his fingers with hers.

"Can you tell me what happened?" he asked.

Susanna nodded. There was no point in keeping the past a secret from him any longer. Everything she had worked for was in tatters. Her plans to build a new life for herself and Rose and Rory were ruined and she would have to start all over again. Better to do so having told Devlin the whole truth, with nothing held back.

"I…" Her voice was hoarse with tears. For a moment she did not know where to start.

"Here." The tea had arrived and Devlin pressed the cup into her cold hands, holding it steady with his own. "Tea is best for shock," he said.

"That's what I told Chessie earlier," Susanna said.

Dev smiled. "I might even have a cup myself," he said. "Ghastly stuff, but its restorative qualities are well-known."

Susanna took a gulp of the scalding liquid and felt her world steady a little. She looked up. Dev was watching her steadily with those very blue eyes. She could see the lines of strain and grief in his face but there was no anger there and no blame.

"From the beginning?" he said.

Susanna nodded. The beginning… She placed the cup carefully on the rosewood table, afraid she might spill it because she was shaking so much.

"The beginning was the morning after we wed," she said. "I decided that it would be best to confess the whole truth to your cousin and ask for his help, so I left your bed and went to Balvenie to speak with him." She felt Devlin start but he did not say anything. "Unfortunately Lord Grant was from home," she said, "but Lady Grant was there. She had taken some small interest in my affairs and so I thought she would be a friend to me." She paused and bit her lip. It was so foolish now to regret her youthful stupidity but still the memories goaded her. She had been so trusting and so easily led. "I told Lady Grant everything," she said. "I thought that she would help us."

Dev shifted slightly. There was an expression in his eyes now that suggested to Susanna that he had probably known Amelia Grant better than she. "It may not surprise you," she said dryly, "to know that far from offering her support, Lady Grant told me that I had done a terrible thing in running away with you." She fidgeted with the fringe of one of the cushions, shredding it through her fingers. "She spoke more in sorrow than in anger but she made me feel so ashamed," she said. "She told me that Lord Grant had that very day procured a commission in the Navy for you and that you would be going to sea, and that your sister depended upon your Navy pay and that Lord Grant would be terribly disappointed in you if you turned it down." She looked up to see Dev still watching her, now with pity and a vivid regret that cut her to the heart. "She said you could not support a wife and that if I loved you I should go…pretend it had all been a mistake, set you free to forge a career and be the man your family wanted you to be." She swallowed hard. "I felt so foolish and so guilty," she said softly. "So I did exactly what she said. I ran away."

Dev shook his head abruptly. "I was going to take you with me," he said. His voice was a little rough. "I know I should have told you but we spoke so little of our plans."

"We were young," Susanna said. She smiled faintly. "I do not think that talking—or even planning—was foremost in our minds," she said ruefully. She drew a painful breath. "I did not wonder at the time why Lady Grant had interfered but later, when I was older and understood more of the ways of these things I wondered whether she had wanted you herself." She stopped, looking at Dev.

Dev pulled a face. "Amelia never tried to seduce me," he said, "but I did sometimes wonder if she was jealous of me." He ran a hand over his hair. "Alex was generous to me and I think that Amelia resented that. She resented the time and the money he spent on me. It was Amelia who petitioned Alex to buy me my Navy commission. It was Amelia who found an elderly aunt to care for Chessie." His smile was cynical. "At the time I thought it was because she wished to help us. Later I realized that what she wanted was Alex's undivided attention. She wished us to be gone from her life. And so she arranged it—" his eyes met hers "—just as she ruthlessly dispatched you, too."

Susanna picked up her cup again. The warmth was fading from the china now but she pressed her hands close about to draw the last of its heat. "I know I should not have listened to her," she said, "but I was young and already scared of the consequences of what we had done." She swallowed what felt like an enormous lump in her throat. "I'm so very sorry, Devlin."

Dev took the cup from her hand and put it down very deliberately so that he could once more clasp her fingers in his.

"This was Amelia's doing, not yours," he said fiercely. "You should not have blamed yourself."

Susanna shook her head. "Do you remember when I told you about John Denham? How I said that if he had truly been steadfast in his affection for his fiancée then no power on earth would have been strong enough to separate them?" She sighed. "If I had been strong enough and had enough faith then nothing and no one could have come between us, Devlin. But I was not." She paused but Dev did not speak and she rather thought it was because he knew she was right. She had been too easily persuaded to give him up.

"I ran back to my uncle's house," she said, "and I wrote to you that it had all been a terrible mistake and that I regretted it. I begged you not to come after me. I said that I would obtain an annulment, and then I tried to pretend that it had never happened. Except—"

She stopped. "Except that you were pregnant," Dev said. His voice was harsh. Susanna shivered and felt the cold lap again at her heart.

"Yes," she whispered. "It was naive of me not to have thought of it."

"You were seventeen," Dev said in the same hard

tone, "and innocent. How could you fail to be naive?" His hands tightened on hers and she almost gasped as the grip hurt her. "I should have thought..." Dev said. "I was as naive as you. And I was not there to protect you..."

With a pang of shock Susanna realized that far from blaming her, he was blaming himself. The discovery brought the hot emotion burning into her chest and stinging her eyes again.

"I do not think," she said, "that you have anything with which to reproach yourself, Devlin. I was the one who sent you away."

"Let's not argue the toss over that," Dev said, and for the first time there was the hint of a smile in his eyes that lit the tiniest flame of warmth inside Susanna. "What happened when your aunt and uncle discovered the truth?" Dev asked, and the warmth faded again and Susanna felt sick and cold.

"I did not realize it myself for four months," she said. She had been frighteningly naive as well as willfully blind, unwilling to admit it because she was afraid. "Then... Well, you may imagine. My aunt and uncle were appalled. They had no notion I was wed. They had been promoting a match for me with the local curate. My pregnancy left their plans in pieces."

"How inconvenient for them." Dev's voice was dry. "Did they have no thought for you, and how you might be feeling?"

"Not really," Susanna admitted. Her uncle and

aunt had been dour people, wedded to duty, bound to keep up appearances. Her behavior had shocked and appalled them.

Dev's gaze sharpened on her. "Did they throw you from the house?" He sounded incredulous. "I thought they were good people. Narrow-minded, perhaps, but not cruel."

Susanna shook her head. "They were conventional. Do not forget that they had taken me in when my mother could no longer afford to provide for me. They had given me a better life so they thought my elopement wilful and ungrateful when they had done so much for me. I never knew that they had told you I was dead, though. That feels very cruel." She felt the weak, easy tears sting her eyes again. "They had planned for me to go away until after the baby was born. Then I was to give her up, give her away, never see her again." She could not help the way that her voice cracked as her throat thickened with tears.

"She," Dev said. "She was a girl?" He stirred, released her hands and stood up, moving a little away. Susanna felt lost without the physical comfort of his touch. She knew this was the moment she had dreaded. Devlin would not be able to find any more compassion for her, not when her foolish actions had caused her to lose his child. His grief would be as fierce as hers—and it was all her fault.

"She was called Maura," Susanna said. She could feel the cold seeping through her skin now, setting her shivering. The darkness hovered at the corner of her mind, blotting out the light.

"That's a pretty name." Dev did not smile.

"She died," Susanna said in a rush. Her words tumbled out now, heedless, ragged and confused. "I would not give her up. No matter what they said, no matter what they did… I could not. That was when they threw me onto the street. I did not know what to do. I was pregnant and I was alone."

Dev did not speak. He was very pale, his mouth a tight line, as though he were hurting inside.

"I tried to find you," Susanna said. "I went to Leith, to the fort, but they said you had gone south to join a ship at Portsmouth—" She stopped and drew breath. What would Dev care that she had gone looking for him, hopelessly, belatedly and only because she had nowhere else to go? Except that it had not been like that. She had wanted him desperately then, needed him. Carrying Dev's child she had felt the love and the awe flower inside her, stronger than fear, stronger than any other emotion. She had found the faith that she had lacked before when she had run away from Devlin the morning after their marriage. But she had awoken to her feelings too late.

"I went to Portsmouth," she said, "but I was too late. Far too late."

"They assigned me a ship as soon as I arrived there," Dev said. "We sailed within the week."

Susanna nodded. "So I was told."

"Did you tell them that you were my wife?" Dev asked.

Susanna gave him a look. "Devlin, I was six months pregnant, dirty and destitute." Her mouth twisted. "I formed the distinct impression that they had heard that story before, many times."

Dev smiled reluctantly. "I suppose so." His smile faded. "So when they turned you away, what did you do?"

"I went back to Edinburgh," Susanna said. "I knew I had to find work in order to eat but I was too weak. I fell ill in one of the tenements there." She shuddered, rubbing her arms to stave off the cold inside. "It was damp and cold and disease was rife. I contracted a fever. I lost the baby," she finished tonelessly. "She was born at seven months but she was dead. I think I knew, even though I hoped with every ounce of strength I had left that she would survive. But of course she could not. She was too small and too weak and I could not save her…" She stopped. Dev would not wish to hear any of this and she could not speak of it anymore. She felt icy-cold, shaking with grief. It filled her whole being, locking her heart into the dark.

Then she looked at Dev. His face was tight with pain, his eyes blank. Susanna felt sick to see such intense misery; the misery of a man hearing of the death of a child he had only just learned had existed.

"I am sorry," she said helplessly, hearing the inadequacy of her words, hating herself for them. "So very sorry."

His gaze game back and focused on her so sharply that she almost gasped aloud. "For what?" He sounded angry. "It was not your fault that you fell ill and Maura died. You had been turned out of your home. You had tried to find me. You did the best you could—" He stopped as though he could not bear to go on. Susanna wanted to touch him, to offer comfort, but the contained stillness of his grief forbade it.

"I am sorry for all that happened," she said. "I am more sorry than you will ever know that Maura died and that there was nothing I could do."

She saw Dev put out a hand toward her, an instinctive gesture both giving and drawing comfort, and her heart leaped. But before she could move he let his hand fall to his side. His expression became shuttered and Susanna knew he had withdrawn even further from her. She had been correct; he could never forgive her for the loss of their child and she could never reproach him for that.

"It all makes sense now," he said. "Your work in the gown shop, your poverty…" He shook his head as though waking from a dream. "Why did you not tell me the truth, Susanna? Why pretend that you had left me to find a richer husband?"

"I had a commission for the Duke and Duchess of Alton," Susanna said. "I could not tell you the truth and run the risk that you would ruin it all. I needed the money. It wasn't just for me. I—" She stopped.

Dev raised his brows. "You have triplets?" he queried ironically.

"Twins," Susanna corrected.

Dev looked comically taken aback. Under other circumstances she might have laughed. "You have children?" he said. "I thought—" Now it was his turn to stop abruptly.

Susanna knew what he was thinking. Against all the evidence he had believed her when she had told him that she had never sold her body. He had assumed she had kept her marriage vows. She felt a tiny shred of warmth at this evidence of his faith in her.

"They are not mine," she said. "I inherited them. They are at school but I pay their fees." She cleared her throat painfully. "I promised their mother that I would look after them—and I do."

Now Dev looked utterly shocked, as though she had pulled the rug very thoroughly from under his feet.

"Who was their mother?" he said. He ran a hand through his hair, disordering it, making him look even more bewildered.

"Her name was Flora," Susanna said. "She was my friend. She died in the poorhouse."

Dev's blue eyes searched her face. "You took on the responsibility for another woman's children," he repeated softly.

"I lost Maura," Susanna said. She tried to find the words to explain. For so many years she had kept all these secrets locked inside, harboring the pain deep within her, never exposing it to the light. "I couldn't keep Maura safe," she said. "But I swore not to fail Rory and Rose. I had given my promise always to care for them—"

"And you did," Dev said. There was an odd tone in his voice. "The money…" he said. His voice sharpened as though he were coming awake. "That was why you wanted the money. That was why you were desperate to go through with the charade with Fitz, why you tried to buy my silence—" He grabbed her by the shoulders. She thought he was about to shake her. "Bloody hell, Susanna!" He sounded furious. "Is there anything else you haven't told me?" His fingers dug into her skin. His eyes blazed. "Do you take a perverse pleasure in trying to make me think the worst of you that I possibly can?"

"No," Susanna said. "I did not intend…" She got no further because Devlin was kissing her, furiously, blissfully, with exasperation and a blistering hunger. For a moment Susanna's heart unfurled and she allowed the need to take her, too, the heat sweeping through her veins like a storm of fire.

"I have debts," she said as his mouth left hers. "That is something I had not told you. And someone else knows who I am and they were trying to blackmail me but I asked Mr. Churchward to deal with that for me and it does not matter, now that the truth is out—"

Dev made an inarticulate sound in his throat and dragged her back into his arms again, kissing her fiercely. "I thought you an adventuress," he murmured as his lips left hers, "and now I find you more in need of protection than any infant."

"I can look after myself," Susanna said. "And once our marriage is annulled none of this will be your burden anyway."

Dev's eyes were a dark smoky-blue. "I've changed my mind on that," he said. "There will be no annulment."

Susanna's stomach dropped. "But we agreed!" she said. "You cannot change your mind!"

"I just have done," Dev said. He smiled at her. "And legally I do not believe there is a great deal you can do about it, sweetheart. You are my wife and you will stay that way."

Susanna stared at him whilst fury and confusion warred within her. This was so sudden and so unexpected, the opposite of what he had said the night before and the complete reverse of everything she wanted.

"But you can't change your mind," she said again, her voice faltering. "Why would you do so?"

"Because I want you," Dev said. He rubbed his thumb over her lower lip, a sweet erotic caress that she felt all the way down to her toes. "You are my wife and I want you in my bed. And this way," he added, "I can make sure that I provide for you—and the twins—properly…that I do my duty. You are all my responsibility now. You need protection and I will provide it."

The cold settled into Susanna's heart. Duty. Responsibility. Protection. She could see that Dev wanted to make sure that this time he took care of matters properly in atonement for what had happened in the past, and that was admirable, and more than she would ever have asked of him given that none of it had been his fault. But the longer she spent with Dev the more dangerous it was. She had already tumbled headlong into love with him again in the full knowledge that he would never love her in return. She would fill his bed and satisfy his lust, and then he would leave her and go back to sea. He would walk away and she might never see him again, and she loved him so much that that would destroy her. Susanna felt again the sick tumbling sensation in her stomach she had felt as a five-year-old child when her mother had told her that she was to be given away, sent to her aunt and uncle to live because there were too many mouths to feed. She had lost her family then, the first of many losses. She shuddered to see Maura's tiny lifeless body in her mind's eye. Sooner or later she would lose someone she loved again. It was the way of things. She had already lost Devlin once. She could not allow him a place in her life again because he was promised to the Navy again now, he would leave—and he might never come back. That would destroy her so she had to go now, first, before it was too late.

The chill and the fear of loss seemed to freeze her to the very heart.

"I won't go with you," she said stubbornly. "I do not want to be married to you. We were married, it did not work and I prefer to learn from my mistakes."

Dev looked at her, a smile glinting in his blue eyes now. It did strange things to her equilibrium. "You are still my wife," he said mildly, "and you will obey me in this if I have to carry you into the carriage."

"I'll see you damned first!" Susanna burst out, thoroughly incensed now by his high-handed manner. "How dare you try to assert your marital rights, Devlin?"

Dev gave her a look that brought the hot blood burning into her face. "You had no objection to me asserting some of them previously."

"That was different!" Susanna said furiously.

Dev shrugged his broad shoulders. "Brute force is not my style," he murmured. "I prefer charm and persuasion, but if they fail—" he scooped her up into his arms with insulting ease "—then I see I have no choice. Margery will send on your bags," he added, against her ear, "but you are coming with me."

DEV HELD SUSANNA AS THE coach took them the short journey to Bedford Street. Once she had accepted that she was to accompany him she had gone very stiff and dignified, her body rigid in his arms. His grip was negligent now; truth was that he enjoyed holding her—he enjoyed it very much—and he wanted to kiss her and feel the tautness in her melt as she yielded to him. But more than that he wanted to offer her comfort. He wanted to be able to banish the misery he sensed in her. It was a new and somewhat bewildering concept for him. He had always been perfectly clear on what he wanted to take from and give to a woman and solace and reassurance had been in no way a part of it. Now, though, knowing how much it must have cost Susanna to tell him about the terrible loss of their daughter, understanding at last all she had suffered, he wanted to hold her close and never let her go.

Maura. The bitterness of the loss closed Dev's throat. He could see how the entire tragedy had unfolded from the moment he had heedlessly pressed Susanna to elope with him. Amelia, resentful of him and wanting revenge, Susanna young, fearful of what they had done, wanting only the best for him and his future, thinking she was doing right. Her aunt and uncle casting her out and the fight she had had to survive. Anger shook him and resentment for what had been snatched away from them but he knew that both reactions, whilst natural, were pointless. They would build better this time, he vowed, and nothing would come between them.

He looked at Susanna's pale set face. He was only starting to understand this complicated, self-contained woman he had been married to for the past nine years. He knew now how hard she had struggled against almost overwhelming odds, how she had survived a tragedy that had almost broken her, how she had found the love and generosity to take responsibility for two orphaned children because she was all they had. He felt so proud of her. She was brave and strong and he admired her very much. For a brief moment he pressed his lips to her hair and felt her stir in his arms. She met his eyes; an invisible thread that seemed to bind them caught tight and Dev felt his stomach drop and an entirely unfamiliar emotion tug at his senses.

"We are here." He saw they had drawn up outside Alex Grant's town house. He cleared his throat, feeling confused, uncertain, as though he stood on the edge of an abyss.

Susanna cast him an unfathomable glance from her green eyes. "Then I would like to walk inside unaided, thank you, Devlin. There is no need to carry me. I shall not run away and I would prefer to greet Lord and Lady Grant standing on my own two feet."

Dev smothered a smile. "Of course," he agreed gravely.

He handed her down from the coach and led her into the house, wondering quite how to broach to Alex and Joanna the fact that he and Susanna—together—needed a temporary roof over their heads. Fortunately Joanna made matters very easy for them, for as soon as she had bustled out into the hall to greet them she grabbed Susanna by both hands.

"Lady Carew!" she exclaimed. "Chessie has told me what you did to help her." She glanced at Dev then back at Susanna, her blue eyes suspiciously bright. "Poor girl," she said. "I wish she had confided in me but I am so glad that she felt she could turn to you..." A tiny frown marred her forehead. Dev knew she was wondering why on earth Chessie had turned to Susanna but she was too polite to ask.

Susanna, too, had regained her poise. "I hope," she said, "that the Marquis of Alton has been to pay his addresses?"

"He came an hour ago," Joanna said, looking even more mystified. "I must confess that he was very gracious. Chessie is so happy. They are to wed next week." She stopped again. "A pity he is such a scoundrel," she finished, much more sharply. "Really all I wanted was for Alex to horsewhip him from the house, but I suppose that would not do."

"It would not get the marriage off on the right foot," Dev agreed, "tempting as it is."

"I expect you wished to do worse to him than that," Joanna said, patting his arm.

"I did," Dev said. "I wanted to call him out but Susanna stopped me." He smiled at Susanna and saw her blush a little.

Joanna's eyebrows had shot up. "Indeed?" she said faintly. "Lady Carew—"

"Actually," Dev said, "it is Lady Devlin. Susanna is my wife. I apologize for bursting in on you like this," he added, "but we had nowhere else to go. Is Alex free? I must speak to him."

"Devlin," Susanna said, and Dev felt a very odd possessive thrill to hear her speak in tones of such wifely reproach. "Lady Grant, I do apologize. Men are always so blunt and so very intent on marching straight to their objective with no explanation."

"Well," Joanna said cheerfully, slipping her hand through Susanna's arm, "I am sure we can manage without him." She turned to Dev. "Alex is in the library, Devlin, but I fear he has Lady Brooke with him. She came looking for you, in fact. I understand that she has lost Lady Emma, whom I thought—" asperity colored her tone briefly "—was your fiancée." She turned back to Susanna. "Forgive me, Lady… um…Devlin, but is your marriage of recent standing?"

"Nine years," Dev said. He saw that Susanna was blushing even harder now. He realized that she was nervous and felt a rush of protectiveness. Who would have thought that his brazen adventuress had an ounce of nervousness in her? The thought made him smile. He found he was staring at her like a callow youth transfixed by a beautiful woman and tried to pull himself together.

"Did you say that Lord and Lady Brooke had lost Emma?" he asked.

"Lost to Gretna Green," Joanna said, trying not to smile, "and to that dangerous man Tom Bradshaw." She shook her head. "Lady Brooke is not amused."

"Emma's eloped?" Dev said incredulously.

"Three days ago," Joanna confirmed. "But Lord and Lady Brooke have only just noticed." She shook her head. "They thought she had the headache."

"Good God," Dev said. The door of the library burst open at that moment and Lady Brooke appeared, followed closely by an extremely harassed-looking Alex Grant.

"Devlin!" The Countess of Brooke addressed him directly for the first time that Dev could remember, thereby proving that she had known his name all along. "I sent to you at Albany." Her face crumpled. "The most shocking thing...Emma has eloped with a man who works for a living!"

"Might I suggest that we return to the library to talk?" Alex intervened. "It will be a deal more comfortable than out here in the hall."

Joanna turned to Susanna. "Lady... Ah—" She saw the pitfall before she fell into it. "Susanna," she said, "would you care for tea whilst the gentlemen sort this matter out?"

Dev caught Susanna's hand. "Joanna will look after you," he said in a low voice. "I will see you shortly."

Susanna nodded. For a moment her fingers clung to his and he wanted to hold her and reassure her. "Everything will be all right," he said, and she gave him a tiny smile and a nod.

Lady Brooke was frowning at the exchange. "Emma said that you knew that woman," she said disagreeably. She turned to Alex. "Don't trust her, Lord Grant. She is an adventuress."

"The library," Alex said hastily, catching Dev's thunderous expression. "My commiserations on your broken engagement, Devlin," he added, his face impassive. "Joanna has told you the news?" He glanced at the Countess. "Apparently Lady Emma and Mr. Bradshaw left for Gretna several days ago but Lord and Lady Brooke have only just noticed her absence."

"I thought Emma was ill!" the Countess snapped. "Naturally I did not disturb her. Her maid was attending to her needs, or so I thought."

"It sounds as though Bradshaw was attending to her needs," Alex murmured, low enough that only Dev could hear him.

Lady Brooke rubbed her forehead, setting her turban askew. "Where could she have met such a person as this Bradshaw?" she demanded. "And why would she want to marry him? He is illegitimate and he has no money and he is even more ineligible than you are." She looked accusingly at Dev. "I cannot imagine where she has developed this taste for low company." She snapped open her reticule. "Anyway, there is little more to be said. I cannot pretend to be sorry to lose you as a future son-in-law, Devlin, although the alternative is infinitely worse." She took a letter from the bag and held it out to Dev. "My butler informed me that you left this for Emma several days ago. I fear she never read it so I am returning it to you. Good day, Devlin." She nodded to Alex. "Lord Grant."

Dev took the letter and weighed it on his palm, smiling a little. "I wish Emma all the luck in the world," he said as the door closed behind Lady Brooke. "She is going to need it."

"Bradshaw's a dangerous scoundrel," Alex said. "Farne has been looking for him ever since he tried to kill Merryn and now he runs off with an heiress..." He shook his head. "I doubt we have all heard the last of him." His gaze fell on the letter. "You have the luck of the devil, sometimes—"

"I know," Dev said, "especially since I find I already have a wife. Brandy?" he suggested, seeing his cousin's winded expression. "I know it is early but sometimes nothing else will suffice."

CHAPTER EIGHTEEN

"I AM VERY SORRY," Joanna Grant said, her blue eyes wide and apologetic, "but I fear there is nowhere else to put you. My sister Lady Darent has the blue room and Chessie is in Merryn's old room and I am redecorating the rose chamber…" She made a vague gesture. "And this is only a small house, of course. I understand that you hope to persuade Devlin to agree to the annulment, but in the meantime you are still married, so—" She gave a charming little shrug.

"That's perfectly all right," Susanna said, knowing it was not and wondering why she was not making more of a fuss about Devlin having the adjoining bedchamber to hers. The reason was not far to seek—Joanna Grant was lovely, and simply too kind to upset. She had welcomed Susanna into her home with an unquestioning friendship that had made her both grateful and humble.

"You have been more than generous in offering me a roof over my head at all," Susanna said, "and it does not matter for soon I shall be gone." She felt her spirits drop at the thought.

Joanna looked relieved and distressed at the same

time. "Well, I am grateful that you see it like that," she said, "but does Devlin know that you plan to leave so soon? I beg your pardon," she added, catching sight of Susanna's expression. "That is none of my business."

"I'm sorry, too," Susanna said. She had had a long and difficult day and tears of exhaustion and emotion were not far away. "Forgive me," she added. "It is for the best."

Joanna gave her a spontaneous hug. "I know that Devlin can be frightfully dense at times," she said, "but alas, all men can. They cannot seem to help it. And I do believe—I really do believe—that he cares for you."

Susanna's sore heart contracted a little. She knew that Devlin wanted her. She even knew that he wanted to protect her and offer a better future to her and the twins and she loved him all the more for that. But it was not enough. Sooner or later he would hurt her. She would come to love him utterly, she would let down her defenses and allow that love to permeate every part of her soul, and then she would lose him again and it would be intolerable. Everyone left. It was the way of the world. First her father when she had been no more than five years old, going to war never to return. Then she had lost her family when her mother could not afford to keep her and her brothers and sisters together. Then Devlin and Maura…

So she had to leave first, be strong and forge a new

life again. She had already planned it. At dinner she had heard Alex telling Devlin that the Lords of the Admiralty wanted to see him tomorrow. They had made a decision on his commission, Alex had said, and wished to discuss it with him. Susanna had felt cold and bereft to hear the words and had felt even lonelier as she saw the joy with which Devlin had greeted the news. The vivid excitement was back in his eyes. The challenge was what he wanted. She had encouraged him to seek the life that he needed and now he had to go. He was an adventurer, an explorer who was only alive when he had the world at his feet. She understood that but she could not live with it, could not live with the anticipation of loss.

So tomorrow, when Devlin was at the Admiralty, she had decided she would leave. She would tell Alex Grant that when Devlin had the annulment papers he should send them via Mr. Churchward the lawyer. She would leave Mr. Churchward her direction. He would be the only person who would know where to find her. And she would leave her wedding ring with Alex, too, to pay for the annulment. She would leave it to set Devlin free.

At least they had separate bedchambers, she thought as she looked around the room and noted the paucity of her few belongings that Margery had set out for her. There was no key in the connecting door, at least not on her side. It was inconvenient but she would manage. To think of Devlin on the other side of the door would probably torment her all night long, but if she were to lose him she did not want to make love with him again. She could not bear to feel so close to him yet know it would be the last time.

Margery came to her to help her get ready for bed. She heard Dev come up, heard him talking to his valet, Frazer, a dour old Scot who was more than a little intimidating. Frazer had seemed unsurprised to discover that Dev had a wife, commenting only on being introduced to her that it was exactly what he would have expected. Susanna was not sure whether that was a good or a bad thing, nor what the man would say on discovering the next day that Dev's wife had run away. Perhaps he would have expected that, too.

Susanna gave a sigh as she eased herself between the cool sheets. It would not do to get too fond of these people, of Chessie, so happy now that her future with Fitz was settled, and Joanna Grant with her loving generosity, or Alex, incisive but kind, or Shuna, their adorable three-year-old daughter whom Susanna had fallen in love with on sight. Shuna had taken Susanna's hand in her tiny, warm one and it had felt as though the pain would slice her in half even as the love wrapped about her. She had seen Dev watching her and had had to turn away because she knew her emotions were far too naked. These people would not be her future life. She had to let them all go.

After several hours tossing and turning, thumping the pillow, turning it over to press her face against the cool linen, she knew she was not going to sleep and reached out to light the candle. The room leaped into a warm glow.

A moment later the connecting door opened a crack and she heard Dev's voice.

"Can you not sleep?"

"No." Susanna turned to look at him. "You?"

"No." He came forward into the room. The candlelight gilded his tawny hair. He was wearing a dressing gown of gold and sapphire in a stunningly flamboyant design. Below it his legs and feet were strong and bare. Susanna blinked. She imagined that the rest of him was naked, too—and wished she did not remember quite so vividly how that felt, his body against hers, his scent, his touch.

He sat down beside her on the edge of the bed. "What troubles you?" he asked.

"Everything," Susanna said honestly. "Maura." She hesitated, watching his face. "I am sorry, Devlin," she said. "She was your child, too." She saw the shadow in his blue eyes and this time she dared to raise a hand and very gently touched his cheek. After a moment he caught her hand in his. She thought he was going to move it aside and braced herself for the rejection but instead he held her softly then turned his lips against her fingers. She felt his breath on her skin like a caress.

"Does it ever pass?" he whispered. "The grief?"

Susanna felt her heart crack a little. "I learned to live with it," she said. "Somehow. Slowly."

He nodded. A moment passed. Then another. Susanna felt as though she were hanging on the edge of a precipice. The warmth of Dev's hand against hers was so sweet, so comforting. In time such warmth might even go some way toward healing that cold break in her heart, except that time was what they did not have.

Dev slid an arm about her, slipped into the bed beside her and then he was cradling her against him and it felt so soothing that she felt her body relax automatically as she burrowed closer to his side, feeling the slide of the silken dressing gown and through that Dev's warmth.

He turned his head slightly. "Tell me about Rory and Rose," he said, and Susanna felt a rush of gratitude and pleasure that he had remembered their names. "I look forward very much to meeting them."

"They are fourteen now," Susanna started. "They both have auburn hair and freckles and the most beautiful dark eyes." She smiled, conjuring the twins' faces there in the darkness. "Rose is a tomboy...she loves to ride and to play games as well as to read and study. She is an interesting mixture. Rory—" She sighed. "Rory has grown tall and gangly in the past year," she said. "He is truculent—everything seems to enrage him. He will like it that you are not English," she said, turning her head to look at Devlin. "You're not Scots, but Irish is almost as good."

The candle flame quivered and then she remembered. Her spirits sank. Devlin would not be meeting Rory or Rose. When she left on the morrow she would go to visit the children and try to explain why the promise she had made them could not be honored, that for a little they would have to stay at the schools they hated whilst she started all over again to try to carve out the life she wanted for them all. Rory, she thought, would be monstrous angry. She felt helpless and distressed to think of it. Rose's misery would be quieter and more self-contained but no less sharp for that.

But Devlin was speaking again. "Both children will be better when they have a settled home," he said. "I am sure of it. That was all Chessie and I ever wanted after our father died." He was stroking Susanna's hair gently, talking of his childhood, telling her things that they had never spoken of before, not even in those heady first days when they had originally met and had spent every moment that they could snatch together. Susanna tried to resist the seduction of his words. It was a different temptation this, the desire to belong, the need to be part of a loving family. She had never known that for herself. She had wanted to build it for Rose and Rory and in the end build it she would, but she could not take the route that Devlin offered.

Dev's words washed over her, conjuring images of Ireland in his childhood and the Navy when he first joined as a young midshipman. Susanna held him tightly, feeling herself slipping and sliding toward sleep at last. When she woke, some hours later, both the dressing gown and her night rail had somehow been lost and Devlin's long, hard body was entangled with hers in an intimate, erotic bundle, his hand on her breast, his leg pressed between hers, his erect length against her thigh. Susanna came awake to the demands of her body in the same moment that she opened her eyes to find Dev watching her, a spark of wickedness in the blue depths of his. She could see the stubble dark against his cheek and the shadow cast by his lashes. Sensual awareness crashed over her, making her heart race.

Dev saw the reflection of her desire in her eyes. He exerted the tiniest pressure between her thighs at the same moment as smoothing the pad of his thumb over her nipple. Susanna groaned and he captured her lips with his in a kiss deep and drugging and sweet. His head fell to her breast, his cheek deliciously rough against the softness of her skin. Languorously he nudged her thighs apart and entered her, his mouth at her breast, his shaft deep within her, the pleasure exploding through her in a shimmering tide. Susanna ran her hands down his back and over his buttocks, pulling him into her, reveling in the damp, hot touch of his skin, hearing him groan as he emptied himself within her.

She did not wake again until it was full daylight and Frazer was knocking on the door to tell Devlin that he would be late for his appointment at the Admiralty. Dev kissed her and for a moment she clung to him, knowing that this would be the last time. She lay in the warm nest of the bed until she heard Dev leave, heard his brisk step on the pavement outside, and then finally she got up and, with slow movements, started to pack her bag.

IT WAS LATE THAT EVENING when Dev ran up the steps of the Bedford Street house and threw open the door. He had spent the entire day at the Admiralty thrashing out the details of his commission. Now he ached to share that news. He had barely been able to reach home fast enough.

"Where is Lady Devlin?" he demanded of the startled footman before the door was barely closed behind him.

"She is out, Sir James," the man stammered. "Lord Grant is in the library and wishes to speak with you immediately—"

With a slight frown Dev hurried across the diamond-tiled floor of the hall and knocked on the door of the library. It was just possible, he thought, that Joanna might have persuaded Susanna to accompany her and Tess to an evening engagement but it seemed unlikely given the uproar that currently engulfed the family. Emma's elopement was now common knowledge, as was Chessie's betrothal to Fitz. Fitz had also seen fit to announce that Dev and Susanna were married. The gossip occasioned by such a rich scandal would keep the ton talking for months.

Alex was sitting in an armchair by the library window, reading the *Gazette*. Dev tossed his commission down on the table before his cousin.

"They want me to teach," he said. "You could have warned me!"

"God help us," Alex said, "if the Admiralty think that you are a fit person to train the next generation of the Navy. They'll turn out a bunch of pirates." But he was smiling and he got up to shake Dev by the hand. "You are an admirable choice," he said. "You have the skill and the judgment and the flair that they need."

"I am to be based in Scotland," Dev said, "and work with the Scots and Irish Squadron. I thought Susanna would be pleased to be going back home—" He stopped dead, looking at Alex, as the curious atmosphere in the room communicated itself to him. Something chill wreathed about his heart. "Where is Susanna?" he demanded. "I assumed she was out with Joanna and Tess…" But even as he spoke he felt the hollowness of loss.

"Susanna has gone, hasn't she?" he said slowly.

Alex nodded. "She left this morning, Devlin," he said. "I did try to persuade her to wait and speak with you but she refused." His mouth tightened. "I'm very sorry."

Dev felt the ground shift beneath his feet. Last night, he thought numbly, he had held Susanna and they had drawn comfort from one another and he had felt so close to her, bound in an intimacy as sweet and profound as he had ever experienced. And tonight he had been full of the promise of the future, aching to tell her the good news of his commission and how they could settle in Scotland and build a home there for Rory and Rose, too… But Susanna had not waited to hear it. Susanna had run from him again as she had done once before.

"Why," he said slowly. "Why would she do that?"

"I suspect," Alex said dryly, "it was because you did not give her a good enough reason to stay, Devlin."

"But I…" Dev looked down at the commission. "Susanna knew that I wanted to be married to her," he said. "She knew that I wanted to provide a home for her and for the twins!"

"She did not know that you loved her," Alex said. He got up and crossed to his desk, opening the top drawer. Dev saw him take out a small package.

"Susanna came to me this morning," Alex said. "She left me the direction of her lawyers so that you could send the annulment papers when you had them drawn up as she was sure you now would." He paused. "She also left me this." He held the tiny velvet purse out to Devlin.

A moment before he opened it, Dev felt an extraordinary sense of premonition. He could see himself standing before the altar at the church at Balvenie, holding Susanna's hand, sliding onto her finger the ring that had been his mother's and her mother's before her, a golden band studded with tiny seed pearls. His hands shook a little as he opened the purse and the ring rolled out into his palm and lay there glowing softly.

"I did not realize she still had it," he said quietly. "I thought she must have sold it years ago."

Alex's gaze was very dark and steady. "I do not believe that Susanna knew that it belonged to our grandmother," he said. "She gave it to me to give back to you." He stopped. "I have no doubt," he added very deliberately, "that when she did so her heart was breaking. She did not want to go, Devlin, but she thought she was doing the right thing to set you free to go back to sea. She knew it was what you wanted."

Dev stared at him. "I do want it," he said, "but the future is nothing without Susanna to share it with me."

"I'm not the one you should be telling," Alex said. He smiled. "You may remember that when I let Joanna go you told me I was a bloody fool. You were right. Well, it is my turn now, Devlin. If you do not go after Susanna and tell her that you love her and convince her that you are worth being married to then without a doubt you will be a complete bloody fool."

"I've already been that," Dev said, "but it isn't too late." He would find Susanna, he thought, tell her that he loved her, and then he would hold her against the world, against the future, and never let her go again. Love. He had never thought to feel it again after the disaster of his youthful marriage. Yet now he felt ridiculously excited at the prospect of finding Susanna and claiming her once and for all. He knew his emotion must be vivid in his face because he could see that Alex was trying not to laugh at him. But damn it, he did not care.

Alex's voice arrested him before he was out of the room. "Before you set off to find your wife," his cousin said, gently ironic, "you might wish to deal with this." He passed Dev a note. "It is from Churchward," he added. "I understand that Susanna asked him to act on her behalf in the business of her debts and also in a certain unpleasant matter of blackmail. As it turns out—" Alex grimaced "—the two are connected."

Dev perused Churchward's note rapidly. "Bradshaw," he said softly, through his teeth. "I might have guessed."

"The man does have an unpleasant habit of turning up like a bad smell," Alex agreed. "You will see him?"

Dev folded the letter. "Of course."

"And pay him?" Alex queried.

Dev paused. "I'll pay him what he deserves."

There was a silence. "Don't tell me more," Alex said with a faint smile. "Then when the Runners come asking questions I can plead genuine ignorance." His smile broadened. "How are you going to find Susanna?" he asked. "You know Churchward will never break her confidence."

"I have no idea," Dev said honestly. "But I will not stop until I find her."

Alex jerked his head toward the door. "So what are you waiting for?" he said.

DEV HAD BEEN IN PLENTY of low taverns in his time in seaports from Southampton to St. Lucia, and the clientele in The Bell Tavern in Seven Dials was very much as he had imagined it. There were three men he guessed to be footpads, a half dozen pickpockets and at least two highwaymen. They all stared at him as he ducked under the lintel. They looked from his face to the sword at his side and then to the bulge of the pistol in his pocket, and then they turned away and resumed their conversations.

Bradshaw was not in the taproom. Dev took an unobtrusive seat in a corner and watched the clientele come and go. The room was crowded. Dev drank one pint of ale and ordered a second. He was about to leave when a man came in, a man who was tall and broad-shouldered and looked at first glance at least like a gentleman. Dev felt the atmosphere in the taproom change as though a charge had run through the air like a lightning strike. The man smiled, cocked his head to the landlord for a drink and came across to Dev's table.

"Sir James," he said as he slid into the seat opposite. "I was expecting your wife."

"And you got me instead," Dev said coldly. "Not much of a bargain." He shifted. "If it comes to that,

I did not expect to see you, either, Bradshaw. I had heard that you were in Gretna Green with Lady Emma Brooke."

Bradshaw laughed. "Gretna was too far to go," he said. "I found a priest to marry us here in London, no questions asked."

"I'm not sure that that is legal," Dev said politely, "but that is, of course, your business."

Bradshaw's teeth gleamed in a smile. "And the business of my doting parents-in-law," he said. "They are happy to accept the match—for the sake of Lady Emma's reputation."

"I'm sure Lord and Lady Brooke are very happy for you," Dev said.

Bradshaw took a long swallow of his ale. "You should congratulate me, Devlin," he said. "I only did what you wanted to do—marry a fortune." His dark gaze was mocking. "Except that I did it with a great deal more ruthlessness than you will ever possess. To the winner the spoils, eh?"

Dev felt the prickle of antagonism down his spine. He knew this was all for show, to provoke him, but he could feel his temper rising.

"Absolutely," he said smoothly. He could feel the tension tight across his shoulders but he was not going to show Bradshaw any weakness. "Which brings us rather neatly to business," he said. "I believe you have bought up my wife's debts—after your attempt to blackmail her failed?"

"If one course fails then another will always

present itself," Bradshaw agreed. "I'd done some work for Hammond so I knew all about Lady Devlin's past." He smiled, but it was without warmth. "I planned to blackmail her by threatening to tell Alton her identity."

"What did you want from her?" Dev said. "You knew she had no money."

Bradshaw gave him a look that made him itch to take the man by the throat and throttle the life out of him. "What do you think?" Bradshaw said. "I wanted a taste of her. She's so beautiful what man would not? I wanted to—"

Dev's hand moved to the pistol in his pocket. "Be very careful, Bradshaw." His tone was rough.

Bradshaw shrugged. "Well, she thwarted me by telling Alton herself." He shook his head like a man confronted with an impenetrable mystery. "Why would she do such a thing?"

Dev smiled slightly. He could feel his temper easing as he thought of Susanna's warmth and generosity. "To put right a wrong," he said, "and to help someone she loved. You would not understand."

"Damned right I don't," Bradshaw agreed. "Terminally stupid thing to do when she could have won the whole game." He shrugged, sliding a hand into his jacket. "Here are the papers. I bought Lady Devlin's debts up with the promise of part of Emma's marriage settlement." He laughed. "Ironic, is it not, Devlin, when you have been living off that same expectation for years?"

Dev's lips thinned. "Most entertaining, Bradshaw." He perused the papers briefly. Susanna's debts were substantial, though nowhere near as great as his own. He glanced up. "Do you intend to foreclose?" he asked.

"Unless you pay me," Bradshaw agreed.

Dev sat back in his seat. "You know that I have debts of my own and no money to pay them," he said. Bradshaw nodded, his eyes bright with amusement. He was, Dev thought, a man who enjoyed the game, enjoyed making his prey suffer. It gave him pleasure. Now it was time to puncture that self-satisfaction a little.

"You'll get no cash from me," Dev said briskly, "and if you insist on claiming the money all that will happen is that I shall be thrown in the Fleet and still be unable to pay you."

The bright spark of amusement faded from Bradshaw's eyes. "Whilst I would quite like to see that," he said, "I would like the money more."

"Of course," Dev said. He put his hand in his pocket and took out a little box. He pushed it across the table. "Which is why I am prepared to offer you this," he said, "in return for these." He tapped the papers.

Bradshaw shot him a suspicious look before opening the box a crack.

"Don't show it around in here," Dev advised. "The room is full of thieves and criminals."

Bradshaw's eyes had widened as he took in the

contents of the box. An unholy gleam came into them. "I'll be damned," he said.

"Indubitably," Dev said.

"I'd heard about this," Bradshaw said, risking another look, "but I didn't believe it."

"You can believe it now," Dev said. "It's yours—if you are prepared to accept it in return for Lady Devlin's debt."

Bradshaw's head came up. "How do I know it isn't a fake?" he demanded. "Since you're so strapped for cash why did you not sell it years ago?"

Devlin laughed. "I couldn't," he said. "I came by it through means that were—" he hesitated "—not entirely legal. If I had tried to sell it, questions would have been asked—questions I could not afford to answer when I was betrothed to Emma and wanted to make my way in the ton."

A reluctant grin split Bradshaw's face. "So it's true you were a damned pirate," he said. "I almost like you for that, Devlin."

"The feeling is not mutual," Dev said coldly. "Do you want it or not?"

"I won't be able to sell it for the same reason," Bradshaw said, staring into the box as though transfixed. "But it's a hell of a thing to possess..."

"And you like to own expensive things, don't you, Bradshaw," Dev said gently. "Beautiful women, jewels beyond price..."

He could see the greed and the calculation at war in Bradshaw's face and tried not to hold his breath.

Then Bradshaw's hand closed over the box and it was gone, into his pocket. Dev smiled and gathered up Susanna's promissory notes, ripping them in half, throwing them into the open fire where they shriveled and curled to ash in the grate. He stood up.

"A word to the wise, Bradshaw," he said softly. "Keep Emma close. Treat her well. At the moment you are untouchable because you have the protection of a rich wife and titled connections. But fortunes can change. And when yours changes—" he paused "—there will be a great many of us waiting to bring you down."

He saw Bradshaw's expression darken, saw him reach instinctively for his pistol, but before he could draw, Dev's sword was at his throat. There was a concerted gasp from the entire population of the taproom, chairs scraping back, men on their feet. Dev shot them a smile.

"Keep back," he said. "Mr. Bradshaw wants to return intact to his beautiful bride."

The atmosphere quivered with violence. Then Bradshaw raised a hand and the men fell back and conversations restarted as though nothing had happened at all.

"Ruthless enough for you?" Dev asked politely as his blade rested against Bradshaw's Adam's apple. "On your feet. You will oblige me by walking to the door with me now so I get out of here alive. Oh, and Bradshaw." He smiled. "Be sure to keep that box safe. Who knows, the treasure might be real."

Bradshaw's gaze spat hatred. It was clear he had already started to have second thoughts—but he was too late.

"If I find you have cheated me—" he started to say.

"You'll never know, will you?" Dev said as they stepped out into the darkened alley. "As you said yourself, you'll never be able to sell it. All you can do is look at it and wonder if it's real." He sketched a bow as he stepped up into the waiting carriage. "And now that doubt is sown in your mind you will never stop wondering," he said. "Good night, Bradshaw."

CHAPTER NINETEEN

IT WAS HER WEDDING ANNIVERSARY and it was a beautiful day.

Susanna stood behind the counter in Mrs. Green's gown shop and stared out of the wide bow windows across the harbor and the sea beyond. When she had returned to Scotland she had not wanted to go back to the teeming streets of Edinburgh. There were too many memories there. Instead she had chosen this little town on the west coast with its view across to the Isle of Skye and the sharp black peaks of the Cuillin Mountains. There were taverns aplenty here in Oban where she could have got a job, and inns that catered to the trade provided by the fishermen and the drovers. Fortunately, instead of having to go back to serving pints of ale and singing ballads, Susanna had gained employment in Oban's only modiste's shop. Mrs. Green prided herself on the superiority of her clientele and expected a similar level of quality from her staff. She had liked Susanna's elegance and her pretty manners.

In the three weeks since Susanna had left London she had been to see Rose and Rory and had difficult interviews with each. Rory had stormed out when Susanna had told him that he was not, after all, to be leaving Dr. Murchison's and that they could not set up as a family together anytime soon. Rose had been quieter, reproachfully silent, and in both cases Susanna had seen the unhappiness in them and had felt she had failed them again. Nor had she heard anything from London from Mr. Churchward. Perhaps it was too soon but she was certain that Devlin must have started the process of having their marriage annulled so that he could return to sea with the whole matter put behind him. She wondered if she would read of his exploits in the scandal sheets, read of him capturing a king's ransom or more likely, knowing Devlin, ravishing a king's mistress. She felt another little piece of her heart breaking.

She had cried when she had discovered that she was not pregnant with Devlin's child, and then cried again because she had not understood why she was crying. She had thought that she would be glad to sever all links with the past. She had chosen to be alone and to start afresh because she had been so afraid of losing Dev that she had wanted to make that break before it was too late. But now she realized that it was already far too late, had been from the moment that she had fallen in love with him all over again. Twice now she had not had the faith to risk all on loving him. There could be no third chance.

The bell on the door of the shop pinged loudly. Susanna looked up from the bales of muslin and cambric that cascaded over the counter and felt the ground shift beneath her feet. Devlin was standing in the doorway of the gown shop. He looked incredibly handsome in Navy uniform. Susanna felt as though the room was starting to spin, slowly, giddily, as though she was about to faint. She watched as Devlin stepped inside and closed the door behind him by which time the entire female clientele was staring with undisguised fascination. The youngest of Susanna's fellow shop assistants forgot herself sufficiently to dislodge an entire bale of superfine onto the floor. Dev caught it and restored it to her with a smile and a quick word, and Susanna thought the girl was very likely to swoon with excitement.

Dev came forward to stand in front of Susanna. There was a faint smile in his blue eyes as he looked at her. Her throat dried to sand. Her heart started to race.

"Susanna," he said. Just that one word and Susanna thought that she might very well swoon, too. She took a deep breath and grabbed the edge of the counter to steady herself.

"How may I help you, sir?" she said, very politely. "Are you interested in the merchandise?"

Dev's smile was laced with pure wickedness. "No," he said, "but I am interested in you. I would like to make you an offer."

There was a little gasp from Miss Alison, the shop assistant who was standing to Susanna's left.

"I'm sorry, sir," Susanna said, very cool. "This is not that sort of shop and I am not that sort of girl."

Dev's smile deepened. "Oh, I think you are," he murmured. He put a hand under her chin and tipped it up so that she met his eyes. "In a moment you are going to walk out of this shop with me and not come back," he said.

Susanna held his gaze. "That would depend on the terms, sir," she said, drawing another gasp of shock from Miss Alison on her left. "I don't sell myself cheap."

Dev looked at her for a long, long moment. There was wickedness and challenge in his eyes, and another emotion that made Susanna's heart tumble over and over.

"I love you, Susanna Burney," he said. "I loved you when we met nine years ago, I loved you in London and I will love you until I die. Are those terms good enough for you?"

Susanna heard Miss Alison make a noise between a sigh of lust and a little moan of pure envy. She shook her head, ignoring the battering of her heart. "Those are the sort of words that lead a good girl into trouble," she said, "especially from a handsome gentleman like you, sir."

"But when you already know me intimately," Dev murmured, his lips now no more than an inch away from hers, "you know just how sincere I am. I have never, ever wanted to be married to anyone but you."

Susanna drew back. “That is not true,” she said. “You wanted to marry Emma.”

“I wanted to marry Emma’s fortune and Emma’s title,” Dev corrected. “I did not want to be married to Emma herself or I would have done it long since.”

“How heartless you are,” Susanna said, unable now to fight the smile that was starting to curve her lips.

“My heart is yours,” Dev said. “You know it, Susanna.” He took her hands. She could feel that he was shaking a little and the knowledge of his emotion shook her, too.

“No one can predict the future,” Dev said, “but if you trust yourself to me then I will always have something worth coming back for, Susanna. As long as I have breath in my body I will be yours and your star will guide me home.”

Susanna blinked back the sudden hot rush of tears. “You understand,” she whispered.

“I understand that you have been afraid,” Dev said, “and I will do all I can to make sure that you will never feel so alone again.”

He leaned across the counter and kissed her, and Susanna felt her heart expand with blazing happiness. “I love you,” she whispered against his lips and felt him pause, and smile, before he kissed her again.

“Miss Burney!” Mrs. Green rustled out of the back room to take in the sight of her newest assistant in a passionate embrace with a Navy captain. “What is the meaning of this?” she spluttered. “This might well do for Edinburgh but we do not behave like this in Oban!"

"Well, at least you are using your own name this time, Susanna, rather than someone else's," Dev commented as he released her. He bowed elegantly to Mrs. Green. "How do you do, ma'am? I am Miss Burney's husband, Sir James Devlin. So in point of fact—" he smiled at Susanna "—she is actually Lady Devlin."

"Lady Devlin?" Mrs. Green shot Susanna a deeply suspicious look. Susanna could see that she was now torn between disapproval and the fear that Dev might actually be speaking the truth and that she was about to alienate an influential member of the gentry. "Lady Devlin is working in my gown shop?"

"Not anymore, I fear, ma'am," Dev said cheerfully, "but I do thank you for providing her with respectable work, unlike her previous trade."

"Devlin!" Susanna said, turning scarlet, digging him hard in the ribs. Dev smiled at her, another of his brilliant, wicked smiles and Susanna saw that even Mrs. Green was not immune. The modiste had turned slightly pink and was actually fluttering her eyelashes at Devlin.

"Well," Mrs. Green said. "I suppose I must wish you happy, Sir James."

"Thank you," Dev said. He held out a hand to Susanna. "No more running away, sweetheart," he said softly.

Out in the street, in the keen breeze and the

shadow of the harbor wall, Susanna stopped and put one hand against his chest. "Devlin," she said, "are you sure? Twice I have lacked the faith..." She stopped.

Dev covered her hand where it rested against the dark navy-blue of his jacket. "You don't have to do everything on your own, Susanna," he said quietly. His face darkened. "Rory told me about you losing your father to the wars. I understand now why you were so afraid of risking everything for us all those years ago and why you ran from me in London."

"Rory told you?" Susanna echoed.

"I saw him on my way here," Dev said with evident satisfaction. "He was the one who told me where to find you. Nice lad," he added. "We played cricket together. He can't wait to be out of that house. He only granted me permission to marry you again on the understanding that we would go and fetch him and his sister immediately after our honeymoon."

"Marry again?" Susanna said. "Honeymoon?"

"Your conversation suddenly lacks sparkle," Dev murmured, brushing his lips against hers. "You do nothing but repeat what I say." He grabbed her hand again. "Come on."

"But where are we going?" Susanna gasped as he pulled her along at a pace approaching a run. Dev shot her a smile.

"It is our wedding anniversary," he said. "Or had you forgot?"

They reached the ruined chapel on the headland

just as the sun was dipping behind the distant mountains to touch the sea with molten silver. Dev opened the door and they slipped inside. The air was cool here, the dust motes dancing in the light from the stained-glass windows.

"There is no one here to witness our vows," Dev said as he drew her forward to stand before the altar, "but I do not think that the words will go unheard."

He took the wedding ring from his pocket and slid it back onto Susanna's finger.

"A beginning and an end," he said. "An eternal circle." He kissed her again, and this time it was a kiss of love and promise and benediction, and then for a long time they stood on the sun-warmed stone outside the church door, watching the sea as the sun went down.

Presently Dev stirred, tucked Susanna's hand though his arm and steered her through the rickety gate and up the stony path away from the town. They walked slowly, heads bent, very close together.

"We have three days before we go to collect the twins," Dev said. "Then we travel up to Invergordon where I take up my command."

"You are already become a dictatorial husband," Susanna scolded, running her fingers along the line of his jaw, feeling the stubble against her fingertips and reveling in the roughness of it.

Dev turned his head and kissed her fingers. "I am," he murmured. "And now I want to make love to you and I fear I am going to be dictatorial about that, too."

"I lodge in a most respectable boardinghouse," Susanna started to say, and saw Dev smile.

"Fortunately," he said, "I have taken a little cottage just up here on the hillside. I wanted some privacy for us because I do not intend for us to be respectable at all."

"But how could you afford it?" Susanna said. "Together we must have sufficient debt to sink a battleship."

"Not anymore," Dev said. "I have paid them all."

Susanna drew back a little. "But how?"

Dev was looking rueful. "I had one thing left of great price," he said. He looked down into her face, grinned. "Well, two things, but only one that I could sell."

"You sold the pearl," Susanna whispered. "Oh, Devlin!"

Dev laughed. "I didn't sell that pearl," he said. "I kept that one for you. There were two of them." His smile turned wry. "They were a symbol of my past life," he said softly. "For a long time I was very attached to them because they represented the life I had adored and lost, the excitement, and the adventure…" He stopped and cupped Susanna's face in his hands. "They no longer matter," he said, "because I have a new life with you." He released her and laughed. "Actually, I tell a lie. There were three pearls in all but one of them was counterfeit. I gave it to Tom Bradshaw in payment of your debts." He shook his head. "I'll tell you all about it some other time."

He was already kissing her as he drew her over the threshold of the cottage and closed the door very decisively behind them.

"You always wear such frustrating clothes," he muttered as he started to unfasten the row of tiny buttons down the front of her dress. "This is a very respectable gown," he continued, muffling a curse as his fingers slipped with haste. "Just what I would have expected for a lady working in Mrs. Green's shop."

"I'm a very respectable girl," Susanna said.

"No," Dev said, "you are not." He folded back the material at the base of her throat and pressed his lips to the hollow he had exposed. "No respectable girl," he said, against her flushed skin, "would be pleasured with a pearl from an Eastern potentate's treasure."

A delicious shiver rippled through Susanna's stomach. "Then perhaps I prefer being wicked," she murmured.

The bodice of the respectable gown gaped suddenly as the last button was undone. Dev slipped his hand inside. "Ah, the virtuous gown has submitted at last," he said. His palm was warm against the side of her breast. He pushed the bodice back and lowered his head to pull on her nipple, his teeth grazing her through the fine lawn of her shift. Susanna gave a moan as a shaft of sheer delight pierced her. The bodice of the dress fell, a crumpled shell, to the floor and Dev pulled on the ribbon that fastened her skirt so that it, too, fell away with as much eagerness as Susanna was feeling herself.

"I think," she gasped, "that this will end as it usually does with me naked and you still fully clothed."

Dev laughed. "Maybe not this time." He pulled her up the narrow tumbling stairs and into the bedroom above.

"Goodness, how beautiful," Susanna said, distracted by the huge window facing the west and the golden sunset that now cloaked the sea.

Dev stepped behind her and slid a warm arm about her waist, nuzzling her neck through the silky strands of her hair. She could feel his lips against her nape, tracing a delicious path down her spine, feel, too, the hard, hot press of his erect length against her. She turned in his arms so that she could kiss him properly and freed herself briefly from his embrace only to make short work of the Navy uniform.

"You looked very fine in it," she teased, admiring the firm musculature of his body in the sun's golden light, tracing a finger down the curve of his shoulder, "but right now I prefer you out of it."

The intense light in Dev's eyes made her breath catch. "I am yours to command," he said. He ran his hands into her hair, cupped her head and kissed her again, tasting, savoring, pent-up longing mingled with worshipful desire. It felt different, Susanna thought as her lips parted beneath the demand of his, less driven but no less urgent, the edge of anger between them banished now by love.

The bed was swathed in pure gold and crimson as Dev drew her down to lie beside him. "I truly am yours to command," he murmured, his fingers toying with the strands of black hair that now spread across her shoulders in silky abandonment. "Only yours, Susanna, now and always."

"As ever you speak well," Susanna said, smiling, as she stroked a lazy hand down Dev's spine, enjoying the shudder of response her caress drew from him. "But can you match actions to words?"

They lay for a moment looking at one another, so close, almost touching, a mere hairsbreadth apart. She saw the amusement in Dev's face change to taut desire then he rolled her beneath him and sheathed himself in her in one long thrust, taking her mouth with his even as he took her body. She gasped at the invasion, her breath lost in his, as his hands moved over her, evoking the most sublime pleasure. The spiral tightened, burning out the pain and misery of their lost years, drawing them together with desire now transmuted into love and tenderness. Susanna clung to him as the exquisite climax took them both together. She could feel the tears hot on her cheeks, felt, too, Dev shift slightly to cradle her in his arms as he brushed them away with gentle fingers.

"Darling..." He sounded shaken. "Please don't cry." He rolled over onto his side, drawing her with him, still intimately entwined. "I love you," he whispered against her hot skin. "I will love you always."

"I'm only crying because I am happy," Susanna said, smiling radiantly at him. "I love you, too, James Devlin. And I think," she added, "that I will like being married to you very much."

Dev started to kiss her again. "That's good," he murmured, "for we have a great deal of time to make up."

* * * * *

Tantalizing historical romance from
New York Times and *USA TODAY*
bestselling author

JENNIFER BLAKE

The Three Graces of Graydon
are well-born sisters bearing an ominous curse—a man betrothed without love to any of them is doomed to die.

Coming August 2011

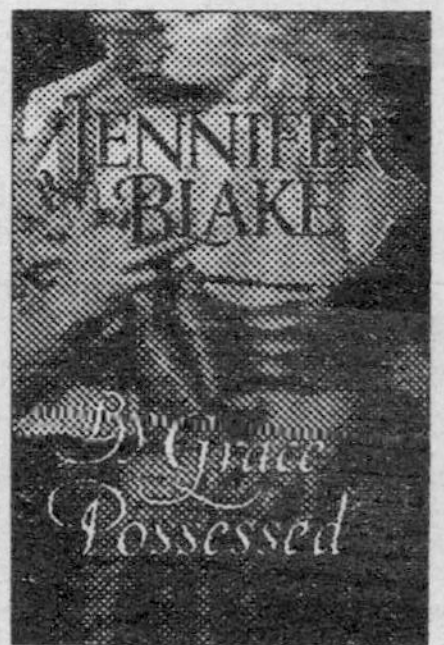

Coming September 2011

Coming October 2011

**Available soon
wherever books are sold!**

MJBTRI11R

HQN™
HARLEQUIN®
www.Harlequin.com